The Lady Confesses

The Hellion Club, Book Nine

by Chasity Bowlin

ARE YOU SIGNED UP FOR DRAGONBLADE'S BLOG?

You'll get the latest news and information on exclusive giveaways, exclusive excerpts, coming releases, sales, free books, cover reveals and more.

Check out our complete list of authors, too!

No spam, no junk. That's a promise!

Sign Up Here

www.dragonbladepublishing.com

Dearest Reader;

Thank you for your support of a small press. At Dragonblade Publishing, we strive to bring you the highest quality Historical Romance from some of the best authors in the business. Without your support, there is no 'us', so we sincerely hope you adore these stories and find some new favorite authors along the way.

Happy Reading!

CEO, Dragonblade Publishing

Pirates of Britannia Series
The Pirate's Bluestocking

Also from Chasity Bowlin
Into the Night (Novella)

This work contains brief descriptions
of addiction and past domestic violence.

Prologue

Joss Ettinger floated in a haze of pain. It felt as if the right side of his body was on fire. Curiously, his left arm was entirely numb. He felt nothing at all. Fragments of memory penetrated the fog in his brain. The carriage racing through the countryside, the fear and adrenaline as they were being chased by Bechard. While there were things he hadn't known about the man, he'd known enough that the thought of him getting his hands on any of the females occupying that coach with him—be they young or old—had made his blood run cold.

The sound of a pistol firing reverberated in his mind. The splintering of wood as he'd been propelled backwards into the wall of the vehicle had been deafening. Soft, cool hands had touched him, but then they'd put pressure on his wounds and the agony of it had been unbearable. Still, he'd fought. He'd managed to drag himself up onto his knees at least, pistol drawn. Then another shot had rung out. The last memory he had was of Effie Darrow—no, Effie Montford, now—issuing sharp instructions to the young women in that carriage. Then the world had gone black.

The second shot. It had struck him in his shoulder, high up. Nowhere near his heart, but he didn't doubt it had done damage. How much?

Despite the pain, Joss raised his right arm and draped it across his body. What he'd feared—that his left arm was gone entirely—was not true. It was there, but he felt nothing. No pain, no tickling or tingling sensations. It was just curiously numb. Experimentally, he tried to move it. He couldn't lift it from the bed, but at least his fingers drew into a fist. It wasn't completely useless to him. Just mostly.

"You're awake."

He knew that voice. He'd heard it often enough in his life. Cracking one eye open and wincing at the bright light of day flooding through the windows, he found himself staring into the slightly haggard face of Vincent Carrow. Joss noted one thing about his long acquaintance: for the first time in all the years that he had known the Hound of Whitehall, he was happy to see the bastard.

"The duchess?"

"Safe," Vincent answered. "As are Alexandria and Louisa. They are all well and in your debt."

"I did nothing. She was still taken."

"Yes," Vincent agreed. "But you slowed the bastard down. You gave us the time we needed to track her and to retrieve her before the unthinkable could happen . . . and you damn near died for your efforts."

Joss asked the question that he most feared the answer to. "How bad is the arm?"

"Not good. Still there, at least. That was a battle. Damned sawbones wanted to lop it off. Bloodthirsty bastard. I put a stop to that."

For once, Joss was grateful for just what a terrifying son of a bitch his sometimes-friend could be. "How?"

The Hound grinned, but it was not at all a friendly expression. "Told him for every part of you he chopped off, I'd be taking an equal amount of flesh from him. He changed his tune then . . . as to the arm. Bow Street is done for you now. How much use you'll have of it is anyone's guess."

Joss nodded. "I want to get back to London. I'm not good

here in the country."

"Soon enough, yes. But you're not fit to travel just yet. Give it a few weeks. Rest now. I'll make arrangements to get you back to London as soon as you're able to make the journey."

Joss watched the other man leave. Alone, he struggled into a sitting position and swung his legs over the edge of the bed. He wasn't foolish enough to try to stand. Not when just that small bit of effort had left him wheezing like an old man. Still, he sat there for a while, flexing his hand—willing some sensation into it. Nothing happened. He moved it, lifting his arm clumsily, trying to grasp the blankets and pull them aside. He had limited success with either. In the end, all his experiments produced was more frustration.

The door to his room opened once more, admitting a woman of middling years with a round, florid face and an ample figure. "Mr. Ettinger! It's so good to see you awake. And sitting up on your own! My heavens, but you are an ambitious one."

"I'm sorry, but who are you?"

"I'm Mrs. Cheavers, dear boy. His grace, the Duke of Clarenden, has let this small house near his estate and hired me to oversee your convalescence. He'd have moved you to his own home, but it's miles away yet and—to be quite frank—no one thought you'd make it that far. Dark and dire days, sir. Dark and dire!"

Her pragmatic answers were at odds with her almost elfin appearance and the singsong way she communicated them. "I see. Thank you, Mrs. Cheavers."

"Oh, don't thank me yet. While you're awake, I'll help you to the chair, and that way I can change the bed without rolling you to and fro like a log. Heavens, but you're a heavy one!"

That he had to lean so heavily on that small, round woman as she aided him to a chair that had been placed by the window was lowering. More than lowering. It made him angry. All the pain, frustration and fear bubbled up inside him to such a degree that he was fighting with all his worth not to lash out at her.

"There," she said, huffing out a breath as she plopped him in that chair. "I'll just get you a blanket."

Moments later, a blanket was tucked around his legs like he was some sort of invalid in a Bath chair. Still, he held his tongue as she went about the business of tidying up. When it was all done, she bundled the soiled linens into her arms. "I'll be back in a moment with something for the pain. You look a little pale, Mr. Ettinger."

He wanted to protest, but he didn't. It would be churlish. Instead he just nodded and sent her bustling from the room. It was less than ten minutes before she returned carrying a small tray with a pot of tea on it and a bottle. "A bit of laudanum in your tea. It'll do the trick," she said, pouring the cup and adding a few drops of the potent liquid to it. "Drink up now."

He did, downing the scorching liquid as quickly as possible. Then the haze returned, and he found himself thinking that he rather liked it, having a veil between himself and the harsh reality of his present and the uncertainty of his future.

A part of his mind protested. He knew the dangers of opium all too well. And what was laudanum but opium in its liquid form? Still, he couldn't quite muster the wherewithal to think about giving up that blessed numbness, that escape.

Chapter One

Four months later . . .

JOSS WATCHED THE ship bobbing in the middle of the Neckinger River. It was little more than a death trap. Leaky, broken down, dirty, and staffed with sailors that even other sailors would have called unkempt. Of course, he knew what that boat was. Calling it a ship was an insult to ships everywhere. That boat was used to transport women. Girls from the north who were foolish enough to believe the promises of good-paying work and free room and board in the city of London. Of course, no one ever told the poor dupes most of the work would be done on their backs and most of their pay would be kept either by the pimps or abbesses that bartered their services. He didn't blame the girls. Most were from the country, uneducated and sheltered by their families. It was hard for him to understand how anyone could be so innocent or trusting, but he'd seen it time and again.

As he watched the ship from his position crouched behind a stack of barrels, he heard the hue and cry. Then he saw her. Her skirts were billowing behind her as she ran full speed toward the aft of the ship. There was nowhere for her to go. In the moonlight, he could see her face clearly. It was etched sharply with fear. Fear of the men who chased her, fear of the water below and of the jump that could well kill her.

With a curse, he crept from his hiding place and, just as she went into the water, so did he. The sound of her splash camouflaged his own.

The water was frigid. Cold enough to make his bones ache and to set his left arm on fire. The numbness he'd experienced at first had slowly receded. What was left in its wake was constant pain that was only intensified by the freezing water.

He was up to his chin in the water when the current carried her in front of him. Reaching out, he grasped the coarse fabric of the dress she wore and hauled her against him. She was completely limp. The moonlight filtered through the boards above them, and he could see a dark rivulet snaking down her forehead. She'd struck her head. And she was unconscious. It was freezing cold, and he wasn't certain he had the ability to carry her.

Suddenly, she began to struggle. With footsteps overhead, he couldn't afford for them to be overheard. Placing a hand over her mouth, he leaned in close to her ear and whispered a shushing sound. "They are still scouring the wharf for you. Until they've moved off we must remain where we are. Nod if you understand."

Her terror was a palpable thing. Of the men above, the water, or him? That remained to be seen. But at last, she gave a brief nod, and he removed his hand from her mouth.

She glanced back at him over her shoulder. "Who are you?"

"My name is Joshua Ettinger. I'm a private inquiry agent—formerly of Bow Street. Your sister—indirectly—retained my services."

She was not entirely satisfied with his answer. He could sense it. There was no rush of relief through her to alleviate the rigid tension in her muscles. Instead, she remained stiff in his arms.

"Did you find her?" The voice drifted down from above. It wasn't the sort of voice he'd expected. Not rough. No cockney accent or street cant. It was cultured, educated . . . and it belonged to a gentleman.

"No. No sign of her. She likely drowned. Hobson told us she

was fearful of water." *That was the servant answering.* It was obvious from the subservience that infused his voice.

"Then I want a body," the gentleman growled. "I need one. She saw me. She knows my face. I'll not swing for this."

The second man sighed, subservient but losing his patience. "We don't have enough men to be scouring the Mint for a lone woman. We'd as like get shot as not."

"Then hire more goddamn men! I will not dangle at the end of a bloody rope because that bitch managed to get past the men you trusted to be on watch, *Captain!*"

The men parted, one returning to the ship and another heading into the Mint. When he could no longer hear their footfalls on the boards above, he dared to speak, "You hit your head. You've been in and out for the last few minutes. I need to know if you're with me before we go ashore. If you're not fully conscious or if you're still unsteady on your feet, I need to know. If I tell you to run, I need to be certain that you can and will." Because much as it pained him to admit it, he wasn't certain he could carry her. Certainly not for any extended length of time.

He felt her shudder against him, a small and involuntary response that told him just how frightened she was. "I can do whatever it takes to get out of here." She took a steadying breath. "I want my sister. I just want to go home to her."

If it was the bloody last thing he did, he would get her there. Because there was something about her—about her fierce determination to survive, to escape her captors, even when facing her worst fears—that spoke to him. "All right. Let's go then. Quiet is better than quick. No thrashing about. We can't afford to disturb the water. Go piling to piling under the wharf."

There was a slight hesitation in her, then she admitted, "I'm not a strong swimmer. I can barely tread water."

"That's all you need to do here. Hold on to me. I'll get us there."

She placed her hands on his shoulders, holding onto him, as he began to make his way back toward the embankment. Slowly, inch by inch, they crept toward the river bank. But there was no guarantee of safety there. And there were even greater complications still to come. They were both wet, freezing, and the night air was growing colder by the minute.

Stay hidden. Stay warm. Stay alive. Those were the objectives. There was no place in that for any sort of tender feelings or admiration for her just because she'd shown such remarkable courage. There was no room in his life for a woman he admired. Certainly not if that woman was another man's wife, and a lord's at that.

HETTIE WAS STRUGGLING. Her teeth chattered while her body was wracked with shivers. Her sodden clothes were clinging to her skin as they slipped from alley to alley in a part of London she hadn't even known existed, much less ever visited. Even in her charity work at the hospitals and in the rookeries, she had never seen anything like it.

Refuse of all manner littered the streets. What had once been beautiful and stately homes were now decaying shambles. And vice was present in every alcove, alley or doorway. Bawds, both male and female, plied their trade. The opium eaters were not in their dens here, but out on the cracked and crumbling sidewalks for all to see. Cockfighting, dice, and other games of chance carried on in abandoned buildings.

Then there were the dogs. Dirty, diseased, scrounging for scraps in the detritus. Rats and other vermin were rampant.

"Keep moving."

Her rescuer's voice was gruff. Not mean, but certainly brusque. He had to be cold as well, she reasoned. He'd been in the water as long as she had, and they were both now exposed to the elements. "I'm trying," she said. "I really am."

"I know. It isn't much further," he said.

"Where are we going?" she asked.

"I don't wish to say . . . not where we might be overheard. And in this place, there are eyes and ears everywhere."

Another shudder raced through her, this one not prompted by the cold. Danger was ever present, and not just from the men who were in pursuit of her. She'd often heard people refer to the rookeries they traveled as cutthroat, and they certainly could be. But she'd never been as frightened there as she was in their current location. The very air around them crackled with menace and danger.

Another step forward, and something sharp stabbed the bottom of her foot, causing her to stumble. She would have given a cry of alarm, but he caught her, his hand covering her mouth once more to muffle any sound.

"Are you badly injured?" He hissed the question next to her ear.

"No. It's all right. More startled than anything, I think." Still as they continued to creep forward, she couldn't deny that it hurt. She tried not to limp, tried to disguise the pain, but she was certain that she was failing miserably.

"It's just up ahead," he said, once more keeping his voice pitched low. "That large brick structure with the arched windows."

It was a warehouse, a massive one from what she could see. The doors and windows were all boarded up, but she could still see the arches he'd indicated. But as they neared the building, he didn't pry the boards from the windows or doors. Instead, with a grace that was somewhat shocking for a man his size, he slipped between the gapped boards that covered the arched opening in front of the doors. Tucked into that small space, he picked the chained lock with some tool or other he'd fished from his pocket.

When the door swung inward, he turned and helped her navigate the boards until she too could ease through into the darkened interior of the building. Once inside, she took a moment. It was quiet. The double layers of brick insulated them from any of the sounds from outside.

"Up those stairs," he said, pointing to a rickety wooden staircase in the far corner.

Moving as swiftly as she dared in the darkness, Hettie shuffled toward those stairs on her near-frozen and terribly battered feet. Running barefoot through the filthy streets of the Liberty of the Mint was not something she had ever imagined that she would do. Of course, she also hadn't imagined that she would be the victim of an abduction either. There were many tragedies in her life that had not been foreseen. Her farce of a marriage numbered amongst them. She was hardly alone in that predicament. So many women found themselves married to men who were not as they should be. But then, given what she'd endured for the last two days, was any man what he should be?

Chapter Two

J OSS BUSIED HIMSELF lighting the stove in the small room. Lady Marchebanks' bolt hole in the Mint had been quite a find all those months back. That it remained undisturbed was a blessing. There was no food, no provisions. But there was a stove for warmth and blankets. They could get by there till the morning.

Once the fire was blazing inside the little stove, he lit one of the lanterns perched on a table. Then, with light, he turned. What he saw made him curse. She was no longer shivering. Henrietta, Lady Ernsdale, was positively purple with the cold that had seeped through her sodden clothing. Without preamble, he barked a single command. "Strip."

She looked mutinous for only a split second before making her very best effort to do as instructed. But every attempt to free the buttons of that coarse gown was foiled by her stiff, frozen fingers.

"Damn it all!" Even as he was uttering the curse, he was moving towards her. It had been a very long time since he'd undressed a woman. That he was undressing her now for such very unpleasant reasons did not stop his body from stirring. Even near frozen, dirty from the river, and haunted by what she had endured, Lady Ernsdale was one of the most beautiful women he'd ever seen.

"I'm sorry," she mumbled, her speech sluggish and slurred.

That effectively dampened his ardor. He was beginning to realize just how severely the frigid water had affected her. "It's the cold," he explained. "It clouds your brain. It can drive you mad if you cannot get hold of yourself. But first things first, we need to get you warmed up."

As the rough fabric of the dress slithered to the floor, he realized that she wore nothing beneath it. Logically, he understood that every garment she'd been wearing at the time of her abduction had been stripped from her and sold by the vultures who'd taken her. But even with the cold that had tinged her skin an unnatural shade of blue, he could see where the rough fabric had abraded her delicate flesh. There were bruises, scrapes, and scratches all over her. It infuriated him. It was also more than just his natural inclination to be protective of women, and particularly innocent ones such as Lady Ernsdale. His response to her was something different—other. *Proprietary. Something he had no right to be where she was concerned.* Whatever the hell it was, it was a waste of energy. They were worlds apart, and it ought to stay that way. It *would* stay that way.

He glanced at her face and saw a slight smile curving her lips. "What is it?" His voice sounded gruff, his tone too sharp to have spoken to her thusly.

"I was afraid to drown," she managed. "But there are worse ways to die. Freezing to death might be one of them."

"Fuck." The moment he said it, he regretted it. That wasn't the sort of word he ought to use in front of her. "You're not going to freeze to death. I won't allow it." To be certain of that, he draped one of the blankets about her shoulders and maneuvered her closer to the small box stove which now provided a cheery blaze.

"What is this place?" she asked.

Telling her that it was a former hideout for traitors and murderers seemed like it would not be for the best. So he offered an abbreviated explanation. "It was the home of a dead woman." He moved away from her then, leaving her in front of the stove as he moved behind her to remove his own soaked clothes. He would use one of the blankets to cover himself solely for her benefit.

"Oh, that's terrible. Did she die here?" She sounded so utterly horrified by the possibility.

"No. She was already dead before she moved in," he answered as he pulled his shirt over his head. He didn't bother to explain that she'd been dead from the first moment she'd elected to betray her country for nothing more than a bit of coin.

Once he tossed his filthy shirt to the floor, he removed his boots, then dropped his pants. As he rose, he looked back at her over his shoulder. She was no longer facing the stove, but was looking at him in a way that—well, it wasn't good for either of them. Admiration was one thing. Attraction was another altogether. But awareness, the tension that developed between two people when those other feelings were both mutual and acknowledged, that was dangerous.

Still, he took a moment to study her. The curve of her shoulder, the slope of her breasts barely concealed beneath the blanket, the length of her pale, slim legs—it was all bared to him. And none of it should ever be for his eyes. She was not for the likes of him.

To break the spell, he joked, "Careful, Lady Ernsdale. You'll put me to blush."

"I don't think so. From what I can see you have absolutely nothing to be embarrassed about."

Like the male of any species, he had his vanity. And she'd certainly stroked it, whether that had been her intent or not. He couldn't say whether or not she had been purposely flirtatious or if he was simply hearing in her words what he wished. What was the adage? If wishes were horses, then beggars would ride. He was very much the beggar in their situation. It wasn't a fact he could afford to forget.

Turning away from her, he spread their clothing out over the other pieces of furniture in the room so that it would dry during what was left of the night. And then he turned back, forgetting for just a moment that it wasn't simply his nakedness which might be shocking to her. Her sharply indrawn gasp was all the reminder he needed.

He turned once more, but this time what she saw made her gasp not in appreciation but in horror. He knew what she'd seen, of course. He saw it every time he dressed or bathed. The large chunks of muscle and flesh torn away at his shoulder from Bechard's pistol ball. All the smaller scars that surrounded it from where the fragments had to be cut out. Highcliff had informed them at a later date that it was Bechard's practice to use iron rather than steel to promote fragmentation. He crafted those pistol balls in such a way that they would break apart and do as much damage as possible. As a result, his shoulder was simply ravaged. Through sheer force of will, he had some use of his arm, but not enough. Not enough to do and be what he once had been.

"It's ugly as hell, but I don't have the luxury of covering it right now." The explanation came out short and sharper than it ought to have. He was reluctant to meet her gaze, reluctant to see her face etched with either pity or disgust.

Hesitantly, she asked, "Does it pain you still? The scars are still very red . . . and very new."

He dared glance up at her then, and he didn't see either of the things that he had feared. Concern, curiosity, appreciation. All of those things were plainly visible to him on her far too expressive and revealing face. And they only further complicated the unfortunate attraction he had developed for her. Not simply because of her courage or her beauty, but because of all that he'd learned about her while retracing her steps. She helped others. She genuinely cared for the wellbeing of those most in society would have snubbed entirely, including those like himself. Bastards from the street who'd thieved, pickpocketed, and done all manner of terrible things for the sole sake of survival. Yet, from everyone he had spoken to of her, he'd heard only of her kindness, of her lack of judgement. The simple truth was that everyone talked of charity, while few ever truly displayed it. But she did.

Attraction. But not simply that. No. There was desire there. It fired his blood when he looked at her, and not even the chill in that small room could prevent his body's response to it. "I'm learning, Lady Ernsdale, to ignore all manner of discomforts. Now lie down before the fire. I'll get us some blankets from the chest, and we'll stay here until our clothes are dry and you've thawed a bit. Once day breaks, we'll make our way out of the Mint and get you back to your sister."

HENRIETTA DID AS he said. Not because she didn't wish to continue looking at him. She did. So very much. Long limbs, sinewy muscle, broad shoulders that tapered to a slightly leaner waist. There was no fat on him. Not an ounce of it. Nor would a tailor ever need to pad his clothes to make him look like a truly prime specimen of masculinity. The Scottish nanny they'd had as children would have called him a braw, bonnie man. And she would have been very, very right.

By virtue of being a married woman, she'd been permitted to see certain works in the British Museum that, as a younger and still unwed lady, she had been previously denied. And she understood why. In truth, she hadn't thought men could actually look like that. Her husband, on the very few occasions when he had actually made an attempt to consummate their marriage, had certainly born no similarity to them. But he did. Mr. Joshua Ettinger. Private Inquiry Agent. And no mere fig leaf would have served to conceal his masculinity.

There was no small amount of curiosity in her about the act that should have no longer been a mystery to her. But alas, she was married to a man who could never show her such things. Even if he could, she certainly wouldn't want him to. And she could only imagine that the differences in such an intimate experience with Mr. Ettinger—versus one with her husband—would be tantamount to daylight and dark. They were not simply opposite in appearance, but in every way that a man might be measured.

She wished she knew more of such matters, that she could speak with another woman about them. Honoria would be of no aid to her. Her sister's marriage had been just as wretched as her own. As for the women they associated with, the so-called ladies of the night, they could speak to pleasure and had often done so. But that was only part of it, wasn't it? The strange awareness, the crackling connection that seemed to exist between them, that was something else entirely. And the transactional nature of what those other women experienced when with a man seemed to be very far removed from her present experience.

How long had it been since she'd been intrigued by a man? Not since she had been a much younger and infinitely more hopeful woman. In truth, she'd been nothing more than a girl then. It was the loss of innocence which marked the passage from girlhood to womanhood, and there were, sadly, more ways to lose one's innocence than simply sacrificing virginity.

It seemed a lifetime ago that she'd been a young woman just moving into society. There had been flirtations, of course, and some degree of interest in her. In some cases, there had been reciprocity of that interest, but nothing that compared to what she currently felt for the man who occupied this small room with her.

Was it simply because he'd rescued her? That was likely part of it. She wasn't so foolish as to think it had not swayed her. Life and death situations forged deep bonds. Any man who'd been to war would certainly agree with that assessment. But it was more than that. He'd been so steady, so constant since that first fraught meeting while she'd battled her fear and the river itself. His calm had seeped into her, had let her feel secure in a way that she never had with anyone else.

When he laid down behind her, his large frame wrapping around her, she became conscious of the heat of his body, of the firmness of muscle under skin that was surprisingly soft when everything about him appeared so very hard. He covered them with one of the moth-eaten blankets, and his arm remained draped over her. Though he made no other move, it was the most natural thing in the world to relax against him. The rightness she felt at letting him shelter her completely as she absorbed his heat and strength was a problem to be picked at and dissected another time.

The river hadn't claimed her. Neither had the cold. Somehow, against all odds, she had survived the ordeal and would be reunited with her sister soon. And in the meantime, she could pretend. She could pretend that she wasn't married to a man like Ernsdale. That, instead, she was married to a man like the one who now held her cradled against his broad chest.

With that thought playing in her mind, she drifted to sleep. It was the first peaceful sleep she'd been blessed with in a very long time.

Chapter Three

I T WAS NEAR dawn when he awoke. His shoulder ached, his neck would likely remain at an unnatural angle for some time to come. While a morning erection was not unusual, he'd never woken up harder in his life—with no sight of relief in the future, near or far. Making some attempt to adjust himself so that at the very least he wasn't poking and prodding her with his rebellious cock, he had to stifle a groan.

Whether it was the sound he'd made or the movement, she stirred in his arms and turned from her side to her back. This new position offered him a moment to study her, to truly take in everything about her. There was some light seeping in through the boarded up windows, and some still from the stove. It was enough. Even in the darkness he'd thought she must be impossibly beautiful. But in his wildest imaginings, he could not have envisioned a creature so perfect.

Even under the remaining grime deposited by the river, her skin was like porcelain—pale, smooth, unblemished. The color of her hair was lighter than he'd imagined. Not a coal black like her sister's, but a soft brown with hints of gold and red buried within it—strands which seemed to capture the light, or what there was of it, and amplify it.

Against his will, his gaze drifted to her lips. The cupid's bow shape of them was exaggerated by the lush plumpness of her lower lip. It turned out in a slight pout, even as she slept peacefully. Despite his best intentions, the thought of kissing those lips was inescapable. He couldn't put it from his mind, try as he might. And then her eyes opened. He was caught. Completely mesmerized by those emerald depths, he could not look away.

"You're staring," she said. But it wasn't accusatory or scathing. It was simply an acknowledgment of the fact.

"So are you," he replied. And it was true. Her gaze roamed him like a caress, and his body responded to it as if it had been an actual touch.

"You did it first."

His lips twitched with the hint of a rare smile. "I can't help it. You are a remarkably beautiful woman, Lady Ernsdale."

"Don't call me that. I detest that name."

Her obvious disgust at the moniker was a surprise to him. The man? No. He could easily enough understand why she would revile her husband. But the title was what most women aspired to. But then again, it wasn't difficult at all to see that she was quite different from anyone else he had ever known. "Then what would you have me call you?"

"Hettie . . . that's what Honoria has always called me. It's far preferable to either Henrietta or my husb—to *his* title."

Not just any "him," but her husband. She had one of those, a fact he could not afford to regret. Not only that, but the man was a peer. He was a worthless ass who didn't deserve to be called a man, much less a gentleman. But under the eyes of the law, she belonged to him. That was an inescapable truth.

He turned to roll away from her. "We should dress and get out of here as soon as possible." As he started to rise, he felt a hand on his arm. "Don't. Not just yet."

He glanced back at her. It would have been easy enough to dislodge that staying hand, to dismiss whatever it was she felt she needed to say to him in that moment. And yet, he could not make himself utter the words any more than he could remove her hand from his arm. "This is hardly the kind of opulence one should luxuriate in."

"It is," she said. "We are warm and dry. I don't have to be afraid."

Joss frowned. "Must you be afraid at your own home?"

"More so there than anywhere else," she admitted. "Ernsdale is—well, he is not a good man. Nor a kind one. He has a foul temper and is very quick to mete out his punishments. This . . . this very humble room is the first place I've felt truly safe in a long while. My husband would never dare to come after me here, not in such a place. And the men who abducted me have, I can only hope, given up by now."

It saddened him that she would want to stay in such a place, that it would be preferable to her to her comfortable and luxurious home in Mayfair. "Ernsdale is a right bastard, that's for certain. Always knew that about him. Never knew just how much of one he was, though."

Behind him, she sat up. "How do you know him?"

"I worked for Bow Street for many years. We've encountered one another from time to time." Usually outside gaming hells or brothels where his temper had made him a nuisance, or something worse.

He felt a whisper of a caress on his shoulder, the faint trailing of fingertips over the ugly scars that remained. "Is that how this happened? During your work for Bow Street?"

Joss glanced back at her. "Something like that . . . you're playing with fire, Lady—Hettie. Be careful you do not get burned."

"Mr. Ettinger—"

"Joss," he corrected. "If I'm going to use your name, at least here in private, you should use mine."

"Joss," she corrected. "Would you do something for me?"

"More than likely," he agreed. At this point, if she kept looking at him like that, he'd commit murder for her.

"Would you kiss me?"

He was so stunned by the request it took him a moment to even process it. But she saw his hesitation as reluctance and uttered one last compelling argument. "No one has kissed me in a very long time."

He could more easily have stopped his own heart from beating just by willing it to than to refuse her. Turning quickly, he pulled her against him. It was a mistake. The instant he felt her breasts crushed against his chest, his hands pressed to the silken skin of her back—it was like a match to tinder. The simmering tension and awareness that had been present almost from the first moment had been replaced by an out-of-control blaze.

When he touched her lips with his, a delicate brush, he felt the shiver that raced through her. Her breath rushed out, fanning over his own lips, and it was all he could do to keep the touch gentle, light. Especially since all he wanted to do was to take. To claim. Conquer. He wanted not just compliance but eagerness from her. He wanted her to be mindless with need for him. Because he was fast approaching the point of mindlessness himself . . . and he didn't want to fall into that abyss alone.

It had been ages since she'd been kissed, but it might as well have been the first time. Nothing that had come before could even compare. The two men who had kissed her hadn't even really been men yet. Just boys. Young swains who had trailed after her during her first and only season like foundling puppies. There was no comparison.

Heat surged through her. At every point of contact between their bodies, her skin tingled. The feeling of his firm chest and the light dusting of hair that covered it teased the tips of her breasts into hardened peaks. It was stunning to realize that she wanted him to touch her. She wanted to feel his hands on her body.

His mouth moved over hers slowly, hypnotically. Never

rushing. He kissed her as if they had all the time in the world and as if there was nothing more important to him than learning every contour of her lips. When he licked gently at her lower lip, she let out a soft moan of pleasure. And that was his invitation. His tongue swept between her parted lips, sliding sensually against hers with a gentleness that belied his impressive strength. For a man who towered over her, who had the strength to crush her if he chose—he touched her as though she were delicate, fragile and precious. *As if she were cherished by him.*

Sliding her hand over his shoulder and into his hair, she held him to her, terrified that he would end the encounter, that sanity would intrude. But he had no intention of going anywhere, as evidenced by him laying her back down on the hard floor, cushioned by his strong arms. The weight of him on top of her was something she hadn't known she had needed, or even that she could need. But it felt glorious to have his body pressed against her head to toe, for every inch of her to be inflamed by that contact. She never wanted it to end.

The sensual dance of that kiss continued. It was impossibly intimate, but it wasn't enough. She wanted more. Every touch intensified the craving for him. Those caresses burned her like a brand.

As if he'd read her mind, his hand slipped from her back, skating over her ribs and around to the fullness of her breast. He cupped it with that large hand, his strong fingers stroking and kneading the tender flesh. Her back arched, lifting her breast more firmly into his hand. Then he broke the kiss, his lips trailing along her jawline and down the column of her throat. The little licks and nips at her collarbone and the hollow of her throat set her on fire. But that was nothing compared to the storm that swirled inside her when his lips closed over the taut bud of her nipple.

There was no stifling the cry of pleasure. She hadn't even known she was capable of feeling such things. Clinging to him, her hands moving over his back and down to his lean waist, then his firm buttocks, she mapped the hard planes of his body and committed them to memory. The hard ridge of his arousal pressed against her thigh, and she was shocked by how much she wanted to touch him there, to explore all the mysteries of his perfect masculine form.

His mouth left one furled nipple and moved to the other as his hand slid down her belly to the dark curls at the juncture of her thighs. He slipped one finger inside her, just barely. Just enough to stroke a part of her that made her see stars. No one had ever touched her there. Even her husband. His fumbling attempts to consummate their marriage had ended in failure each time. The feeling of his soft, flaccid member pushing against her was nothing at all like what she was currently experiencing. They were worlds apart, in fact.

She wanted to know what desire truly was. To feel that sweeping passion that she'd read about in books and heard other ladies whisper about was something she had dreamed of experiencing. It was also something she had given up on entirely. So long as her husband lived, such things would never be in her reach. But he would not be her husband for very much longer, would he?

Shifting slightly, she parted her thighs for Joss, a blatant invitation for him to do what he wished—to show her all the wonders that could be had between them.

Chapter Four

TOUCHING HER SILKEN skin was like a dream come true. Watching her face as she discovered her passion, that was a gift. One he would never forget. Stroking the tender bud nestled between the petal-soft folds of her sex, he found what she liked. He knew what made her gasp, what made her moan, what made her shudder, and what made her nails sink into his flesh.

Every touch was a discovery, every sound was like music to him. And when he felt her belly quiver beneath his hand and her thighs tense to the point that they trembled, he knew she hovered on the brink. Dipping his head to her breast once more, he scraped his teeth against the hardened bud of her nipple. It was the thing that pushed her over the edge. The strangled cry of pleasure that escaped her was gratifying, but not necessary for him to know that she'd found her pleasure. Her body clenched around him, even as that delicate pearl fluttered beneath his fingertip.

He didn't withdraw his hand immediately. Instead, he continued to stroke her—soft, soothing touches that would ease her down. Kissing her tenderly, he waited until her ragged breathing had settled into a more even rhythm. Only then did he pull back.

"What you've made me feel," she whispered, "is beyond anything I could have ever imagined. But there's more, isn't there?"

"There is," he concurred.

"Show me . . . please?"

"Are you certain? There is no going back, Hettie. You're a married woman, and this will make you an adulteress. Are you prepared for that?"

There was something strange in her expression. Her gaze was shuttered, and he knew, without question, that she was keeping something from him. But she'd offered him her body and not her secrets. It wasn't his place to pry.

Finally, she said. "I don't care. To be a good wife, one should have a good husband and I . . . well, I do not. I want you to make love to me."

He ought to correct her. What they were doing was not making love. He wasn't even certain such a thing existed; it was a pretty term for a primal act—something to make people feel less guilty about their perceived sin. But for whatever reason, he couldn't force the words out. If that was what she wanted, he determined, he would certainly try to give it to her. He was capable of being gentle, of being tender with her. And after everything that she had endured, surely she deserved that much regard from him.

"Please, Joss?"

Was there a man on earth strong enough to resist such a tempting offer? He didn't think so. If there was, he was not the one.

Lowering his head once more, he claimed her lips in a kiss that seared them both to their very souls. He felt her shudder against him, felt the bite of her nails on his flesh as she dug her fingers into his back. His own hands tangled in the fall of her dark hair, tilting her head back to give him greater access to her mouth, to deepen the kiss. The soft, sensual glide of her tongue against his as she kissed him back was like a victory. He could have shouted it from the rooftops—she wanted him. Scarred, half-wrecked from the wounds he'd sustained, dirt poor, and literally without a pot to piss in, she wanted him. And he'd never wanted anything more in his life than he wanted her in that moment.

Trailing hot kisses down her neck, to the swells of her breasts, he worshipped her with his lips, his tongue, his teeth. And he was rewarded with soft moans and cries, gasps of pleasure that had her lifting against him, arching her back and offering herself to him completely. He accepted greedily, hungrily. But it wasn't enough.

Levering himself up, he positioned himself between her parted thighs, their bodies aligned perfectly. Easing into her, he immediately recognized that she was not very experienced. But when he pressed deeper, he realized instantly that something was very wrong. This was not an experienced woman. This was not a married woman who understood the full span of physical intimacy. The woman who had taken such pleasure in his arms, who had pleaded with him so sweetly to make love to her—as if she knew precisely what that entailed—was a virgin. Or rather, she had been. Because even as that fact had registered in his mind, his body had been very much in control. Though he'd gone entirely still, the damage was done.

"Hettie?"

"Don't," she said. "Don't. It doesn't matter . . . and I'd so much rather it be you."

It did matter. That she thought otherwise told the glaring truth of just how the men she'd known in her life had treated her. A commodity to be bartered and sold rather than a woman to be cherished. Resentment welled inside him—resentment for men like Ernsdale who deserved nothing that life had given them and resentment toward fate that had put her in his path when he knew she would never be his to keep. Nothing that passed between them could be more than temporary.

IT HAD BEEN much nicer before. That was the thought that kept circling in Hettie's mind. When he'd been kissing her, caressing her, touching her so intimately—it had been glorious. She'd felt like she was floating. Now, it was simply uncomfortable and a bit awkward, and part of that, she knew, was her own fault. Had she told him that, despite her status as a married woman, she'd never lain with a man before—well, he likely wouldn't have believed it. After all, who would?

She'd been married for more than six years. Her husband had never managed to successfully consummate their union. Not that she wished him to do so. And she'd never had the courage to take a lover for fear of discovery. It seemed that her abduction and running for her life after the fact had somehow tapped a well of courage not yet known to her.

"It gets better," he promised solemnly.

She certainly hoped so, though that hardly seemed like something she ought to say to him. It was terribly unflattering. Rather than say anything at all, Hettie simply nodded.

"You look doubtful," he observed. "Understandably so. This is hardly the way it ought to have happened. You should be in a bed draped with fine linens, and it ought to be any man but me. A man who can give you the world."

"I have a husband who could offer me the world, but he never has—he never will. I don't want anyone else," she said. "I just want you. And you want me . . . me. Not the fortune, not the connections, not the fashionable debutante that I was. I'm at my worst, and you still make me feel beautiful."

"You shouldn't need me to make you feel beautiful." As he spoke, he slipped one hand behind her knee, drawing it up so that it rested against the firm muscles at his side. "That's something you simply are. Now. In a decade. In a century, should we live so long. You'll always be that."

Hettie didn't reply. She couldn't. When he'd shifted her, adjusting their joined bodies just so, something miraculous had happened. There was no longer even a hint of pain or discomfort.

And the fullness from before was no longer something she was simply aware of. It was what she needed. In the same way that she needed air to breathe and sustenance for her body, she needed him—that intimacy and connection.

He withdrew, easing his hips back, and she wanted to protest, to beg him to stay with her. Before she could utter a word, he'd surged into her once more, flexing his hips against her. In that moment, the entire world simply fell away. She lost sight of where they were, of the danger they'd faced, of everything that had led her to that place where she currently lay in his arms. Whatever she might have endured had been well worth it to achieve this one perfect moment in time.

With every stroke, Hettie's thoughts fractured, drifting away from her until she could do nothing but cling to him with mindless need. Her body tensed and coiled as she felt that once-foreign tension deep inside her. It built and built, every muscle drawing taut. And then, without warning, that tension snapped. Sensations she couldn't hope to describe washed through her, wresting a sob from her lips as she quaked beneath him. Then he went still, his body shuddering against hers as she felt the flood of warmth inside her. His release.

Now, she understood. She knew why women made fools of themselves, why they fell from grace. But like all things beautiful and perfect, she knew it would be fleeting. There was no room in her world for happiness. Not when freedom was now further away than ever.

Chapter Five

JOSS LAY ON his side, curled around her as she pressed her face against his chest. He traced lazy circles on the curve of her hip, marveling at the velvet-soft texture of her skin. There had been a shortage of beautiful things in his life, of perfect moments. From the rookery where he'd started out to the workhouse where he'd eventually wound up, he'd spent his whole life fighting and struggling.

Fate had intervened in the form of a fateful, failed attempt to pick the pocket of Vincent Carrow. When he'd failed, he'd run like a pack of hellhounds were chasing him. But Vincent had caught him easily enough—found him in an alley, beaten and bloodied from the trouncing he'd gotten earlier that day. It was that moment that changed everything for him.

The Hound had cleaned him up, fed him, dressed him, and plunked him in a school to learn and make something of himself. When he'd been encouraged to go into Bow Street, he'd done so readily enough. It seemed a small enough price to pay for everything that had been given to him. And he'd liked his work. He'd liked the notion that he was making the streets somewhat safer for others. If there were things he had to turn a blind eye to, so be it.

Losing Bow Street, losing his purpose, had left him vulnerable in a way nothing else had. He'd sunk into the oblivion that laudanum, and then opium, could provide. Somehow, he'd pulled himself back from the brink of ruin, but there were still times he woke up in a cold sweat, craving the sweet relief the drug could provide. But he imagined that opium had been replaced. If he woke up in the middle of the night with a craving, it would not be the haze of the drug for which he longed. It would be for the woman in his arms. The woman he was about to lose forever.

The sun was up. It had been for some time. And the real world, the one waiting for them outside the Mint, was calling. It could not be put off any longer. So he uttered words that he knew would break the perfect spell between them.

"This was a mistake," he said.

She pulled away instantly. It stung. No. In fact, it cut to the very bone. As she sat up, there was no hint of the passionate woman from only moments earlier. There was a coolness about her now, a thin layer of ice covering any warmth that she might normally exude.

"Very likely," she agreed. And then with a bitter smile, she added, "Most of my interactions with men have been."

Joss said nothing further, but rose from their pallet on the floor and began inspecting their muddy, dried-stiff clothing. It hurt to look at her. It hurt to see that he'd dimmed the fire in her eyes, even if it was the best thing for them both. Quickly, he donned his breeches before turning to her and tossing her the hideous dress she'd been forced to wear. "It's a shame, but it'll have to do for now."

THE ROUGH FABRIC of the dress had not been improved by the river mud deposited on it. Still, it could have been a sack, and she'd have donned it gladly. Being naked in his presence after everything that had transpired between them—and everything that had not—was too much for her. "Turn around."

One dark brow lifted in what appeared to be bemusement. Then he gave a shrug and turned his back to her, indulging her request for modesty. Humoring her. *Patronizing her.* If she'd had a weapon she'd have thrown it at him. Preferably it would be heavy and very pointy. She wasn't normally a bloodthirsty person, but she'd like to draw a bit of his.

She'd been frightened of men in her life, for a variety of reasons. From her father's thundering verbal assaults where he called them all manner of ungrateful wretches to her husband's petulant, spiteful rages—men had shown her the worst of themselves. They'd left her bruised and exhausted. But none had ever truly hurt her, not that inner part of her which she showed to no one save Honoria, not the soft and tender underbelly of her very person. She'd never shared that with anyone else. Not until Joss Ettinger had looked at her with those soulful dark eyes. And now, not only was she hurt, but also embarrassed. She felt like a fool.

If all that had transpired wasn't humiliating enough, she now had to stand before him wearing a garment not even fit for the rag pile. With the hideous gray-brown dress once more hanging off her body, she squared her shoulders and prepared to face him. "Alright. I'm dressed now."

He turned back to her, his expression schooled into one that was completely impassive. They might have been strangers passing on a sidewalk for all that she felt in his gaze as he casually swept it over her. In retaliation, she did the same, letting her eyes roam over his broad, tall frame. While she'd been dressing, he'd donned his shirt and jacket. Only his boots remained, in his hands. They were probably not dry and would likely not be salvageable at all. With a pettiness that shocked her, she hoped they were his favorite pair.

"Take one of the blankets, wrap it about yourself like a cloak and cover your head with it. Walk like an old woman, hunched over and appearing as feeble as possible. That will make your skirts drag the ground and camouflage the fact that you have no shoes."

"Why should that matter?" Henrietta demanded.

"Because your abductors know precisely what you were and were not wearing when you left that ship. They know you were shoeless, cloakless, and wearing that ugly smock which doesn't deserve to be called a dress," he replied. "And when we are outside, you do what I say. No questions. No hesitation. I don't care how bloody mad at me you are."

"I am not angry with you." She was furious with him, but madder still at herself. Her pride was wounded. And despite everything, she still had that in abundance. Giving herself to him, no matter how right it had seemed at the moment, had been a terrible mistake. As Honoria would say, she should have known better. "And I will do what you say when you say because, contrary to popular opinion, I am not foolish. I am out of my element here and dependent upon you for survival. Whatever my feelings about you are at this time, I can trust that your objective—to return me to my sister—has not changed."

It sounded so cold, so detached. As if they hadn't been locked in a passionate embrace only moments earlier, as if she didn't know the intimate details of his body and he did not know hers. But the answer apparently satisfied him. After a tense moment, he gave a curt nod and made for the door. She was left to either stay behind or fall in step following dutifully after him.

Chapter Six

IT HADN'T BEEN a smooth getaway. Not at all. Their last few hours in the Mint had involved taking a circuitous route to the gates separating that lawless place from the City of London. Ducking into alleyways, weaving their way through refuse that didn't require any sort of identification beyond filth, it had taken far longer to travel such a short distance than it ought to have. But there had been no help for it. The sailors from the ship where she'd been held were still scouring the Mint for her, and Joss knew that if they caught her, she would not escape again. And while she recognized that he could likely best one of them, maybe even two, if the others were nearby, it would be for naught. So they hid, evaded, avoided, and concealed themselves whenever possible. In short, it was slow going.

They worked silently to make their way toward the Mint's gate and the freedom to be had just beyond it. All Hettie wanted was to get back to Honoria, to see her sister and to know that—for the time being, at least—they were both safe. And she wanted to be far from him. She wanted to forget that anything that had transpired between them had ever occurred. And with every touch, even the most casual and necessary sort, she recognized that it would be impossible to do unless all ties were severed permanently. She would never see him again. It was the only way.

"Wait here."

The gruffly whispered instruction formed the first words spoken between them since they'd left the warehouse earlier that morning. It belied every tenderly whispered word they had shared before and only confirmed the distance that had grown between them since was insurmountable.

Hettie resented that he seemed to be supremely unbothered by what they had shared. But that, she supposed, was the benefit of being more experienced in carnal matters. Perhaps if she'd had a truer marriage, something where things had progressed in the normal way, then she might not have been so uncertain of how to behave in their very unusual situation. But then again, there was nothing about their situation that anyone could even hope to prepare themselves for.

"Did you hear me? Wait here!" he snapped.

Her jaw firming with anger and her lips twisting in mutiny, she wanted very much to tell him to go to the devil—that she was more than capable of finding her own way home. But that was a lie, and they both knew it. Her best chance of ever returning safely to the life that she had just been plucked from was to put her trust, limited as it was, in the man at her side.

"Yes, I heard you." With that, she moved toward a stack of crates near the end of an alleyway. Concealing herself behind them as much as possible, she watched to see what her rescuer would do next. As far as she could tell, watching him walk out into the open, the man had no fear of anything. But then, unless someone saw them together and recognized her, his part in her escape was still entirely unknown. He had no reason to be afraid.

As he neared the gates, two men emerged from the shadows. She hadn't even been aware of their presence. Nonetheless, her heart leapt to her throat as they approached Joss. *Mr. Ettinger.* She could not afford to think of him so intimately. Never again.

He exchanged words with one of the gentlemen as the other crept up behind him. But she needn't have worried for him. He had clearly anticipated the move. At nearly the last second, he grasped the other man by the throat and spun him around so that the club brandished by his compatriot struck him instead. That man sank to the ground, leaving only one for him to fend off. Having struck down his friend, the second man apparently had a change of heart. He dropped the club and ran off, disappearing between dilapidated buildings.

JOSS TURNED BACK to where Hettie was concealed. "Come on. We don't have much time. He'll be coming back with reinforcements. They guard the gates—normally, it's to keep others out. Today, they've been instructed to keep everyone in. I can only assume that your abductors have paid them handsomely to do so."

He scanned the streets and alleys, watching for any sign of the guard or his colleagues, as Hettie extricated herself from the stacked barrels and crates. They were yards still from the entrance and the relative safety to be had on the other side of it.

By the time she'd reached him, he could see a group of rough-looking men heading in their direction. They'd emerged from one of the abandoned warehouses that lined the street. Joss didn't wait. He scooped her up, tossing her over his shoulder and ignoring the pain it caused him. He sprinted toward the freedom that awaited them through those gates.

With shouts and curses ringing behind them, he ran for all he was worth. When he breached the stone gates that marked the boundary of the Mint, his lungs were burning and his shoulder was on fire. And a bevy of men—men he recognized—stepped forward. The Hound's men had come to their aid.

"Mr. Ettinger, sir," one of them said. "We've got a cart just over there. We're to take you and the lady to Mrs. Blaylock's home."

"Take her to Mrs. Blaylock's. I'll make my own way to the club to meet the Hound."

The man flushed. "He's with Mrs. Blaylock, sir. And I don't think he'll be leaving there anytime soon."

Joss cursed. Of course. She was a menace just like her sister. Neither one of them would give a man a moment's peace. "Fine. Bring the cart this way. Lady Ernsdale's feet have taken enough abuse during our escape."

The horse-drawn cart was moved to where they stood, and Joss reached for her to help her into it. She jerked away from him and instead allowed one of the other men to aid her. That she'd place her trust in a common criminal over him was both telling and deserved. Muttering a curse under his breath, he climbed up as well, making it a point not to touch her. His hands clenched into fists at his sides as he was fairly certain that he'd never touch her again.

Chapter Seven

A s THE SMALL cart rumbled over the cobbled streets of Mayfair, Hettie felt as if there was an insurmountable chasm between herself and Joss Ettinger. As there should be, she thought. It was clearly what he had wanted. Whatever his reasons, he'd decided that their intimate interlude together should have no significance, and pride would not let her argue the point.

When at long last the cart halted before her sister's home, she allowed one of the men who'd flanked it—some on horseback and others on foot—to help her down. As her feet touched the stones, she winced. She'd been off of them just long enough to forget how badly it hurt to put all of her weight on them. There were dozens of small cuts and bruises from running through the dirty streets and stepping on heaven knew what. None of them were too deep or severe, but that didn't make them free of pain.

As she climbed the steps and entered the sparklingly clean foyer, Mrs. Ivers, her sister's housekeeper, let out a sharp cry. "Heaven be praised! They've brought you home!"

Within seconds, the door to the small sitting room flew open and Honoria appeared in the doorway. With her hair wild and her clothing rumpled, she looked a mess. Well, a mess for Honoria, who never had a single hair out of place. Her wonderfully organized and fastidious sister wasn't the sort to appear in public without everything being just so. But she was a welcome and beautiful sight.

Honoria took another step forward and her expression shifted. Hettie sighed.

"It was the river," she explained, referencing the dank smell that accompanied her. "I'm not even certain it could be classified as water given the degree of filth it contains."

"Mrs. Ivers, have a bath run for my sister, please, and have one of the maids get her something of mine to wear," Honoria requested. Even then, she didn't stop. Instead, she kept moving forward until she wrapped her arms about Hettie.

More moved than she cared to admit and afraid of becoming an overly emotional wreck, Henrietta protested, "I'll make you smell, too!"

"I don't care," Honoria insisted. But she wrinkled her nose a bit. "Well, I care. But not enough to let go of you. Not just yet. I've never been so afraid in all my life."

That made two of them, Henrietta thought. And speaking of fear brought another one to mind. "Where is my husband?"

"He's at his home . . . and you will stay here. This will be your home going forward," Honoria answered with steel in her voice. "Now, let's get you upstairs. We'll get you bathed, we'll get you some clean clothes, and then we'll sort it all out."

Honoria stepped back, and Hettie knew the moment she had seen Mr. Ettinger. Honoria left her side and walked toward him. Much to his chagrin, no doubt, her sister grabbed him in a tight embrace. Honoria said something to him, the words pitched so low that Hettie had no hope of hearing them. But she could tell from his expression that whatever it was had left him very uncomfortable. His cheeks flushed with color, and he was so stiff and obviously discomfited by the exchange.

Joss HAD NO idea what to do. He had river mud dried on every inch of him; his clothes were caked with it. And Mrs. Honoria Blaylock, a woman who was never anything less than perfectly tidy, had just wrapped her arms about him and murmured her heartfelt thanks for something that she ought not have had to ask for to begin with—someone to save her sister.

"You do not have to thank me. It's my job," he answered. The words came out stiff and somewhat sharp.

She stepped back from him, a smile on her face that gave her the beatific expression of a madonna. "I do have to thank you. Whether it's your job or not, I am grateful. And if there is ever anything I can do for you, Mr. Ettinger, you have but to ask. It's yours."

No wonder the Hound felt she needed looking after. "That's a dangerous sort of promise."

Honoria nodded. "Yes. That's a testament to just how important it is to me . . . how important she is to me. And now, you are as well. You are no stranger here. You were family already to Mr. Carrow, and now you are family to me."

Unable to answer, he simply nodded and turned on his heel to leave. It wasn't a question that he would be followed.

"What the devil has gotten into you?" Vincent demanded as soon as they'd cleared the front door.

The details of the night—and the morning—were not something he ever intended to share with his friend and employer. "It was a long night, and I spent half of it freezing my bollocks off in the sewer that is the Neckinger River. The remainder of it was spent trying to avoid all the people who wanted to kill us and trying to keep *her ladyship* from freezing to death."

The Hound's eyes narrowed with suspicion. "How did you manage that? Keeping her warm, that is."

Joss shrugged. He had no intention of answering such a question. And he didn't think it was any of the other man's business. What had happened was between him and Hettie, and should it ever arise, her bloody husband. "Lady Marchebanks' bolt hole in the old warehouse. No one else has yet discovered it, and the box stove and furnishings, as well as the blankets, remain relatively untouched."

"Mm-hm. I know the quickest and most effective way to warm a person who is half-frozen, Joss. It's not a fucking blanket, either."

He bristled visibly in response, his shoulders drawing back and his jaw firming. Challengingly, he fired back, "She's home, isn't she? I found her. You've got the ones responsible for the deaths and for her abduction now."

"In theory. Did you—" he broke off. Beginning again and clearly striving for patience, the Hound said, "Prior to this abduction scheme, Lady Ernsdale was a virgin. It's not common knowledge, but it is a very important fact as she plans to seek an annulment from her shite husband."

Dread. That was the only word that could adequately describe how he felt.

The Hound continued, "But if she's no longer chaste, if her virginity cannot be proven, then she'll have no grounds for it. And you know that bastard will not simply accept it quietly!"

Joss shoved his hands angrily into his pockets. He was mad at her. He was mad at himself. He was furious with goddamn Ernsdale for even existing, much less making her life more difficult. "Whether or not the lady is a virgin is something you'll have to take up with her. My bit in all of it is done. And now, I'm going home. You'll be getting my bill soon enough. My very, very hefty bill!"

Joss turned and stalked away. He knew the Hound was watching his every step, but it didn't matter. What had been done could not be undone, and there was no fixing the muddle they'd made of it all. Why hadn't she told him? Why would she take such a risk knowing what was at stake? Because she hadn't been thinking, of course. Because she'd been through something traumatic, and like it would for anyone else, the rush of adrenaline and the need to in some way affirm that she yet lived had superseded all common sense. And whether he wished to admit it or not, he'd taken advantage of that because it aligned with his own purposes. Because it had given him what he wanted. In his own way, he was as bad as Ernsdale and her father. That sentiment did not sit well with him at all.

"Bloody hell," he muttered. "Bloody everlasting hell."

Chapter Eight

Hettie had scrubbed at the washstand as best she could before getting into the tub. After all, she'd hardly be able to get clean if the water was thoroughly polluted by whatever dried muck from the river remained. She had just stepped into the tub, sinking down in the blissfully hot and perfectly perfumed water, when she heard the door open. There was the sound of scurrying footfalls and then her sister's crisp stride. The servants had been sent away, and only Honoria remained with her.

Opening one eye, Hettie looked over at her sister, who stared at her with concern. "What?"

"I won't ask questions. You will tell me what you wish for me to know," Honoria replied in that calm and reasonable tone.

"Oh, I hate it when you do that!" Hettie said with exasperation.

"Do what?" Honoria asked innocently.

"When you sound all saintlike and patient. Ask, Honoria. Just ask."

Honoria watched her for a moment, then gave a curt nod. "Fine. Did you have an intimate encounter with Mr. Ettinger?"

Hettie tensed. She'd told her to ask, but that was far more direct than she'd anticipated. "Define intimate?"

Honoria shook her head. "I do not believe that is necessary. There is only one thing that can create the sort of tension between two people that I recognized between you and the investigator today. I recognize it because I have recently experienced it myself."

Hettie sat up, water sloshing over the side of the tub. "Mr. Carrow?"

"He's asked me to marry him," Honoria said. "And I've accepted. There will be . . . ramifications."

"There always are," Hettie said softly. "Can you live with them?"

"Yes. Can you? This will complicate your desire for an annulment. I'm certain that Vincent can help, but it will be difficult."

"I'm not going to get the annulment," Hettie declared decisively. "I have earned this title. I have paid for it with more blood and misery than I care to think of. I will enjoy the position that title affords me . . . and the degree of protection that it will also extend to you. And like all young wives with wretched old husbands, I shall simply wait patiently for his dissipated life to take its final toll."

Honoria's eyes widened with shock and no small amount of horror. "Hettie, you cannot! The man is detestable. He fully intended to let them kill you rather than part with the ransom. Such a man—I cannot accept that you will be tied to him in such a way."

Hettie smiled. "Don't you see, Honoria? His actions have given me power. I know the most dishonorable secrets that he holds—his impotence, his greed, his willingness to sacrifice me for the sake of coin. And, if need be, I shall invoke the name of my new brother-in-law. I've little doubt that Arthur fears him enough to restrain his temper where I am concerned. So, I will stay here long enough to recover, and when I am at my best once more, I shall return home and take the reins of my household. And it is mine. Because I have paid for it with money, blood, and very bitter tears. He doesn't own me now. I own him."

Her sister's silence prompted Hettie to once more open her

eyes. She could see the concern etched on Honoria's face. "I understand him, Honoria. I do. There is nothing he fears so much as public ridicule, and between what I know of him and your betrothed's connections, he has no hope of keeping his secrets unless I choose to let him. Trust me."

"I do trust you. Implicitly. But I worry what this will do to you . . . not physically, but you have always had a tender heart. To be this cold and calculating is not in your nature."

Hettie sighed. "My nature has altered to accommodate the life our father sold me into. Do not fear for me, sister. I will be fine. Whatever the outcome, I will be fine."

Honoria didn't argue the point further. Likely because she recognized that Hettie's mind was set and there was no changing it. In some regards, they were very much alike. Their obstinance was certainly a point of similarity.

HONORIA LEFT HER sister in the tub, hair freshly washed and skin glowing from the vigorous scrubbing it had received. The maids would see her out of it and dressed for bed. Mrs. Ivers would see that Hettie's feet and other injuries were taken care of. Her greatest concerns had little to do with her sister's physical wellbeing at that moment. Honoria was more worried for the sake of her sister's tender heart.

She found Vincent in the breakfast room. Mrs. Ivers was feeding him along with several of his men, all of them served with heaping plates of bread, cheese, sausages, and hearty pudding. "I see Mrs. Ivers is taking very good care of you."

Vincent looked up at her, his eyes seeing far more than she likely would wish for him to. "Indeed, she is. But alas, I fear I cannot eat another bite. Delicious as it is, I am quite full. Come to the sitting room with me, Mrs. Blaylock; there is something I would discuss with you."

"Yes, of course. I daresay our concerns are in alignment," she concurred and exited the breakfast room with his booted footsteps echoing behind her. When they'd reached the sitting room, she turned to him. "They are lovers."

"I suspected as much," he conceded softly. "But we are in no position to take the moral high ground, Honoria. They are both adults. And she knew the potential costs of such an action even when he did not."

"I know. I do not blame him. I do not blame her," she said, wringing her hands. "It's more about the decision that she has made to remain with Ernsdale. She thinks that between your knowledge of his misdeeds and hers, he can be held in check."

"He can to a degree," Vincent agreed. "But not forever. The man consumes spirits as most of us consume air. Eventually, drink and temper will win out over his fear."

"I know," Honoria said. "I know. Will you help her?"

"You need never ask for such a thing. I will always do what is required to see to your happiness. I will protect Henrietta to the best of my ability . . . but you understand better than anyone, what happens behind closed doors between a husband and wife cannot always be easy to discern."

Honoria moved toward him, resting her head against his chest and taking comfort in the strength and warmth of him. "I do know. And so does Hettie. I cannot understand why she feels she must do this. Not when another option has been made available to her. She means to simply wait for him to die."

"Perhaps she knows something of his condition that the rest of us do not," he mused. "He is not a man of robust health, that is certain. But whether he is hovering at the brink of death, I cannot say."

"Will it send me to Hell to pray that is so?"

"If that's all it takes to send a person to Hell, my darling, it will be filled to overflowing. Now, it's been a very long night. And I want nothing more than to take you to bed."

"I'm exhausted," she admitted. "But I haven't a hope of sleeping."

"I want to take you to bed, Honoria. Sleeping was never part of the equation."

Her lips quirked into a sly smile. "Then by all means, Mr. Carrow, please escort me to my chamber."

Chapter Nine

Four weeks later

"I SEE THAT you have finally decided to return home. I thought I'd need to seek a divorce on the grounds of abandonment. Or perhaps bring suit against your sister and her . . . *paramour* . . . for alienation of affection."

Hettie looked down at her gloved hands. She didn't cower. She didn't apologize or try to placate him. The silence grew, stretching between them as she tugged the leather gloves off, one finger at a time. Slowly. As if there was no rush to do anything.

"There is no affection for them to alienate," she finally said. "You despise me . . . but not nearly so much as I despise you."

His face purpled with rage. "You will not speak to me—"

"I will," she said, her voice calm, cold, and commanding. "I am through being tormented by you. You will not strike me. You will not harangue me. You will not browbeat and belittle me. Because if you do, I shall tell everyone the awful truth."

"What truth is that?"

"That you are a drunken sot, riddled with pox, unable to perform your husbandly duties, and you were perfectly willing to let my abductors murder me to save you the embarrassment that would have ensued when I sought an annulment . . . and before you think to bully me into submission, you should know that there is a new footman in the house right now. An associate of Mr. Carrow's. I have but to shout, and he will come to my aid. And if you think to dismiss him, know that Mr. Carrow will not be at all pleased."

"You mean to let that criminal taint our home?"

At that, Hettie laughed. "This home is already tainted. It's tainted with your wickedness and dissipation. It's tainted with my bitterness and disillusionment. I have a proposition for you, Arthur. And if you have an iota of good sense, you will accept. I will continue to live here with you. In public, I will be a dutiful and loving wife—and you will be a loving and devoted husband. In private, we shall do our best to avoid one another at all costs. I will stay out of your way, and you will stay well out of mine. In exchange, you get my silence. And you get Mr. Carrow's silence and continued goodwill."

"And what do you get out of this? Other than not having to feel the weight of my hand for being an insolent baggage?"

"I get to be Lady Ernsdale. I get to maintain my position in society and to preserve what dignity I still possess. Take the offer, Arthur. Neither of us wishes to have our names further dragged through the mud," Hettie said reasonably. "We will both sleep in this house, but in terms of having a marriage, or any sort of interaction with one another—it's just unnecessary."

He stared at her for a long moment, his lip curled in a sneer. "Fine. Do what you will. So will I. But your sister and her husband will not enter this house. They will not darken my door. Is that understood?"

"Perfectly, Arthur. I daresay they will be relieved to know they are not welcomed by you. Should I feel the need to see my sister, I will simply visit with her in her own home. And while we're on the subject of relatives: Simon. Simon will not be permitted here again."

Arthur's face darkened. "Simon? What the devil do you care if he comes around?"

"I simply don't like him," Hettie answered. "He walks

through this house as if it were already his, as if everything in it somehow belongs to him already. I can't believe I'm more offended by his behavior than you are!"

Arthur's temper settled then. "He's a presumptuous arse. Never did like the boy. It will be no great loss not to have him toadying to me while sizing up his inheritance."

"Excellent. Then we have an agreement. We simply avoid one another as much as possible. Good day, Arthur. I'm going upstairs to take care of some correspondence." With that, Hettie sailed out of the drawing room and made her way up the stairs.

It wasn't until she was inside her own room that she finally drew a breath. Leaning back against the door, she felt positively weak. She'd done it. She'd faced him down, made her bargain, and had the means within the household to enforce it. Arthur would not dare to risk incurring Vincent's wrath again.

Moments later, Foster entered along with the footman, who carried her bags. She was in a house filled with servants whose only loyalty was to the man she'd married. Those two were the only allies she possessed.

"Well, we're in it now, for better or worse," Hettie mused.

"You were very brave, m'lady," Foster said.

The footman, a youngish man with sandy hair and a broad, handsome face grinned. "Indeed, my lady. It was a joy to see. Don't much care for his lordship."

No. No one did. Arthur had lived his whole life alienating others. "Thank you both. I know returning to this house is the last thing you wished to do, Foster. And as for you, James, thank you. Thank you for agreeing to reside in his miserable place to preserve my safety. I am well aware of what you are sacrificing."

James cast his adoring gaze on her maid. "It's not so much a sacrifice. I'm happy to be here for you both."

Well, that was an interesting development, Hettie thought. At least someone's romantic interests seemed to be going well.

SIMON DAGLIESH STOOD in the center of his ransacked rooms at the Albany and felt a frisson of fear snaking up his spine. He was not alone in the rooms. Two men stood in the shadowy recesses while a third man, large and imposing, was seated on the one upright piece of furniture that remained.

"Mr. Dagliesh . . . you have been a very difficult man to track down," Ardmore said. "One might think you were trying to avoid me."

"I've had many obligations, sir. I would never purposely attempt to avoid you," Simon said, his tone falsely obsequious.

Ardmore drummed his fingers on the tabletop. It was the only sound in the room, and it seemed to stretch on endlessly as he weighed the pitifully thin excuse that had just been lobbed his way. At long last, his fingers stilled and he spoke. "Ah, well that is a relief. One might have thought it had something to do with the truly extraordinary amount of money that you owe me. You do remember that you owe me money, don't you, Mr. Dagliesh?"

"Certainly, I remember. And I am making great inroads into securing the means to repay you in full," Simon replied.

"That is an excellent bit of news. But I'm afraid I require more than simply your word. I need to be convinced of your sincerity," Ardmore continued. And then he raised his hand, signaling to the two men in the shadows to step forward.

They were, in a word, bruisers. They were massive, and from their scarred knuckles, their profession was quite obvious. And Simon knew that he was going to have to do something drastic. They'd kill him otherwise. Or simply make him pray for death.

The first one grabbed him by the front of his shirt, shaking him not unlike a rag doll. When he crumpled to the floor, the second man stepped forward and kicked him in the ribs with booted feet. Any attempt to get up from the floor was met with slaps or punches. Only when he lay there perfectly still, completely submissive, did they halt.

"So unpleasant," Ardmore said. "It brings me no pleasure to see you punished so. If only, Simon, there was some way you could return my investment so that I would not have to do these terrible things to you."

One of Ardmore's goons reached for him again, and Simon pleaded. "No. No more. I beg of you. There is a way. There is a way!"

Ardmore stayed his henchman with a flick of his wrist. "I'm listening, Simon."

"I will inherit everything from my uncle when he dies," Simon rushed out quickly.

"When," Ardmore said. "When he dies. But I don't know when that will be. I could well shuffle off into the great beyond before he does. No. I need something more definite than that."

"And you'll get it. I do not mean to wait around for natural causes to solve this problem," Simon explained. "But it's only been two weeks since his wife's abduction and rescue . . . to act against him now? There is too much attention on both my uncle and Lady Ernsdale. Once the gossip has died down, then my uncle will meet with some sort of accident or tragic event that will result in his death."

Ardmore raised his hand once more, and the two men stepped back, giving Simon enough space to actually draw breath. They obeyed him like trained hounds. It was terrifying.

"Two months. That should be an adequate amount of time for interest in your uncle and his marital woes to have died down. Two months, and you will have everything you owe me, plus ten percent interest, delivered on a silver platter . . . or you'll be begging for mercy as your very blood drains from your body. Do you understand, Mr. Dagliesh? No more reprieves. No more concessions or extensions. This is your last chance."

Simon watched as Ardmore rose and exited his chamber. The two men followed. Even when he was alone, he did not immediately move to get off the floor. He wasn't certain he'd be able to, not without casting up his accounts. So he lay there, contemplating how he might manage to end his uncle's miserable life. There was no question he'd do it. His very survival depended upon it.

Chapter Ten

HETTIE WAS SEATED in Honoria's drawing room. Spread out on the table before them were ledgers and correspondence as they tackled their various charitable obligations. It had been two weeks since she'd returned to Arthur's home, but she'd found herself spending several afternoons each week with her sister. It was to the point where Hettie feared she was becoming a burden. After all, Honoria and Mr. Carrow were newly married. They intended to leave London soon to visit his country estate. What would she do when there was no safe harbor for her?

Of course, she knew that provisions would be made and they were only going to be gone for a week. Vincent would do what was necessary to ensure her continued safety until their return. But it wasn't that which she feared. It was the loneliness that threatened to engulf her. And that was not her sister's burden to carry. If anyone deserved to focus only on their own happiness for a time, it was certainly Honoria.

"The hospital is requesting additional funding," Hettie said, reviewing the last letter. "Unfortunately, we have exhausted every potential donor. But perhaps we could do some sort of event? An auction or a conscripted party? Though, I daresay we are neither of us in a position to host such a thing. Is there someone else we could enlist to do so?"

Honoria sighed. "I don't know. Possibly. I'll have to give it some thought and send out some inquiries."

"I'll do the same."

"Hettie, are you . . . are you well?"

Hettie met her sister's concerned gaze. "I'm perfectly fine, Honoria. Why do you ask?"

"You do not seem quite yourself. You have been so quiet and subdued. I understand, of course, that you went through something quite traumatic, and I cannot imagine that it would not have some lingering effect. I worry that there is more to it, however. Perhaps more to do with Mr. Ettinger than with your abduction . . . or is it Ernsdale? Is he making your life there a misery?"

Shaking her head, Hettie took her sister's hand. "You are very sweet to worry after me so. But no, strangely enough, Arthur and I have reached a truce of sorts. I stay out of his way, and he stays out of mine. Occasionally we dine together, speaking the bare minimum of words to one another, and then we go our separate ways. We have settled into a society marriage . . . perfect from the outside but cold and lonely within. Not that I'd want anything else with Arthur."

"But you do want more for yourself," Honoria guessed. "Perhaps with a very large, broad-shouldered, handsome former Bow Street Runner of humble origins who has an overabundance of pride and stupidity?"

Hettie pursed her lips in displeasure. "Is it really so obvious? And I have no notion why I ought to still be mooning over him. It was one night. Only one."

"Yes, but one night where you saw one another both at your best and your worst. It complicates matters when you have a bond forged in fear and danger."

She wasn't wrong, Hettie thought. Her very survival, the very fact that she was still alive and well to have a conversation with her sister was due to Joss Ettinger. And despite his rejection of her that morning, she couldn't forget the way he'd looked at her in the darkness or the almost reverent way he'd touched her.

Those remembered pleasures were her only company at present. "Perhaps that is it. Over time, as I continue to heal and recover from all that I went through, that bond may become lessened. It certainly hasn't been an issue for him. I've neither heard from him nor seen him since. And it doesn't matter. I'm not free anyway, am I? At the end of the day, I'll still be Arthur's wife. Perhaps when he is gone, then I will find a man to love me the way your Vincent loves you."

"I want that for you. I didn't know how much I needed that until we found one another. And it isn't that I wasn't content or that I didn't feel like I had a purpose in life. But contentment is not happiness," Honoria said wistfully. "And you should have happiness."

Hettie felt those words reverberate within her. Honoria wasn't wrong. But wanting something to be did not make it so. Getting to her feet, she gathered her things. "We are becoming a maudlin mess. I should go before we both wind up in tears."

As she turned to exit, the drawing room doors opened and Vincent walked in. But it was the man beside him who made her halt. Joss Ettinger stood there. Their gazes locked, and Hettie would swear that the very air crackled between them.

"Lady Ernsdale," he said, his tone stiff and cold. "You are looking well."

Hettie forced a polite smile to her lips. "Thank you, Mr. Ettinger. I am well. Quite well. Good day." With a nod to Vincent and to her sister, she then simply walked out as she completely ignored the fact that she could not properly expand her lungs and that her knees were shaking.

JOSS WATCHED HER walk out, and it took everything he had in him not to go after her. He wanted to chase her down, pull her into his arms and kiss her till they were both utterly senseless with it.

But he had no idea how such an advance would be welcomed. Likely, it would not. He'd made his choice, for better or worse, and his cold treatment of her would not be easily forgiven. Hettie was a woman with a great deal of pride. It was one of the many things he admired about her.

"Excuse me," Honoria said. "I'm going to see my sister off." Then she sailed from the room, leaving him alone with the Hound.

"Go after her," Vincent urged him quietly. "It's patently obvious that you are both miserable."

"Why?" Joss asked. She'd still be married to a worthless shite, and he'd still be poor as a church mouse and working for a living. "There's no way it ends well. We are both imprisoned by our current stations in life. I'm too poor, and she's too married."

"It isn't a real marriage, a fact of which you are very well aware. Besides, he's old. He's sick. And he won't live forever."

"Maybe not. But despite any lapses in judgement on my part, I'm not the type to make a cuckold of a man, even if he is a son of a bitch," Joss replied. "Leave it alone. I don't meddle in your affairs of the heart. I'll thank you to stay the hell out of mine."

"Is it?" Vincent asked.

"It is what?" Joss fired back, confounded by the whole conversation.

"An affair of the heart?"

Realizing he'd said too much, revealed too much, Joss shrugged. "It's not anything. Not anything at all. Now tell me why the hell it was so urgent that I come here."

"I need you to take over for me. Just for a week while we are away in the country. And only at the club. Honoria and I mean to go to the countryside for an extended stay eventually, but we need to take the measure of the house first, see what needs to be done to make it fully habitable."

"When do you intend to leave the city for good?" Joss asked. He was ambivalent about it. Vincent was his friend. The Hound was his employer. Sometimes separating the two was very difficult.

"I think sooner rather than later. As for the club, I need someone there I can trust."

"You have Stavers," Joss protested.

"Yes, but he can't very well do it all, can he? I need you, Joss. I need you to manage things for me, and if you do, you will be very well compensated."

"How well compensated?"

"Two hundred pounds?"

"Five."

The Hound stared at him for a moment, then shook his head. "Fine. Five. And while you're at it, you can consider whether or not you'd like to do it permanently."

"I'm not a gamester, Vincent. I'm a private inquiry agent."

"A poor one. You wouldn't be poor then, I'd make you a partner. Me, you, Stavers. Everything would be split in thirds."

It was tempting. Very tempting. "I'll think about it. But I'm not a criminal."

"A gaming hell isn't criminal either, not when it's well run and honest. Mine always has been. My hands are plenty dirty, but that establishment is quite clean."

"I'll think about it," Joss repeated. And he would. Because the financial freedom that offered him would put him on better footing. But he was likely just pissing in the wind. He could be rich as Croesus, and Hettie would still be married to another, and even if widowed, far beyond his reach.

Chapter Eleven

HETTIE'S HANDS WERE still trembling by the time she reached her own home. It had been bound to happen, of course. Given how close she was to her sister and his association with the man her sister was now married to, their running into one another at some point had been inevitable. Knowing it would happen and being fully prepared for the jolt of seeing him—well, those were very different things.

She resented him. She resented that he was so stoic and so removed from the situation. Perhaps it did bother him to see her, but one would certainly never know it to look at him. His expression had remained inscrutable, and his polite tone had conveyed nothing of his emotional state. Did he have an emotional state?

It was hard to balance the two sides of him she had seen. When he'd rescued her initially, he'd been patient. He'd been comforting and solid and had offered her—what had he offered her? Nothing. Not really. But she had presumed to believe he had some regard for her. In the end, with his cold dismissal after their intimate encounter, she didn't know who he truly was. Was he the kind man who'd plucked her from the water or the cold-hearted cad who cared not a whit for anyone's feelings?

The footman, James, employed by Vincent, helped her down from the carriage. He acted as her guard of sorts, keeping her safe from threats both inside the home and out. His presence was a comfort to her, as it deterred any unpleasantness from Arthur. But as she climbed the steps to the front door, she heard shouting from within.

Then the door flew open and Simon appeared directly in front of her, his face twisted into an expression of complete fury.

"You are responsible," he snapped. "Barred from my own uncle's home! A home that, since you are worthless as a woman and cannot even provide him an heir, will one day be mine!"

"Yes," she said. "I have asked that you not be given entry to my home. And Arthur has agreed. All the servants have been informed that you are not welcome here."

"What reason could you have?"

"You drink and gamble so recklessly that any association with you is unwise. And others may not realize that you were thick as thieves with the Walpoles, but I know. *I know.* And perhaps I cannot prove that you aided them, but I will not be dissuaded from believing it. You should leave, Simon. You're creating a scene."

He pushed past her, nearly knocking her back down the steps. Had James not been behind her to catch her, she could only imagine that she would have been gravely injured by such a fall on the hard stones. She also could not imagine that such injury had not been Simon's intention all along.

When he was gone, she smoothed her skirts and then stepped through the open door into the foyer. Arthur's face was all but purple with rage, and for the first time since their marriage she knew beyond question that it was not directed at her.

"Insolent puppy!" He spat. "How dare he speak to me the way he did! If I could, I'd disown him entirely."

As it stood, he would only inherit the title and a very small amount of money to maintain his estate. Everything else would revert to her when Arthur died. "I find that I am very tired after that ugly scene, Arthur. Excuse me as I retire for a rest."

He said nothing, just continued fuming and griping to the

empty entry hall about his nephew's worthlessness. Climbing the stairs, Hettie entered her room and closed the door behind her. Then she leaned back against the cool wood and tried to still the tremors that wracked her.

Simon's words rang in her mind. *Worthless as a woman. Unable to provide an heir.* He didn't know that his uncle's impotence was the cause. More so, Hettie had the terrible realization that she could very much provide an heir, it just wouldn't be an heir of Arthur's blood.

It had been nearly six weeks since Mr. Ettinger had rescued her. Six weeks and her courses had not come.

"Oh, dear sweet heaven," she whispered.

Could it be?

It was surely the only explanation. And it was about to make her life very, very complicated.

⇥⟫⟪⇤

SIMON DIDN'T RETURN to the Albany. He was half afraid to. What if Ardmore was waiting for him again? The deadline the money-lender had given him was fast approaching, and he was no closer to snatching the title and fortune from his uncle's dying grasp than he had been when he'd made the foolish promise.

There would be no further extensions. There would be no more grace. And, terrifyingly, Simon knew that death might be preferable to whatever they would do to him.

If he couldn't get to his uncle in his home, then he'd just have to get to him elsewhere. Because not getting to him, not ending the old bastard's miserable life, was no longer an option. And he might take it upon himself to get rid of Lady Ernsdale, as well. If for no other reason than she had insulted him so terribly. As if she had the right to bar him from a house that would one day be his!

"That bitch will pay, and so will Arthur," he murmured to himself.

He needed a plan. A strategy. And since he couldn't watch his uncle's movements twenty-four hours a day, then he would need to enlist some help. There were any number of places in the city where such an accomplice might be obtained. One in particular was The Cock & Crow. A dockside tavern, dark and seedy, it was the sort of place where one's name and face were forgotten as soon as they left. Given that he was about to embroil himself in a conspiracy for murder, being forgettable was vital to his continued existence.

Chapter Twelve

Two weeks later

HETTIE STARED AT the food on her plate as if it might actually try to bite her. It had been days since she'd eaten anything of consequence. Days enough for her to come to terms with the shocking realization that had come upon her only weeks earlier. She was with child. One indiscretion. One gloriously passionate moment followed by so much regret, and now she faced the ultimate consequence from such an encounter.

How long would it be before one of the servants told Arthur that she had not bled? How long would it be before he demanded to know who the father of her child was? Would he denounce her? Would he proclaim the child a bastard and cast her off? It was certainly possible. And regardless of how reprehensible his behavior had been from the very outset of their marriage, her one sin, in the eye of both society and the law, would far surpass the plethora of his.

She would have to tell Honoria the truth, and Vincent. He could not protect her when he did not know what she required protection from. But would he tell *Mr. Ettinger*? And she forced herself to think of him thusly. As Mr. Ettinger. Thinking of him as Joss allowed the memories of their night together to creep in. And those memories were a weakness she could ill afford.

Would Vincent tell him? Likely, she supposed. If positions were reversed, she would. And he did have some entitlement to the knowledge, regardless of what he chose to do with it. But she wasn't ready to face it. Not just yet.

"The duck is not to your liking?" Arthur asked. "Perhaps we should hire some French chef . . . more fashionable than our English cooks. Can't abide their rich sauces. Frogs and snails. Slimy things." The last was accompanied by a shudder.

Hettie had to place her hand over her mouth to keep from retching. It wasn't even Arthur's fault. In his own way, since her abduction and subsequent rescue, he'd been at least a tolerable husband. They'd struck their bargain, and he was adhering to it. He left her alone most of the time. They only ever saw one another for dinner or social engagements that they were both required to attend. Those were few and far between. Given the scandal of her abduction and Honoria's marriage to the veritable king of London's criminal underbelly, they were no longer high on anyone's list of exalted guests.

"Arthur, my head is positively splitting," she said, "Would it be too terribly difficult to just eat this meal in silence?"

He bristled at the question. Shoving his chair back from the table, he rose and tossed his serviette onto the linen table cover. "Fine. You wish to enjoy your meal in silence, I will simply take my leave of you . . . I liked you better before."

"You didn't like me at all before," she pointed out.

"And less so now," he countered before stalking out of the dining room. Moments later, the front door slammed. He would go to his club or to one of the gaming hells he frequented. He would drink and lose heavily and return home in a foul mood, likely the following morning. But he'd stay far from her, and that was all she could ask for.

Hettie pushed her plate away from her, unable to bear the sight of it any longer, and signaled for a footman to take it away. When the food had been removed, she rose and retreated to the small morning room which she'd taken as her own personal respite. It was the least objectionable room in the house, likely because it had never been redecorated by Arthur's first wife. Apparently, the previous Lady Ernsdale's taste had been atrocious. Everything in the house was fussy and overdone—too ornate, too gilded, too everything, really. But that room, with settees and chairs upholstered in a soft blue offset against darkly stained wood and a cream and blue carpet, offered up a peaceful spot in an otherwise often chaotic home. And she needed a bit of peace. Desperately.

Taking a seat at the small writing desk near the window, she began to pen a letter to her sister. She hated to do it, as they'd only just returned to town and were likely exhausted from their journey. But she'd never needed her sister's counsel more.

ARTHUR DAGLIESH, LORD Ernsdale, muttered to himself as he strode down the dimly lit street toward his favorite gaming hell. Well, not favorite, really. He was no longer permitted entry at his favorite. There had been an unfortunate disagreement and nasty allegations of cheating. A duel had only narrowly been avoided. Since then, he was no longer welcome in that lovely establishment. The same could be said for any number of others. It was getting to the point where he was running out of places where he was welcome. Of course, none of that had been aided by his wife's sister marrying into the criminal class. Now, due to his unfortunate and quite involuntary association with the Hound of Whitehall, he was looked on as suspect by many.

Sympathy should have been with him, he thought bitterly. After all, following Henrietta's abduction and rescue, it was quite clear that he was the injured party. What man wanted a wife who may have been defiled by others? The truth of it was that he'd have been better off had they managed to kill her. Not that he cared one whit whether she lived or died beyond how it might benefit or bedevil him. If she had died, then he'd have access to the entirety of her fortune and not just the small bit that the trustees her father had named chose to dole out. It was galling that he'd only married the chit for money and discovered too late he'd only get his hands on it in piecemeal fashion.

The establishment he'd chosen for the evening's entertainment was only steps away. The Plum Pearl dealt primarily in cards and dice, but there were other avenues of entertainment in there, as well. In particular, there were hidden passages that allowed one to observe the bedchambers many of the "ladies" used to entertain their guests. Watching had always been his preferred pleasure, and many of those ladies specialized in very specific types of pleasure. His introduction into that world of bondage and restraints, the deprivation of pleasure to the point of agony, had been enlightening, to say the least. Was it any wonder that he couldn't feel any sort of excitement at the thought of bedding his frigid, virginal wife?

"Ernsdale?"

Arthur's steps faltered. But he didn't stop, nor did he turn. He wasn't a man who was well liked, and he knew it. There were many who would do him harm, and since this person was following him, rather than waiting to speak to him in the club or calling on him at home, it indicated that it was not someone whom he would want to deal with.

Picking up his pace, he had just reached the steps, one foot poised to push up when he felt it. One hand grabbed his shoulder, pulling him back. And then there was just a small sting, a slight prick of pain followed by a spreading coldness. Dropping his head, he saw the crimson stain spreading over the front of his waistcoat.

The blade had been so thin it was almost painless. It had slipped easily between his ribs. But then pain exploded when that sliver thin blade was turned, twisted brutally inside his chest, and then yanked free. His blood steamed in the cold air as it seeped out, the little puffs of white silhouetted by the gas lamp that burned beside the door of the establishment that would have offered him solace.

He stumbled, turning to face his attacker. But he never saw him. He never saw the man who had killed him because he was already gone, vanished into thin air. Another glance showed that the front of his waistcoat was now entirely saturated with blood. The deep crimson appeared almost black in the dim light.

The world was spinning, the darkness around him growing, creeping in ever closer. He fell, pitching forward into the street. He never heard the carriage wheels or the beating hoofs that approached. And before the first one had struck him, he had already breathed his last.

Chapter Thirteen

J OSS LEANED BACK against the cold bricks of the building and watched his quarry. The woman in question emerged from the pawnbroker's, patting her reticule as though she were inviting a robbery. When she was out of sight, he rose from his casual stance and fell in step behind her, at a distance, of course.

The young bride of a much older gentleman, she'd taken to selling off the gifts he lavished upon her. Two weeks earlier, she'd fired a bevy of household servants after accusing them of thievery—which might have gone without notice, had she not done the same thing months earlier. The gentleman might be aging, but he was hardly a fool. There had been little doubt in his mind that it was his wife who was pilfering her own jewels and bartering them. But he'd wanted to know why. And thus came the distasteful part of Joss' employment. Follow her, observe her. Report back that she was selling her jewels to either pay a blackmailer or support a lover. In his estimation, those were the only viable reasons for her surreptitious divestment of assets.

Near the end of the street, the woman climbed into a hack and made for her posh Brooke Street home. It was not difficult to follow on foot. Given the congestion of London's streets, it was more difficult not to get ahead of the carriage rather than to simply keep up. When the conveyance halted before the gates to Hyde Park, Joss took note. It was the wrong time of day for a lady to be in the park. The evening hours tended to cater to vices rather than promenades. If he intended to find out what she was about, he had to move quickly.

Crossing behind the carriage, he dodged traffic and the steaming evidence of horses' hearty diets. But he managed to catch up to her. And he was completely stunned by what he saw. It wasn't a lover she was meeting. It was a woman—very young, very pretty, and very heavily with child. He hadn't solved his mystery at all, but simply added another layer to it. He also had the sneaking suspicion that his client might not be the wronged party after all.

Not for the first time, Joss thought how much easier it had been to do his work when Vincent had been a more noticeable presence in town. The man had but to whisper and information flowed like a raging river. But then money and power had always had that effect.

Walking away from the woman and her secret meeting, he headed back the way he'd come. Perhaps the pawnbroker knew something. It was at least a place to start. He highly doubted that either his client or his client's wife would be in any way forthcoming.

He walked, lost in thought, as the crowd thickened around him. It was only then that he became aware of a commotion up ahead which had prompted the assembly of gawkers. In the distance, he could see a crowd gathered, watching from the sidewalks The wagon which held their rapt attention was one that he was all too familiar with. On the flat surface of the wagon's bed, a body was laid out and wrapped in sheeting. It wasn't as if the sight of a corpse being paraded through Mayfair truly shocked him. After all, murders happened every day in London. Most people just lived their lives blissfully unaware of the fact. It was the decided lack of outcry from those surveying the wagon which left him puzzled. There were no tears, no one appeared outraged. Half of them seemed somewhat bemused by it all.

When he neared the crowd, he saw a familiar face—a shop boy whom he had often paid well for information. "Thomas, who is under that shroud?"

"Lord Ernsdale, Inspector Ettinger, sir," the young man answered. "Cut down in cold blood on the street outside a gaming hell. Never seen so much blood!"

Joss felt as though his heart had fallen into his stomach with the same force as a rock falling from the top of a mountain. It left him reeling. "Ernsdale?"

"Aye, sir. Not been too long ago that there was another scandal . . . his lady wife abducted in broad daylight! Do you think they're connected?"

He sincerely hoped not. If they were, his efforts to avoid Hettie Dagliesh would be effectively at an end. Because regardless of what had passed between them, and what had not, he would not see her in danger.

"I don't know, Thomas. But I mean to find out. You hear anything and you let me know. Same arrangement as before."

The boy's eyebrows lifted. "But you're not with Bow Street no more!"

"No. But Lady Ernsdale's sister is now married to someone we both know . . . a certain Hound who would not want his sister-in-law to be in any sort of danger." Joss hedged around the real reason for his interest.

With his eyebrows now having climbed fully to his hairline, the boy nodded vigorously. "Oh, aye, Inspe—I mean, Mr. Ettinger, sir! I'll let you know the very minute I hear anything at all."

Joss watched the wagon roll on by, noting the blood that had seeped through the white linen. And a terrible thought occurred to him. Had she done it? Or hired someone to do so? If she had, he could hardly blame her, but others would not look so kindly on it. And if that terrible possibility had crossed his mind, others would begin to wonder, as well. Hettie faced more danger than just simply the potential threat of her husband's murderer. She might well be labeled a murderer herself. The law was unforgiving of any woman who dared rise up against a tyrannical man.

"Fuck," he muttered. "Bloody fucking hell."

HETTIE STARED AT the man before her with a kind of shock that defied reason. "I'm sorry. But . . . what did you say?"

"Your husband, madame, Arthur Dagliesh, Lord Ernsdale, is dead," Inspector Maurice Bates answered coolly.

Hettie rose. She wasn't sure why or even where she intended to go, but in the face of such news, it hardly seemed like she should simply sit calmly. Immediately, she realized the error of her decision. The room began to swim alarmingly, and her vision began to dim. Just as suddenly, she found herself once more plunked into the chair she'd recently vacated.

"Do not faint, madame. We haven't the time if we are to catch those responsible for your husband's demise."

"Responsible?" She parroted the inspector's word. "Are you suggesting that my husband's death was . . . it was murder?"

"Stating, Lady Ernsdale, without question," the investigator said, his tone very firm and his expression grim. "He was stabbed and left to bleed out into the street."

Hettie couldn't speak. It wasn't grief. Shock, yes? Most assuredly. While she certainly hated that he'd met such a terrible and violent end, she did not feel any grief at the prospect of his loss. In truth, lurking beneath the shock, relief was flooding through her. Relief and the promise of freedom. "Footpads? Was it a robbery?"

The investigator stared at her for a moment, his gaze assessing. "No, madame. As a general rule, footpads in Mayfair are a rare occurrence . . . and footpads do not typically stab a man in the back with a needle-like blade. It was a high quality rapier, well forged."

"Then you think he was intentionally targeted," she surmised.

"Indeed. And I must ask, Lady Ernsdale, if you have any notion who might want your husband dead." He looked up then, his gaze leveled on her with distinct hostility. "Other than you, of course."

He wasn't there to inform her of her husband's death at all, Hettie realized. He was there to gauge whether or not she was already aware of it. "I did not want my husband dead, inspector. My husband and I were not a love match, most assuredly. We certainly had our disagreements at times, but I had made my peace with our marriage, however it came to pass."

"Until you were abducted by ruffians and he refused to pay the ransom to get you back . . . or did you think I was unaware?"

Hettie shook her head. "No, inspector. To my great humiliation, everyone is aware of Arthur's miserly response to my abduction. Luckily, I was not dependent solely on him for my safe rescue. But I'm certain you know that, just as you know who was ultimately responsible for my rescue. Does *he* have any notion that you are standing in my parlor and accusing me of murder?"

"He does not . . . but then I don't answer to him, just like he don't answer to me. Not every Runner is in the Hound's pocket, madame, nor are we all cowed by the behemoth who worked for him."

There was an animosity there, Hettie thought. The inspector harbored a grudge. Against Vincent Carrow or against Joss Ettinger? It ultimately didn't matter. He would use her as a tool to wage war against a man who had very few weaknesses. It was a complicated situation and becoming more so by the minute.

"If there is nothing else, Inspector, I should like you to leave. I am very tired, and the news has been quite upsetting. I'll bid you good day, sir," Hettie said, uttering each word with icy politeness. "I will expect, that if there are further questions, they will be asked by someone else who does not share your bias. Whatever your past interactions are with my sister's husband, or those in his employ, they have no place in your investigation into the untimely death of my own husband."

Hettie rose from her seat and tugged at the bell pull near the door. "Milford will show you out," she added as the butler entered the room. Without waiting for them to depart, she sailed out of the room and made for her chambers upstairs.

Once inside her room, she leaned back against the door and let out a shaky breath. She was in a great deal of trouble. And the only way to get out of that trouble was to determine who was actually responsible for Arthur's death. She needed an investigator. A private inquiry agent whom she could trust.

One name came to mind, and though she might want desperately to dismiss it, she could not. She would need to enlist the aid of Mr. Ettinger.

Chapter Fourteen

J OSS FOUGHT BACK a yawn. It had been a sleepless night, consumed with thoughts of a certain woman who was now a widow. And her newly eligible status eliminated one obstacle, but certainly not all of them.

Looking around, he took stock. His office occupied one of the two rooms he had rented above an apothecary's shop in Cheapside. The shingle hanging outside read simply "Private Inquiries." Business was not booming, but he had more than enough to keep him busy and to keep the rent paid. And he was doing it without any aid from Vincent Carrow, a fact that he was quite proud of.

As he settled deeper into the creaking leather chair behind his desk, he perched his booted feet atop it and considered all the things he'd seen the previous evening. But nothing at the forefront of his mind had anything to do with his actual paying client and whatever it was that his pretty young wife was up to. No. On Joss's mind was the death of Lord Ernsdale, and more particularly, the widowed state of Henrietta Dagliesh.

Unbidden to his mind came the image of her—naked, her body gilded by the dim light of that simple box stove. It was a memory that tormented him often. And he strongly suspected that it would do so for the remainder of his days.

As if his thoughts had summoned her, the door to his office

opened, the small bell hanging above it tinkling lightly. Silhouetted in the doorway, wearing a green dress with a matching pelisse and bonnet, she looked every inch the wealthy and titled lady that she was.

"No," he said. The word came out immediately and without thought. It hung in the air for a moment and then settled over them like a thick fog, unpleasant and unwelcome.

"No? You do not even know why I am here," she said, ignoring his protest and stepping into his office regardless. The door closed behind her with a kind of finality that told him she had no intention of leaving until she'd said her piece. Part of him was grateful for her tenacity. She wasn't for the likes of him, no matter how much he might have wished otherwise. But having a moment longer just to look at her—to drink in the sight of her—soothed his soul.

Clearing his throat and shaking his head to banish such asinine romantic notions, he said with cold detachment, "Fine. Tell me why you're here so that I can give you my well-informed refusal and send you on your way."

"My husband is dead," she said simply.

"Congratulations would be more apropos than condolences," he said without any inflection at all.

She stepped deeper into the room and settled into the chair that faced his desk. Clearly, she intended to be there for a while. As she straightened the fabric of her skirts, dust stirred around her, reminding him that he had yet to hire a woman to clean because he couldn't damned well afford to. Not yet.

"He was murdered," she stated simply, as if it weren't a shocking act of violence. She seemed as unmoved by his death as she was by the low appearance of his office.

He knew it was shabby. The walls needed painting. The surface of the desk was cluttered, the wood finish nicked and pocked from years of use long before it had come into his possession. The chairs were lumpy and not especially comfortable. The floor and walls were utterly bare, devoid of anything that might brighten up the place. And in all of that, he was acutely aware of how it must appear to her. For himself, her presence highlighted one undeniable fact—he was beneath her. In status, in wealth, in manners and breeding, in morality. In every way, she was much too good for him, and he had no hope of closing that chasm. So he focused on the one thing where he felt solid and confident: his ability to take the facts and get to the very root of them.

"As he was universally despised, that is hardly a shock."

"Do you know Inspector Bates?"

It would be that prick, Joss thought bitterly. "I know him well enough."

"He is convinced that I had something to do with Arthur's murder," she replied. Despite her hands folded primly in her lap, there was a hum of nervous energy about her. Something was very, very wrong.

"Did you?" He wouldn't blame her. If any man deserved killing, Arthur Dagliesh certainly fit the bill.

She glanced up at him, her shock at the question easily apparent.

"You had reason, Hettie." It had been a slip, to utter her name, not even her given one but the too-intimate shortened form, as if he had the right. He could only hope she wouldn't notice. "*Reasons.* By the score, in fact. Did you do it?"

"Of course not. Arthur and I had reached an . . . understanding, of sorts. I would not confirm or even acknowledge the rumors about his lack of action when I was abducted, and he would simply leave me be. It's the happiest I have been since we married."

Joss shook his head. "And statements like that, Lady Ernsdale, are what make you a good suspect."

"I didn't kill him. I couldn't. Even if he did deserve it. You know that. But I need you to prove it . . . and the only way to do that is to find the person who did murder him."

He longed to say yes. To play the hero for her once more.

But there was no percentage in it. In the end they'd part ways once more, and he'd be a hollowed-out shell of a man in the aftermath. "No. I'm not getting tangled up in the mess of your life. I've done that once already." And it was eating away at his soul on a daily basis. He couldn't risk being near her, of falling under her spell again.

"I could hang for this."

It would never come to that. Vincent would not let her hang. "That's hardly likely."

"If my suspicions are correct, it's very likely. And growing more likely with each passing day . . . you see, I think that Arthur's heir, Simon Dagliesh, is behind it all. I wouldn't even put it past him to have had some involvement with Gilbert Walpole."

The sixth sense that had always served him so well reared its head then. It wasn't just a possibility, but a probability. Still, he prodded her, "The inheritance is a done deal. He's got the house and the title. You'll go back to your sister and everything will be fine."

She looked down at her primly folded hands. In fact, she locked her gaze there and would not look up at him again. And when she spoke, her voice was pitched so low that he had to lean in to hear her.

"No. No, it won't," she said softly. "Because I'm with child . . . and if that is discovered, he will see me dead. Because if he does not, he risks losing the thing he has already done murder for."

The air seized in his lungs. He couldn't breathe, couldn't speak. Because he knew just what the implication was. After all, she'd been untouched until the night they'd spent together. "With child?" he finally managed to ask.

"I DON'T EXPECT anything from you in that regard. You've made your feelings about me, or rather your lack of them, abundantly clear. But I am asking for you to help me to at least prove my innocence. I don't wish to bear my child in a prison and go to the noose immediately after . . . and Simon will stop at nothing to see that happen." She stopped talking, realizing that her words were tumbling out in such a rush he could likely make no sense of them. Taking a deep calming breath, she studied his face. It was impassive. Whatever he was thinking or feeling regarding her confession, she would never know until he chose to tell her. *If* he chose to tell her.

Continuing, Hettie explained, "When I am gone, there will be no one to protect my child. And no one turns a hair at the death of an infant, do they? It's commonplace enough to go completely unremarked upon. He'll still have everything he wants, it will simply be delayed. In short, Mr. Ettinger, I am in more danger now than ever before . . . and the stakes are infinitely higher."

Hettie was left once more waiting for a response. She waited for him to say something in response to all that she'd just shared with him. But he remained seated, his face an unreadable mask as the stony silence closed in on them. The longer that silence drew on, the more her hope faded. He'd saved her once, but it did not seem that he was inclined to do so again. Still, she waited. She waited until the very last shred of her hope left her.

After an interminable moment, and with no response given, Hettie gave a curt nod and rose. Turning on her heel, she made for the door. Before she could even grasp the doorknob to make her escape, he was there. His large hand slammed against the wood directly in front of her face, holding the door closed.

She didn't look back at him. She didn't dare. If she did, he'd see the tears in her eyes, and she wasn't ready to be that vulnerable before him. Never again. "Let me go. It's quite clear you have no desire to help me, and I have no desire to be a burden to anyone. I will ask Vincent. I'm certain he will know someone else who can look into the matter."

"Give a man a damned second to think, Hettie," he whispered gruffly. His breath was warm on her neck, ruffling the hair at her nape in a way that made her shiver.

"Let me go," she said.

He continued as if she hadn't spoken at all. "That's a hell of a thing to hurl at me and then just expect me to take in stride."

She knew that. It had certainly been a great deal for her to come to terms with, as well. And it wasn't as if she'd been keeping that secret for months. It had only been two weeks since the reality of it had sunk in for her. But she didn't want to empathize with him, she didn't want to think of his feelings. There was a little part of her, a petty and vindictive one, that still held a grudge over the way he'd treated her that morning—as if he couldn't be rid of her quickly enough.

Somehow, she managed to turn around in that small space he'd left for her without actually pressing her body against him. "I don't have the luxury of breaking it to you gently," she countered. "There is too much at stake."

"I know. I know there is. And I'll handle it. All of it. And once it's done, then we'll come back to this conversation," he warned.

"What conversation? I'm a widow, Joss. No one will bat an eye at my having a child only months after my husband's demise. In fact, it will likely only garner sympathy for me. You truly need not do anything." It was the perfect solution. Well, it was for everyone except Arthur's legitimate heir, but the feelings of Simon—who, at best, was a wretched little man and at worst was a cold-blooded murderer. His feelings could hardly be counted.

Joss leaned in, close enough that she could feel his breath warm against her ear, close enough that she could smell him— wood smoke, a touch of whiskey, and the clean, masculine scent that made her ache to press her face into the hollow of his neck and let that scent consume her.

"Not another fucking word about what I have to do." He bit out the words. They were low and quiet, but no less fearsome. "You don't dictate that to me, Henrietta Dagliesh. I'll make my own decisions. I've been doing so for quite some time . . . and bearing the consequences of them."

Hettie shivered. His nearness, the sheer size of him—it should have been intimidating. She should have been frightened. But she wasn't. All she could think of was how good it felt to be in his arms again, or to at least be surrounded by his arms, even if the goal was restraint rather than passion. The temptation to lean into him, to sink against the hardness of his chest and feel his strength seeping into her was overwhelming.

As if he'd read her mind, his hand slipped from the door and his arm curved around her. He tugged her against him and just held her there. And she let him. For just a moment, she savored the sensation and took the warmth and comfort that he offered her.

Chapter Fifteen

S HE'D HAUNTED HIM since that night. Constantly in his thoughts while awake, the memory of her also invaded his dreams whenever he could manage to sleep. There was no peace. No respite from the feelings she'd stirred in him. One night. A span of mere hours, and she had altered him irrevocably. Of course, when those hours were fraught with danger and the risk of discovery and death at every turn, was it any wonder?

In times such as those, one learned things about a person that went far deeper than simply their favorite color or favorite tune. One learned what that person was truly made of, both their character and their heart. And if there was anything he had discovered about her that night, Hettie was a woman of remarkable fortitude and bravery. And if ever a woman was capable of taking on the challenge of raising a child entirely by herself, it was her. But then, she should not have to. And he would not let her. Whatever came, she would not face it alone, because a child changed everything. *His child changed everything.* He'd not abandon his own flesh and blood as his own father had done. Thoughts of being good enough, or fearing that he was too far beneath her, suddenly seemed insignificant in light of everything else.

He longed to tell her those things, to justify what she perceived as his rejection of her. But the temptation of her was too much to resist. He tightened his arms about her, pulling her close even as he took another step forward until her back pressed against the door. There was no token protest. Before he'd even dipped his head to claim her lips, she was rising up on her toes, her mouth seeking his.

Like that first time, the heat was instantaneous. It flared like a match to dry kindling. He cupped her chin, tipping her face up to his to deepen the kiss. The silken strands of her chestnut hair peeking from beneath her bonnet beckoned to him. Loosing the ribbon, the elaborate piece of millinery fell to the dusty floor, where it was promptly forgotten. Hair pins scattered as he slipped his hands into the thick tresses, twining them about his fingers.

It escalated too quickly. She pressed herself against him, her breasts crushed against his chest and the softness of her body cradling the hardness of his own. Nothing had felt right. Not since that night. Every day, he'd been fighting temptation, fighting the urge to go to her. And if the way she kissed him back was any indication, he wasn't alone in that. It was a clash of lips, teeth, and tongues—there was nothing gentle in it, nothing fine or tender. It was just hunger. Hunger and the desperation that existed inside them both, no matter how much they might wish otherwise.

Abruptly, she turned her face from his, breaking the kiss. The sound of their ragged breathing filled the room. "I didn't come here for this," she whispered.

"I know that. But neither of us, try as we might, can deny it."

Her gaze lifted, her eyes flashing with accusation. "You did. You couldn't be rid of me quickly enough!"

She was hurt—wounded by his cold dismissal of her. And she had every right to be. He had rejected her, though likely not for the reasons she might have imagined. "It isn't what you think . . . I wanted to protect you."

"From what?"

"From yourself, from me, from squandering the only chance you had to be free of your husband—or so I thought. I knew that we could not continue after our one night together in the Mint.

Because our worlds, the lives we live, are too far removed from one another. That became even more apparent when Vincent informed me of your plans to seek an annulment."

But an annulment was no longer necessary. And most of the reasons that he had to avoid her, namely the difficulty it would create in both their lives, had largely been eliminated by her husband's murder. Not all of them, but certainly what had seemed the insurmountable one. That wasn't a fact they could afford to bandy about. Nor was it one that would lend credence at all to her innocence, or to his own, for that matter. There would be ramifications if she chose to be with him. Her place in society would be forfeit. Her late husband's fortune, assuming he still had one, might be forfeit, as well.

She stared up at him, her expression guarded save for the fire of righteous indignation which burned in her eyes. "I've had enough of men deciding what is best for me in my life. Not a one of them has ever gotten it quite right. I'll thank you to let me make my own decisions from now on. You will send word when you've found something?"

He nodded. And that was all she required. She stooped to retrieve her bonnet, ignoring the scattered hairpins altogether, and then swept from his small office with the regality of a queen.

Alone once more, Joss turned to move back to his desk. But the glint of metal on the floor made him pause. Leaning down to pick it up, he realized it was one of her discarded hair pins. There were several others, as well. Once he'd gathered them, he moved to put them in the desk drawer to return them to her later. All but one. That one, he stuffed back into the pocket of his waistcoat, like some sort of talisman. He'd hold onto it for luck. He was surely going to need it.

MAURICE BATES LOOKED at the report from the coroner's inquest and cursed softly. There was nothing of note in it, nothing that would be useful to him in making a case against Lady Ernsdale. Getting a woman convicted of murder—no, getting a *lady* convicted of murder, was no easy task. Fairer sex. Weaker sex. You'd never prove it by him. And Henrietta Dagliesh, Lady Ernsdale, was just the sort he despised. All pious and upright and judgmental. She doled out her charity to the poor unfortunates all while thinking herself far above them.

Had she killed Ernsdale? The coroner's report indicated only that the man had been stabbed, the blade going all the way through. It had punctured his lung, nicked a vein that bled like the very devil. With his dying breath, the man had fallen into the street, likely begging silently for help, only to be run over by a heavy carriage and after having been trampled by the horses which pulled it. As murders went, it wasn't the sort most people would lay at the feet of a gently bred lady. Poison, certainly. A pistol, in rare cases. But to get close enough to a man of superior strength and stab him through and through? It was messy. It was risky. It was premeditated. And he'd have a devil of a time proving it.

The truth was, he didn't truly care one way or another if she was guilty. He only needed a conviction. Making an example of her, getting her arrested, tried, and even potentially executed, would make his career. Scandalous, salacious cases were the making of many a man who worked for the Runners. They paved the way to positions in politics and to opportunities to amass the kind of fortune a man like him would never see otherwise. His position with the Runners was a stepping stone and nothing more. Maurice was a man of many ambitions.

"What do you know about the Ernsdale kidnapping?"

Felix Monroe, the man who shared his office, shrugged. "I know the shite was going to let his wife die rather than pay the ransom."

He tapped his fingers on the desk, drumming them in an impatient rhythm. "What if there was no kidnapping?"

"What?"

"It was never reported to us," Maurice mused. "Surely if anyone had been truly concerned for her safety they would have brought it to our attention? Of course, if the entire thing was a ruse, as Ernsdale had suggested, they would have done anything to avoid our involvement."

Felix shook his head. "That theory doesn't hold water, Bates. The Hound of Whitehall was involved in her rescue. He's the one that gave us the Walpoles for the murders of them women in the rookeries. He'll not take kindly to you casting aspersions on the sister of his new wife!"

Alister sneered. "The Hound of Whitehall . . . bloody criminal. He's lost his power in this city. Moved off to the country with his bloody reformer."

"I don't think that's the way of it," Felix countered. "He's still got the power. 'Sides, he ain't gone yet. I reckon he's got shelves of ledgers—all of 'em filled up with the things others don't want the world to know about them. Secrets is where his power lies, not money, though he's got boatloads of it. Those secrets? He holds 'em by the score."

Maurice knew that. He knew it well. But he was privy to a few secrets of his own. "We'll see. I mean to bring Lady Ernsdale to justice for her husband's murder."

"You really think she done it?" Felix demanded. "I just don't see it. Poisoned? Yeah. Even shot, from a distance, yeah. But women, and ladies especially, ain't usually for the up close kind of murders."

Ignoring the fact that Monroe's arguments mirrored his own assessment, Bates shrugged. "She had motive."

"And an alibi," the younger man said.

"From her bloody servants. She pays them. Of course they would lie for her!"

Felix sighed, as if realizing that any attempt to dissuade him amounted to beating his head against a wall. "Do what you want, Bates. You always do anyway."

Chapter Sixteen

HETTIE KNOCKED ON the door of her sister's home. Honoria no longer resided in the townhouse that had belonged to her late husband. And Vincent refused to allow her to stay in rooms over his club. To that end, he'd bought a house on the very next block—far enough removed from the gaming hell, but still in a very genteel neighborhood. In many ways, he was much more of a stickler for propriety than either she or her sister were.

Stavers opened the door. "Lady Ernsdale! What a pleasure it is to see your lovely face. Do come in . . . I'll inform Mrs. Carrow that you have arrived."

Hettie smiled. "Thank you, Stavers. I do wish to visit my sister, but before that, I need a private word with Vincent—no. I need a private word with *the Hound.*"

One of the butler's silver brows lifted. The other, bisected by a scar, did not budge. Clearly he understood the distinction. Trouble was brewing. "You may wait in the study, Lady Ernsdale. I'll have him fetched from the club."

Hettie nodded and went to the small study off the entryway. Closing the door softly behind her, she seated herself in one of the green velvet upholstered chairs. They were definitely Vincent's taste and not Honoria's. He was a man who appreciated luxury. Honoria would have looked at the velvet and figured out how many warm coats could be made for women and children rather than how many chairs she could cover with it.

They were such polar opposites, she mused. And yet despite their many contradictions, they were so perfectly suited to one another that, at times, it was painful to see. *Because she was envious.*

It was a terrible thing to admit, even to herself. She had wanted her sister to be happy for so long, to be free of her late husband's awful temper and heavy hands. Even as a young girl, long before her own debut, she'd known that something was amiss there. But she'd never known the whole of it. Not until she was married herself. Only then did she understand just how little recourse a wife had against the abuses of a husband.

Now, Honoria was married to a man the world called a criminal. But he cherished her sister. Loved and worshipped her with a devotion that was positively staggering. She would never begrudge her sister such happiness, but was it really so wrong to want a similar sort of happiness for herself? Though she supposed her priorities would have to change now. It was no longer simply about what she wanted and needed. She would have a child's needs to consider.

The enormity of that thought overwhelmed her. Leaning forward, Hettie placed her head in her hands and tried to fight back the headache that threatened to lay her low. She could not afford to give in to such ailments when there was so much to be done.

And that was how Honoria found her, looking as if the weight of the world rested upon her shoulders.

"Are you unwell?" Honoria asked, her concern evident in her voice.

Hettie looked up. "I need to borrow your widow's weeds . . . Ernsdale is dead. And a Bow Street detective believes I killed him."

Joss had been waiting in the office at the club for some time when Vincent finally walked through the door.

"Sorry. Had a bit of a problem on the floor. Beaumont called Mawbry a cheat, and they very nearly dueled with the cutlery," the Hound relayed with derisive amusement. "Children."

"Could be worse," Joss remarked. "A fortnight ago it was Hamstead and Carlisle. Over some insult to Carlisle's wife, I believe?"

"Daughter. Insult to the man's daughter," Vincent replied absently. "Hamstead said it was a damn good thing she's rich because her face won't catch her a husband; it'd barely catch flies."

Joss blinked. "Oh. I suppose that might be worth a fight, after all."

Vincent shrugged. "Hamstead is an ass, but he's not wrong. Poor girl . . . but none of that tells me why you are here, Joss. And you wouldn't be here without a reason. Not when you've been avoiding me since my return so you wouldn't have to answer the question I posed to you before I left."

He'd considered more than a dozen different ways to relay it all. But simply, matter of factly and with a minimum of detail seemed best. "Ernsdale was murdered, Maurice Bates wants to pin it on Henrietta, and she's with child . . . my child."

The Hound stared at him. Then after the longest moment of very uncomfortable silence, he uttered a single vulgarity that summed it all up perfectly.

"Yes," Joss replied. "That is generally how conception occurs."

"Christ, you've really cocked it all up."

Joss just shrugged. He wasn't wrong. "I'm aware. But I can't very well uncock it, so let's do what we can to manage it. Starting with Bates. I need to find out who did actually murder Ernsdale. Hettie has her theories, and she's likely correct. But I don't want to miss something by being so singularly focused. Ernsdale was a very hated man, after all. Most people are murdered for money, love, or revenge—and there is an entire city full of people who would have happily avenged themselves against that shite."

Vincent moved past him and sat down at his desk. There were several ledgers spread across the desktop, most of them chocked full of secrets and scandals that would set the whole of London on its ears. "So why are you here? Just to tell me that you did the absolute one thing you should not have done when charged with rescuing a woman?"

It goaded Joss to admit it. "I'm here because I need your help to do this. And because you once offered me a position managing this club . . . as your partner."

"Ah . . . so you can support the wee Ettinger? You may want to rethink that. Henrietta is a lady. Ladies do not marry men who run textile mills or shipping businesses . . . or even very successful gaming hells." Vincent leaned back in his chair and steepled his hands. "You're going to have to become something you look down your slightly misshapen nose at: a man of leisure."

Joss felt everything inside him recoil at the prospect. He had little respect for men who did no work, honest or otherwise. The idea of joining their ranks, of being a kept man, living off of a woman rather than supporting himself—it was anathema to him. "Bite your tongue. I'll do this my own way."

"You have already. That's why Hettie's with child and without husband."

Joss uttered a curse that mirrored Vincent's earlier one, prompting a bark of laughter from the other man. But the laughter died away when the door opened and Stavers appeared. The very unlikely butler was, to put it mildly, rough around the edges. "Pardon the intrusion, but Lady Ernsdale has arrived at the house and wishes to speak with you."

Vincent kept his eyes trained on him, and Joss, despite the fact that he had a good two stone in weight and nearly four inches in height on him, had to fight the urge to squirm and fidget beneath that penetrating gaze.

"This should be interesting," Vincent mused. "Care to join

me?"

He wasn't about to remain behind. Not when he hadn't seen Hettie since she had come to his office the day prior. They needed to talk. But they couldn't do that with Vincent and Honoria hovering about them as they tried to fix all their problems for them.

Getting up from the chair he'd occupied, Joss reached for his coat. "Let's go."

Chapter Seventeen

H ETTIE STARED UP at her sister, who was still gaping at her. "Ernsdale is dead," she repeated, sounding somewhat dazed by it. "The thing I've prayed and hoped for has come to pass and all it's done is make my life more difficult rather than less. And . . . oh, God . . . I sound like a horrible person. Praying for his death. Who asks God, quite literally, to strike someone dead?"

"Any woman who has had to bear the brunt of a man's temper and rage when the law is on his side," Honoria answered. "Wishing him dead did not make him dead. If it did, then I'd have been widowed on the very day I became a bride."

Despite the truly terrible position she was currently in, Hettie had to smile at that. Honoria could always manage to make her laugh even in the most dire of situations. "Have I told you how incredibly happy I am that you are my sister? If I have not, I've been terribly remiss."

Honoria stepped deeper into the room and perched on the arm of Hettie's chair, wrapping her arm about her sister's shoulders. "The feeling is quite mutual."

"It may not be for very long," Hettie said. "It's naught but one scandal after another. As if your marriage to a somewhat questionable character, my abduction, my miserly husband, now the murder of that same miserly husband weren't enough . . .

now, I am—" She broke off, not quite able to say the words aloud.

"What is it, Hettie? You know there is nothing you cannot tell me."

"I'm going to have a child . . . and obviously, Ernsdale was not the one who fathered this child."

Honoria's eyebrows lifted and she blinked rapidly for several seconds. "Well, that was certainly efficient. The first time, Hettie? Really?"

Hettie fixed a baleful stare in her sister's direction. "That is not helpful, Honoria."

"No. No, I don't suppose it is. What will you do? About Mr. Ettinger, that is. Have you told him?"

Hettie looked down at her hands folded primly in her lap. "I did. Yesterday afternoon. It didn't go well. It did not really go poorly either. We're just—he needs time to make sense of it all." Honoria's hands covered hers as her sister knelt down in front of her. Lifting her head, she met Honoria's sympathetic gaze directly. "Do not feel sorry for me. I could not bear it. Pity would surely send me spiraling into fits of melancholy worthy of Bedlam."

"I do not pity you. I worry for you. That is a very different thing," Honoria said gently. "And I think you should not be so quick to dismiss Mr. Ettinger. It is quite a thing to comprehend. You've had more time to acclimate yourself to the notion than he has."

Hettie laughed, a slightly watery sound that bordered on hysterical. "He said much the same thing. And it's true enough, I suppose. It isn't his fault I have such low expectations of the male sex."

Honoria nodded. "That is quite true. Neither of us had much in the way of an example when it comes to what a man should be. Our father, my late husband, your late husband—but there are men who can be trusted. And you may find them in the most unexpected of places."

There was no time for Hettie to consider her response to that. The door opened and Vincent entered—with Joss Ettinger right behind him. Hettie's gaze roamed over his tall, broad-shouldered frame and felt that familiar stirring. Lust. She wouldn't deny it, not to herself at any rate. Even after everything that had passed between them, his cold rejection of her and all the turmoil that had occurred since, she still wanted him. But she wasn't a child who didn't understand consequences. And courtesy of her husband, she understood all too well the potential disasters that lay in making oneself vulnerable to a man. She might want him, but she'd die before she admitted it.

THE TENSION BETWEEN them was so thick no one could miss it. It filled the air of what was, in fact, a quite spacious room. But all Joss could do was look at her. Since she'd arrived at his office the day before, she did seem to have rested somewhat. The sickly pallor of her face had receded to some degree of normalcy, and she looked more herself with rosy cheeks. The deep shadows beneath her eyes were still present, though less glaring.

It was Honoria who broke the awkward silence. "Vincent, I must discuss something with you. It is vitally important. Let's adjourn to the morning room for a few moments." Turning back to Hettie, she added, "I'll have refreshments sent in while you and Mr. Ettinger . . . become reacquainted."

When the pair of them had departed and Joss found himself alone with Hettie, he couldn't stop the amused chuckle. "Your sister has the subtlety of a cannon."

Hettie did not disagree with him, but she didn't share in the laughter. Based on the set of her shoulders, she was much too tense for that. His amusement quickly faded in the wake of her stoicism.

"Right," he continued. "I'm looking into Ernsdale's murder. It happened outside a gaming hell he frequented. Not one of Vincent's, unfortunately. A less popular one, as most of the fashionable establishments had banned him. No witnesses. No one seems to know a damned thing about it. It's a strange position to be in—trying to solve the murder of a man whose death only gladdens me."

"I'm not glad that he's dead," she replied. "I am happy to no longer have him as my husband, but that is a very different thing from celebrating his death."

Joss nodded. "I suppose it is. Though saying so in front of Maurice Bates will only complicate matters for you. You'd do best, when faced with him, to weep prettily and possibly even pretend to faint. He dislikes women in general, but the stronger the woman appears, the more intense his dislike becomes."

Hettie's lips turned down slightly and her brow furrowed. "So I should lie? Pretend to be something I am not?"

"Men like him do not like to have their beliefs and opinions challenged. By appearing strong and composed, you call into question everything he believes about the fairer sex," he explained. "That makes him uncomfortable, and when he's uncomfortable, he will be more likely to strike out at whomever he sees as a threat . . . whether that's to his beliefs or to his own small corner of the world."

"Then he had much more in common with my late husband than I could possibly have realized. The question, Mr. Ettinger, is how do you respond when someone threatens your world?"

He shrugged. "It's never happened. I wouldn't let it."

A laugh escaped her, but it wasn't humor. The sound was sharp and hard. "Of course it hasn't. You are impervious to everything, I suppose?"

"No. Not especially. It's simply that I've made it a point in my life to never have any sort of attachment to anything. If there's nothing you can't live without, then there's nothing for others to use against you," he answered. "Or at least that's been the way of it till now . . . till you."

The air in the room shifted. It changed into something entirely different. The anger was still there. The hurt pride and the rejection wouldn't go away without significant effort. But the heat was present, as well. The sharp, clawing need that had consumed them both on that one fateful night still pulsed between them.

"Don't," she finally managed to whisper. "Do not offer me things now just because . . ."

"Because you're having my child?"

"Yes," she said. "I've already been with one man who didn't want me for myself. I will not do that again. I will not suffer that again."

Joss didn't hesitate. They were done talking, or at least to his mind they were. Crossing the room in long purposeful strides, he halted before the chair she occupied and leaned down, placing his hands on the chair's arms and caging her there. They were nose to nose when he spoke, his voice low and deep, roughened by emotion and desire. "I don't want you for yourself? I only want you for the child you carry? If that were true, Hettie, you wouldn't have appeared in my dreams every night. I wouldn't have woken up in the wee hours with my cock aching for you. I wouldn't have been tormented by your image every goddamn waking minute! You're not just wanted. You're my obsession . . . worse than liquor. Worse than bloody opium."

She didn't say a word, though her eyes were wide with shock. But she didn't pull back, nor did she push him away. Instead, she simply stared into his eyes for the longest time. Then her gaze drifted lower, settling on his lips. And the hunger—the same hunger that tortured him—was visible in her gaze.

It was the only sign he needed. For two long and lonely months, he'd dreamed of kissing her again. But the kiss they'd shared the day before had only spiked his need to touch her, to taste her. It was a thirst that he feared would never be quenched.

Joss touched his lips to hers—not with the anger and heat that had consumed him the day before. But with all the tenderness she deserved. He poured things into that kiss that he would never have the words to express. That wasn't him. That wasn't the sort of man he was, to wrap it all up and make it pretty and romantic. But not being able to say it didn't mean he was incapable of feeling it. And she stirred things in him no other woman ever had. It was more than desire. More than just attraction. He didn't know if it was love because that was an emotion he'd never experienced before. Not once in his entire life had he known that sort of softness of the heart. Given how much she moved him, it wasn't an idea he could dismiss out of hand.

Chapter Eighteen

SIMON DAGLIESH SETTLED his cool gaze on the solicitor. It was false, of course. There was nothing cool about him. His palms were sweating, and he could feel his heart thumping in his chest. "What do you mean the title cannot be conferred yet? My uncle is dead, and I am his heir."

"Your uncle is dead, sir, but he has a young bride. Until such time as it is proven she is not with child—and your uncle's potential heir—we must simply wait."

Simon tapped his walking stick against the wooden floor of the man's dark, dim and cluttered office. "That is not an option. I cannot wait. I need the title. And I need the fortune. I need them immediately."

"That just simply isn't possible . . . well, it is possible, but unlikely."

He seized upon that one word. Possible. "How? How is it possible? What must occur for this to be resolved?"

The solicitor splayed his hands palm up as he explained, "If your aunt will consent to an examination by a doctor who will confirm that she is not with child, we may be able to expedite the process. The other way such a resolution might occur is if your aunt were to pass away. Though given her youth and state of health, that is unlikely."

It was becoming less unlikely by the minute. "Send her a

letter at once. Demand an examination by a physician. This is urgent and cannot wait."

The solicitor shook his head. "It is not within my power to demand anything of Lady Ernsdale. I will certainly write to her and request that she consider that avenue to quickly settle her late husband's affairs, but you must understand that the bulk of your uncle's wealth is, in fact, hers. She brought it into the marriage, and it will go with her now that the marriage is done."

Simon felt his blood run cold. "How much is left?"

"Four thousand pounds, roughly. The ten thousand held in trust for your aunt will now be hers in its entirety as both your uncle and her father have now passed on. Now, had she preceded your uncle in death, the ten thousand would have been absorbed by the estate."

He'd killed the wrong one first, Simon thought bitterly. "What if something were to happen to my aunt now?"

"I'd have to look into the particulars of the trust and see who inherits it upon her death, but that is an unlikely outcome, sir," the solicitor insisted.

Simon rose, leaning across the little man's desk until they were nose to nose. "I do not need your opinions on the likelihood of her death. I simply need the facts of the inheritance of her fortune. You will send word to me at the Albany when you have it." He turned to go, but as he reached the door, he turned back. "And you'll not breathe a word to anyone about our conversation or the very pertinent questions I asked. Because if you do, you will not live long enough to regret it."

With that final warning ringing in the air behind him, Simon exited the solicitor's office. The door closed quietly behind him, and he exited the building. Outside, he hailed a hack and made for Piccadilly and his apartment at the Albany. It was a fashionable address, one that others recognized as a symbol of his place in society. That his rooms at the Albany were the least desirable the building had to offer—small, dark, cramped, and prone to dampness whenever it rained—was a fact he kept to himself. No one else needed to know that he was scraping by, eking out enough funds to maintain at least the appearance of wealth by cheating at cards. Why? Because all of his life, his uncle had been a skinflint.

When the old sot had married his not quite fashionable but very lovely young bride, he'd thought things might change. Perhaps, with more readily available funds, his uncle would be prompted to a new degree of generosity. But that had not come to pass. Instead, his uncle had grown even more tightfisted. Eventually, he'd cut him off entirely. With his stipend extinguished, Simon had truly only been left with one choice.

London was unforgiving of a man with empty pockets. Higher society was especially so. Without a fortune, he'd never be able to marry. If he could not marry, then he could not add to this fortune. It had been a conundrum to be sure.

There were only two ways a man might obtain a fortune that did not involve sullying one's self with something so crass as work. Money was to be married or inherited. And since marriage was not yet attainable for him, he'd felt inheritance was the more expedient choice.

Simon lifted his walking stick in the darkened interior of the hack and flicked the little latch on the handle. The blade, thin and sharp, sprang forth from the tip, and he smiled. He'd won it in a card game. At the time, it had just been a pretty piece. In the end, it had been eminently useful. But it would have to be retired. Killing his uncle with a blade outside a gaming hell was one thing. But if his aunt were to die by the same means, it would rouse suspicion. No. Aunt Hettie would have to be met by some terrible accident—something tragic and fatal.

JOSS ENTERED THE gaming hell through a side entrance. It wasn't that he wouldn't be welcomed at the front door, but arriving there would raise questions that he didn't want anyone asking. If he meant to find out who murdered Ernsdale, he didn't need any potential suspects knowing of his suspicions.

Hettie was insistent that it was Simon, Ernsdale's nephew. He didn't necessarily disagree, but that didn't mean other possible suspects should be ignored. Once a Runner always a Runner, he thought. For his part, and most of the other men at Bow Street, that was the case. But there were always exceptions . . . like Maurice Bates. He only ever looked at evidence that aligned with his theories. Bates would happily send an innocent man—or woman—to the gallows rather than admit he had it wrong.

Knocking softly on the door of the small office that the club's boss occupied, he turned the knob and entered before being given leave to do so. But the man behind the desk merely raised one eyebrow at that. "Inspector Ettinger . . . or is it simply Mr. Ettinger now?"

"It's Joss, and you bloody well know it," he said, seating himself in a chair that threatened to give beneath his weight. "Jesus, Collinsworth, why can't you get some real furniture in here?"

The man, Jack Collinsworth, simply shrugged as he looked at him with amusement. Collinsworth wasn't much shorter than Joss, but he had a leaner frame. He might have come up from the gutter like the rest of them, but he hadn't been born to it. His speech had always been impeccable, and he gave the appearance and impression of elegance in every mannerism. Those traits were largely responsible for the position he found himself in currently: running and eventually owning a successful gaming hell. "Because that would encourage others to stay, and I'm busy. You're here about Ernsdale, but there's nothing to tell. The man hadn't set foot inside the club that night. No one saw anything."

"I am here about Ernsdale," Joss replied. "But not that Ernsdale. Simon Ernsdale."

Collinsworth frowned. "He's in here from time to time. Don't much care for him. Seems there's always trouble when he's about. Lots of accusations of cheating and of running a crooked establishment. Curiously, the accusations never come directly from him. He just whispers into the ears of others and lets them wreak the chaos on his behalf."

"Is he capable of murder?"

Collinsworth looked at him with an arched brow. "Every man, and woman for that matter, is capable of murder. Do I think he'd be far less conflicted than others to take a life? Yes. I'd say that is true."

"How often did the elder Ernsdale frequent this establishment?"

Collinsworth sighed and closed the ledger before him. "Is this business, Joss? I know you're not a Runner, and last I checked, you weren't working for the Hound anymore—or at least worked for him as little as possible."

Jack was a friend, as much as a man in Joss's position had friends. He would not confess such things to many people but he was certain that Jack would keep his confidence. "It's personal . . . I have a *relationship* with Lady Ernsdale. And Bates is trying to pin this murder on her."

"Did you kill him?"

Joss laughed. "If I'd done it, his body wouldn't have been left on the sidewalk to be discovered by others. He'd have just vanished in the night."

"Vanished. Right. If I hear anything, I will send word to you," Jack offered. "What does it mean when you say that you have a 'relationship' with her?"

"It means just that. I won't say more," Joss said.

Jack nodded. "I see. So that's the way of it, then. Another mighty oak has been felled."

Joss ignored the teasing. Mostly because he wasn't hypocritical enough to deny the truth when it was spoken—even if he didn't like it. "Find out what you can. People talk to you."

"You mean I ply them with liquor and they confess their secrets because they presume I'm not a threat."

Joss shrugged, neither agreeing nor disagreeing. Jack wasn't a violent man by choice, but that didn't mean he was incapable of it. In truth, he was one of the most dangerous men Joss had ever known—mostly because everyone around him thought him too refined to be a threat. But underestimating him was a mistake most people only made once. "Just pass any intel along."

"I will, but it'll put you in my debt," Jack warned. "And at some point or other, I will collect."

Joss considered it. Then gave a curt nod.

"Is she worth it?" Jack asked.

"Ten times over," Joss replied without hesitation before hoisting himself out of the miserably tiny chair and making for the door. By the time he had Ernsdale's murderer, he'd owe his very soul to someone. Assuming that Hettie hadn't claimed it already.

Chapter Nineteen

T HE ONLY GOOD thing about widowhood was that no one expected her to parade herself about in society. It was a relief not to have to put on a show, to keep up the pretense of being a grieving wife to a husband that she couldn't muster much feeling for one way or another.

"Will you be dining alone tonight, madame, or will you have guests?"

From the way the butler sneered when he said guests, she could only surmise that he meant her sister and Vincent, whom he clearly felt was inappropriate. "No guests. And no need for a big fuss. A simple tray in my rooms will suffice."

He dipped his head in a slight bow. There was no outward insolence, but it was quite clear to Hettie that her position in the household was precarious. The servants knew that she was on the way out—or thought they knew. Being with child would complicate matters for everyone. To what degree, she could not yet say. But she knew that Simon would take some sort of action when he discovered it.

Climbing the stairs to her room, she slipped inside and settled herself on a small settee that was flanked by the fireplace on one side and the window on the other. Before her was a small table where she often wrote letters, read her books, and, when the occasion called for it, took her meals. That had been a more frequent event prior to her kidnapping.

It was truly a strange turn of events that the moment where she had faced the most danger, where she had been utterly terrified, had given her more power in her relationship with Arthur than she'd ever had prior. His lack of action on her behalf was scandalous enough, that a rescue had to be mounted by the notorious Hound of Whitehall—well, even if Arthur hadn't met an unfortunate demise, it was quite likely she'd be spending the evening alone in her own home.

Well, it was still her home. At least until Arthur's affairs were settled.

A moment later, her maid knocked softly. "Enter," Hettie called. When the door opened, Foster was there with a tray for her dinner, which she promptly deposited on the table before her.

"There you go, my lady. Is there anything else you need before you retire for the night?"

Hettie looked at the tray. It was roast lamb in a heavy sauce. The very thought of it turned her stomach. She was quickly learning that morning sickness did not only strike in the mornings. "I am not very hungry, Foster. Leave the bread, but take everything else away. And have some tea sent up."

Foster looked up, her expression troubled. "My lady, I don't mean to speak out of turn. But you need to eat. It isn't good for you or for the baby." The last words were whispered, despite the fact that they were the only ones in the room.

Hettie stilled. "Who knows? Who in this house knows, Foster?"

"Right now, it's just me. When I begun to notice that you hadn't had your courses, I took over all your laundry. Wouldn't let the other girls touch it cause I said they ruined your clothes before. I was very mean to them, but I didn't know what else to do. I was afraid he'd kill you if he knew."

It wasn't an unfounded concern. He might have. But someone killed him first. It would only make her appear more guilty if it came out that the child wasn't Arthur's. "It's all a muddle,

Foster. And I do not know how to unmuddle it all."

"You can't," the maid said. She broke protocol by sitting on the settee next to Hettie. And Hettie welcomed it. She needed the comfort of having someone else in that house who understood what was happening. "There's too many folks that know it can't be his. And with the kidnapping, there's questions as to who the father might be. And it doesn't matter what you say to anyone, they're going to choose their own truth . . . and it'll be the one what benefits them most."

There was no denying the wisdom of those words. It was something that Hettie had learned the hard way. "Do whatever you must to keep the secret a bit longer. I know it will come out eventually, but I'd prefer it to be on my own terms. Simon is . . . well, he's greedy and grasping. And dangerous. Whether this child is Arthur's by blood, it is by law. And that makes me and my child a threat to him."

There was no chance to say more. A strange sound at the window halted their conversation. Turning to identify the source, she was stunned to see an all-too-familiar face at her window. Her third story window, at that!

"Good heavens! Foster, let him in before he falls to his death."

The maid just sat there for a moment, blinking owlishly at the window.

"Foster! Let him in," Hettie insisted more sharply.

Instantly, Foster rose and crossed to the window, undoing the latch and letting the casement swing inward. "Good heavens, sir! There's a door downstairs that you could have used!"

"There is," Joss agreed, levering himself into the room. "But then others would know I am here, and that's not good for anyone. Is it, Hettie?"

"No. It isn't. Foster, I think it goes without saying that this should remain a secret."

"Mum's the word, m'lady," the maid replied quickly. "Should I stay?"

"No," Hettie said. "You may go. The tray can be seen to in the morning. I imagine that Mr. Ettinger could use some sustenance."

When the maid had gone, Hettie turned back to him. "What were you thinking to come here this way? Uninvited and slipping in through a bedroom window like a thief in the night!"

"I was thinking to protect you . . . your reputation and your life. If Simon Dagliesh is responsible for Ernsdale's murder, he's likely experiencing some paranoia. My former association with Bow Street is well known. If I were to be seen coming and going, it might prompt him to take action against you."

Hettie's lips parted. "Oh. Well, of course, I hadn't considered that he might be watching us."

"Even if he's not, you can bet money that Maurice Bates is. There's no love lost between us. If he thinks I'm aiding you in some way, he'd be more likely to try and drag you to the gaol."

Hettie shuddered at the thought. "I have been locked in enough small, filthy rooms for my lifetime. I'd really prefer not going to another."

"I know you would . . . I came tonight because I've discovered something. Simon hovers on the verge of eviction from the Albany. His rent hasn't been paid for two months now, and patience with him and his promises of a windfall is wearing thin from creditors both respectable and . . . not so respectable. It is likely that the windfall he has promised them could only be his inheritance from his uncle. I think, Hettie, that you are in more danger from him than either of us had initially imagined, because he's not just greedy. He's desperate."

Chapter Twenty

S HE WAS PALE. That was the first thing Joss noticed about her. The second thing he noted was the tension in her shoulders. And it wasn't simply being faced with his presence which made her tense. Hettie was struggling. The weight of the worries presently deposited on her slim shoulders was staggering. And for two months, she had been facing everything completely alone, including his rejection of her. Whatever his reasons or his honorable intentions, he had hurt her, and that thought pricked at him like shards of broken glass.

"I'm sorry," he said.

"Whatever for?"

"That you were abducted. That you were used as a pawn by others. That you've had to face things completely alone because every man you've ever known—myself included—has proven a disappointment."

There was only silence for the longest time as she stared at him, her head cocked slightly to one side as she considered not only his words, but the whole of him. It was like she could see straight through to the soul he thought had once been sacrificed entirely. It took everything in him not to squirm beneath that steady regard, like a misbehaving child called onto the carpet.

Finally, she spoke. "You owe me nothing. Not an apology, certainly. I knew the risks that night in the Mint. I knew them fully. And I cannot say that I would alter anything about it even if it were possible to do so. I've asked for your aid, and you are providing it. That is more than enough," she said, as if it were that simple.

"Well, it's not good enough for me," he said, shaking his head. "But you've had enough of men telling you what to do in your life. I'm not that sort. But that is my child, and I mean to know it and for it to know me. What's between the two of us . . . well, we'll just have to figure that out as we go along."

"There is no us. We had one night together . . . one night with consequences. And just because we can't seem to keep our hands off one another, that doesn't signify that there is anything there beyond basic attraction. I will endeavor to curb my inappropriate behavior and you should, as well."

"Inappropriate? Hettie . . . I have never met a woman—not in all my life—that burrowed under my skin as you have. We spent one night together, and it has haunted me every moment of every day since. I regret my coldness to you that morning. I regret the impersonal way I left you with Mrs. Blaylock—Mrs. Carrow, now. God above, it's all cocked up. I told myself I was doing what was best for you, but I'm not a selfless man. Never have been. Never will. I want you. And nothing will stop me from trying to win you."

She shook her head, and her expression had shifted into one of sadness. "I'm not a prize to be won. If you want me, I don't need to be wooed. I need to know that I am valued and respected. I need to know that any partnership we have going forward will be just that—a true partnership and not one of us shouting orders or making unilateral decisions for the other. You called me a pawn. And it's an accurate description. For the entirety of my life, I've been naught but a commodity to be traded upon, first for my father and then for Arthur and ultimately for my abductors. I won't be that for you. Not now. Not when I have a choice."

If she only knew that he did already value and respect her. But actions always spoke louder than words. Thus far, actions had only shown that he was a selfish ass led about by his prick.

"There is a chance then," he mused, "that you would consider marriage to such a lowborn person as myself?"

She leveled that same assessing, squirm-inducing gaze upon him once more. When she spoke, her voice was low and soft, but held complete conviction. "If I were ever to marry again, the man would be judged only on how he treated me and how he made me feel. On his true worth and his own merit. I care nothing for birth or station. In truth, I never have. That was my father's obsession—that was what saw Honoria and myself married to men who were little better than monsters."

"I'm not a monster, though I have done monstrous things . . . I've done things that I'd never dare even whisper. But I'll never hurt you."

"You will," she murmured softly. "You likely will not mean to, but you will. And it's just as likely that, should we pursue the madness of trying to have a life together, I will hurt you, as well. It's simply part of it, I think. But those hurts should never be intentional, and they most certainly must generate remorse on the part of the offender. To say we'd never hurt one another means we'd achieve a state of perfection. And I've no interest in being perfect. Not anymore. It is a very lonely way to live."

"You are perfect," he insisted. "Perfectly imperfect. I would change nothing about you, Hettie. Not a single hair nor a thought in your head."

"That you know of. But we do not know one another, Joss. Not in the way we should if we are to build a life together."

"What would you know of me? I'll tell you anything you wish to know."

Her eyebrows arched upward. "Anything?"

"Yes," he agreed, "Anything."

"How is it you came to be in the employ of the Hound of Whitehall?"

Joss ducked his head. He'd expected that question. "When I was naught but a lad, and he wasn't much more than one himself,

I tried to pick his pocket. Well, not tried. I did, in fact, pick his pocket. I just didn't escape successfully. He caught me a few streets over, and that was the end of it."

"Why would you try to pick his pocket?"

Joss shrugged. This was the ugly part of his life, the part he preferred to tell no one of. But she was entitled to hear it if anyone was. "The workhouse is no place for a child, even a sizable one as I was. I was eleven or twelve—I'm not really sure. Regardless, in a place such as that you either need to be able to fight for your share or pay for it. I wasn't much of a fighter back then. I stole his purse to pay for food."

As he finished the explanation, he noted her expression. It was sad, certainly, but it wasn't the piteous one he had anticipated, and for that he was grateful.

"I'm sorry. I know they are horrid places. And reform is hard won for such institutions."

"Indeed. Some would say having them razed might be the better solution."

"Do you?" she asked.

He considered his answer carefully. They were a necessary evil because, at present, they were the only option for many—terrible as it was. But recalling his own experiences, the ones that haunted him, he said, "Only one of them . . . the St. James. That's where I spent most of my time."

She winced. "It is a brutal place. I am so sorry. What happened to your parents?"

"My mother died," he answered. And he said no more on that matter. It was a nagging wound and one, much like his shoulder, that he would never fully recover from. He'd simply learned to get on with life in spite of it. "I never knew my father. It's an old story . . . anyway, that's when the Hound took me under his wing . . . for a price. I worked for him. Running errands. As a courier. And he and Stavers taught me to fight. Then I worked for him as muscle. And the whole while, I was being tutored. Taught to read and write. Because he had a plan for me. The best way to avoid trouble from the Runners was to have allies amongst their ranks."

"That couldn't be easy. Serving two masters." She phrased it as a statement, but there was invitation in her tone. Invitation to expand, to explain, to encourage him to share more.

He'd already shared more than he would have with anyone else. He'd assumed that it was simply in his nature to be taciturn. Now he had to wonder if perhaps it wasn't the absence of any desire to talk so much as it had been the absence of someone to talk with.

Deciding that was a topic to dwell on another day, he laughed. "No. No, it was not easy. I'm grateful to him. And I will never be free of him entirely for that reason. But I've made every effort to extricate myself from his enterprises—the illegal variety, at any rate—as much as possible. Which means, I am quite poor. At least for the time being."

"I am quite rich. The money is all mine, you know? Arthur hadn't a tuppence to his name. And my father, for all his many faults, was certain to ensure that my and Honoria's financial futures were maintained. While we were married, Arthur controlled whatever funds the trustees released to us, which was very little, really. Had I left him, he'd have kept the bulk of it. But now that he's gone, it will all revert to me."

It made him twitchy, the idea that she'd have to support him. He wasn't foolish enough to presume that her money would not make their lives easier, but he disliked the idea that others would view him as a fortune hunter. *Or that she would.*

Somewhat defensively, he responded, "I'm not without pro-spects. Vincent, who is an altogether different entity than the Hound of Whitehall, despite how it may appear, has offered me an opportunity to become more involved in the legitimate business enterprises that he is involved in. But that would mean the taint of trade and the loss of your social standing . . . I say that not to dissuade you, but to be entirely forthcoming. Lies have no place between us at this point."

Hettie folded her hands neatly in her lap and stated very matter of factly, "Well, if Inspector Bates has his way, it will not matter. He will have me arrested for Arthur's murder, and any plans for our future, jointly or separately, will be for naught."

"Leave Bates to me. I'll handle him. In the meantime, I don't want you to go anywhere without at least a pair of armed footmen. If Simon is the culprit, which seems the likeliest of explanations, and he is in such dire straits, I fear what he may attempt to do next."

"Will you stay?"

"Here?

"Yes," she said. "Just for a little while . . . I am very tired of my own company of a sudden."

It was an olive branch, and one he would gladly take. Crossing the room to where she sat, he joined her on the settee. Once there, he pulled her against him, nestled to his side. It wasn't about heat or passion. It was about comfort. Comfort and connection. He supposed that was something neither of them had been blessed with very much in their lives. Both of them had been victims of circumstances—for him it had been poverty that had robbed him of any semblance of affection for most of his childhood, and for Hettie . . . well, she'd been seen as naught but a commodity to be traded by every man she'd ever known.

Filled with a mix of emotions, not the least of which was sheer terror, Joss remained quiet. The enormity of the decisions made weighed heavily on him for the simple fact that he was afraid to fail. What did he know about being a father? What the hell did he know about being a husband, for that matter? On that score, he supposed he couldn't do worse than her last one, though the thought brought little comfort.

"You are very deep in thought," she observed.

"I suppose I am. The stakes are very high, Hettie. For both of us."

She went quiet again, but only for a moment. Then she lifted her head to look at him. "The fact that we are both aware of that should serve us in good stead. I like that you tell me what is on your mind, that you do not simply dismiss me out of hand. That alone, Joss, is a revelation."

He wanted to tell her everything, to simply pour out every wretched detail of his existence. At the same time, he wished to protect her from that—from the filth and poverty of his youth, to the opium dens that had so recently been his solace. Fear held him back, fear that she would come to her senses and refuse him. Fear that she would find him as unworthy as he felt.

The silence stretched between them, each of them lost in their own thoughts, their own doubts and, perhaps, their own hopes.

Chapter Twenty-One

THE DAY OF her husband's funeral started well enough. Hettie was more rested than she had been in weeks. *Because he had stayed with her.* Not through the whole of the night, but well into the wee hours of the morning. He'd held her, never demanding anything. Never taking what she would freely have given him. And the truth of it was that she was strangely grateful for that. Passion and heat had already been proven between them. But the real intimacy, the kind of comfort one could find in being close to a person when speech was not even necessary, when silence no longer caused discomfort, that was something she wasn't sure she'd ever had with anyone. Not until him.

Well rested or not, it did not take long for the day to take a turn. Foster appeared in the doorway of the morning room, her hands clenched tightly in front of her. "There's a man here to see you, m'lady. He wouldn't give his name."

"A gentleman?"

"Not a fine gentleman, but he's more than a shopkeeper or merchant."

It was an early hour for anyone to be calling. And that was warning enough for Hettie that it would likely be an unpleasant event. No one came to call so early without either very good news or very bad news, and good news had been in terribly short supply. "Well, making him wait will not change his reasons for being here. If it's something dreadful, I'd best get it over with."

With that, she followed Foster from the morning room to the study where the man had been shown. Bracing herself for whatever was to come, she found herself almost relieved when it was only the pale-faced, thin-framed clerk who worked for Arthur's solicitor awaiting her on the other side of the door.

"Mr. Batson, I wasn't expecting you. I had assumed I wouldn't hear about any of Arthur's estate matters until after the funeral was completed. Isn't that normally when the reading of the will should take place?" she asked.

"Well, yes, m'lady. It is. And if I were only here for the will, it would be a blessing, I say. A blessing! But I'm not here on behalf of your husband's estate. Well, not directly. I'm here, my lady, in a capacity more related to our understanding."

Their understanding. Mr. Batson had been her ally and her friend. The man, in truth, had taken pity on her after witnessing one of Arthur's more violent episodes. Her husband had struck her in front of the little clerk. But that episode had been enough to garner his support. It had been Mr. Batson who had advised her regarding her previous plan to seek an annulment.

"Our arrangement, Mr. Batson?"

"Yes, m'lady. I always made it a point to keep you well informed of anything occurring in my employer's office that might impact your current or future well being, and I'm afraid that there is something afoot which may well do so! Lord Simon Dagliesh intends to issue a challenge to the estate."

"A challenge?"

The solicitor blushed. "Yes. In light of there being no close male relatives who could advise you on matters of estate, Lord Simon, as the heir apparent, wishes to seize control of the title and estates immediately rather than let them fall into 'disarray.' But that can only be achieved by establishing that there will be no direct heir from your late husband. It's a simple matter of having your physician sign an affidavit—I, say, my lady, that you look most peaked. Are you unwell?"

She could deny that she was with child. But it would be proven for a lie soon enough. And Simon would never accept that she would have no wish to lay any sort of claim to the title or the remnants of Arthur's estates. Not to mention, of course, that the bulk of the actual wealth would go with her—unless she died. They would never be safe from him. If he thought she or her child posed any sort of threat to his position, or his fortune, then he'd stop at nothing to see them eliminated.

"I'm afraid that will not be possible, Mr. Batson. I am with child," she said simply.

The man all but quaked with shock, his lower lip trembling as he struggled to find words. "My lady . . . that is . . . well, I am certain that it must be a balm to your grieving spirit in this terrible hour."

"Indeed, Mr. Batson. It is. Until the child is born and its sex determined, we will not know if Arthur has a direct heir or not. I am afraid that Simon will simply have to be patient." She would have to be mad as a March hare to think that would ever happen. Simon was deep in dun territory. He owed money to everyone, and now, courtesy of Joss, she knew he was on the verge of being tossed out of the Albany. His situation was not merely desperate but untenable.

The clerk nodded. "This development is a decided complication, my lady. I do not think he will be pleased, madame."

"No, Mr. Batson, I dare say that he will not," Hettie agreed.

"In regards to the matter we discussed in the past, the matter of the consummation of your marriage and how it might impact decisions you were making about proceeding in your marriage—I am to assume those issues were resolved?"

"Any child I conceived during the course of my marriage is, by law, my husband's child unless someone wishes to challenge that," she replied. "Isn't that what you once told me?"

"Yes, madame, it is," the little man agreed with a sigh. "Perhaps if you let it be known that the child is not your late husband's . . . well, it doesn't matter does it? When his lordship discovers the division of your marriage settlement and that the bulk of it will return to you, I fear for your safety. Lord Simon has hired a solicitor of his own. A most disagreeable man, really, and not at all the sort one could rely upon to be above board and honest. Though that would be a very costly measure in a different way."

That Mr. Batson knew the truth of Arthur's predicament and that the child she carried could not possibly be that of her late husband, but was still willing to help her—it was beyond touching. But that still didn't negate the fact that he was advising her on the best way to move forward while retaining control of Arthur's title and estates, which she had no legal right to under the circumstances. They were hardly in the position where they could question anyone else's morals. "It would be very costly. And there is no guarantee that Simon would not act against me regardless. I have strong suspicions, Mr. Batson that Simon is responsible for Arthur's murder. I think it likely he would have done harm to him before had we not been so embroiled in scandal that everything about us was under such extreme scrutiny."

"Are you safe here, my lady? Are there servants in this house whom you can trust?"

"Very few, Mr. Batson. And in light of that realization, I think any further business between us should be conducted at my sister's home. I shall stay with Honoria and her Mr. Carrow for the time being. I think it would be the safest way forward."

Mr. Batson nodded his balding head. "Indeed, madame. Terrifying fellow, Mr. Carrow, but most efficient! I will return to the office. This afternoon, I expect that my employer will request a letter be drafted to you regarding the aforementioned physician's affidavit and the exam that would need to be conducted. But I shall not send that letter until late afternoon, thus giving you adequate time to make your way to your sister's home . . . by say, four this afternoon?"

"Yes, Mr. Batson. I will make certain to be safely tucked up in my sister's home by then . . . if you could deliver a message to someone for me, a Mr. Josiah Ettinger. He's a private inquiry agent who is a frequent associate of Mr. Carrow. If you could let him know that I will be taking sanctuary in my sister's home, that would be most appreciated."

"I will see it done, my lady, and as always, mum's the word about our conversations," the little man said. "It wasn't right, you know? The way he treated you. It wasn't right at all. It's one thing to be in a marriage where there is no love, but to be in one where one party is actively cruel to another—I simply cannot fathom it."

There was something in the man's tone that alerted her to a hidden pain. "Do you have a wife, Mr. Batson?"

"No, madame. I was never so blessed as to marry. But I did love a young lady once . . . many years ago. Her father disapproved of my lack of prospects and arranged for her to wed another. It ended very poorly for her. Now, I try to intervene where I can to prevent such a sad fate from striking others."

Overwhelmed with compassion for the poor man, Hettie felt tears stinging her eyes. "You are a very good man, Mr. Batson. And you have done remarkable things in the name of your lost love."

He beamed at her. "Then I have achieved my loftiest goal, my lady. I shall bid you good day now."

Alone once more, Hettie immediately rang for Foster. When the maid entered, she wasted no time with explanations. "I've decided that I shall go and stay with Honoria and Mr. Carrow for the time being. Pack for an extended visit, Foster, for you and myself."

The maid nodded and then rushed away to do as she'd been bid. Hettie then wrote a short note to her sister, explaining what she planned to do, but carefully made no mention of Mr. Batson or his warning in case the missive was intercepted. Her entire life seemed to be nothing but a series of intrigues and schemes. She longed for something simpler. Something easier. Certainly something less lonely.

Chapter Twenty-Two

THE FUNERAL WAS held in the afternoon at St. Paul's. It was not well attended. Arthur Dagliesh had not been a well-liked man. Even members of his various clubs were scarce. The service was suitably abbreviated and subdued. Wearing a simple black gown and veil, the dry-eyed widow was the subject of much conjecture.

"Do you think she did it?" one mourner asked another.

"I think if she did, one could hardly blame her," the other quipped quietly. "He was a bounder."

There were shrugs of agreement from those in hearing distance. Other similar conversations were taking place throughout the small crowd of assembled mourners. But one person was not joining in.

Standing near the rear of the congregation, Joss observed the whole thing with a watchful eye and his ears attuned to every sound. Even then, most of his focus was trained solely on the gentleman who stood near the front: Lord Simon Dagliesh, the soon-to-be named Lord Ernsdale. The visit he'd received that afternoon from a small clerk from the solicitor's office had provided more damning, if circumstantial, evidence against Ernsdale's heir. The man was angling to seize control with undue haste, a sure sign of desperation. And desperate men were always dangerous men.

Movement beside him was Joss's only alert. But he didn't flinch. He knew who it was instantly. The Hound.

"It's a miserable affair for a miserable bastard," the other man murmured.

"So it is," Joss agreed.

"Let's speak outside. There's too much to relay in here."

Together, the men stepped out of the church and onto the busy street beyond. But they stayed close to the entrance. After all, Honoria and Hettie were both inside.

"You've found something?" Joss asked.

"Simon Dagliesh isn't just in dun territory . . . he's the proverbial king of it. The man has amassed more debts than he could ever hope to pay," Vincent explained. "Even with the whole of Arthur Dagliesh's estates and Hettie's marriage settlement, he would be hard pressed to cover even half of it. And he's in deep with the sort of people who do not like to wait for payment."

"Not just shopkeepers and merchants, then," Joss mused. "Moneylenders?"

"Several of them. He's been holding them at bay with promises of a windfall . . . and men like him only get windfall sums when relatives die. That's quite the impetus to hurry along their demise."

"So it all comes back to the money." Joss shook his head. "Not so different from the rookeries, is it? Everyone always trying to come out on top."

"Not so different, but not so simple either. This is more than just his reputation at stake. It's Ardmore," Vincent said the name in a low voice, the word coming out sharp between clenched teeth.

Joss cursed under his breath. Just uttering the name of London's most notorious moneylender was enough to strike fear in the hearts of many. The man was ruthless. He and the Hound had clashed from time to time, but generally gave one another a wide berth. No one wanted an outright war, after all, and between the two of them it could be nothing less.

"I'll speak to him," Vincent continued. "I doubt it will do much good. Like many others, he believes my stepping back from the direct running of my enterprises signals weakness."

"Can you really just walk away from it all? You've been building this empire for decades." It was a fair question. At one point in time, nothing had been more important to Vincent Carrow than his criminal enterprise.

"I can. I want to," Vincent admitted. "There are other things in life more important than simply amassing wealth and power."

"I never had the drive for those things that you did," Joss admitted.

"I'll focus on Ardmore. You keep your attention on Bates. The man is asking questions of all of Honoria's and Hettie's acquaintances. He's all but labeling her a murderer. He means to have her hanged in the court of public opinion whether it happens in actuality or not."

"I'll pay him a visit now. You've got the pair of them?"

Vincent nodded. "I do. I've got men stationed all around the church and along the route to the house. She'll be staying with us for the foreseeable future. You should, as well."

"I'm in no danger," Joss denied quickly.

"You're in danger of being a dunderheaded ass. That might be worse than death in this case," Vincent growled. "You can't very well resolve what's between you if you're never in the same blasted place, can you?"

Joss was silent for a moment. Then he cursed. "Fine. I'll stay. But she and I will come to things in our own way. We don't need the pair of you interfering."

Vincent held up his hands in surrender. "Fine. You do it your way. But there is one thing you need to remember . . . if she's not married to you when the child is born, then legally that child is a Dagliesh. Is that what you want?"

No. It was the last thing he wanted. Bloody hell.

➵➵➵❮❮❮

As the service came to a close, Hettie was very aware of all the stares and whispers. Everyone was looking at her. Not that many were gathered, but that hardly signified. Tales would be carried. Simon glowered at her with barely concealed hostility and suspicion, casting himself in the light of grieving relation rather than the person with potentially the most to gain from Arthur's death. He was painting a picture, all too clearly, for others present. A picture that would be discussed, directed, and given prime placement in every gossip rag in the city.

"It certainly feels as though you've already been convicted, doesn't it?" Honoria asked softly, her voice little more than a whisper.

"No doubt that has been Simon's plan all along," Hettie replied softly. "In the wake of my abduction, he likely worried that I would be too sympathetic a figure. I have to imagine that he waited until a suitable amount of time had passed for everyone to forget that I too had been a victim of violence. He's a wastrel, but that is clearly a choice and not an indication of any lack of intelligence on his part."

"The scheming is exhausting," Honoria noted as she took Hettie's hand and gave it a comforting squeeze. "Being a pariah is shockingly restful."

Hettie felt her lips quirk beneath her veil but resisted the urge, somehow, to smile or laugh. Neither would make her look less guilty of either murdering or conspiring to murder her husband. "Do not make me laugh. It's not a good look on a supposedly grieving widow. Regardless, I imagine I shall find out soon enough."

Honoria's lips pursed as she too struggled to maintain her composure. "Let's get you home. You can rest, put your feet up, have a nice cup of tea, and try to put the unpleasantness of today behind you."

Hettie was fairly certain it would not be even remotely that easy. But escaping the speculative stares of those around her was an appealing option nonetheless.

As they neared the rear door of the church, Simon abruptly stepped in front of them.

"You may have fooled everyone else here," he said, a sneer on his face. His scathing voice was pitched just loudly enough to be overheard by anyone nearby. "But I know the truth. You never held any affection at all for my uncle, much less love. Now he lies dead, and you play the grieving widow."

"Watch what you say, Lord Simon," Honoria warned. "My sister has been a good and dutiful wife to a man who was an absolute failure as a husband. Or did you forget that when my sister was abducted, he meant to let her languish with her kidnappers rather than pay the demanded ransom?"

Simon started to say something in response, but Honoria was not done with him. Not by a long shot. "You, sir, have far more to gain from your uncle's passing than my dear sister does. Perhaps you only cast such aspersions against her to allay any suspicion of yourself. I have found that what men protest so loudly is often not at all reflective of what is in their minds, hearts, or deeds."

Simon drew back in such a fashion that it almost appeared he might strike out at Honoria. But before that could happen, a grim voice spoke from behind him.

"Raise your hand to her, my lord, and it'll be the last time it's raised for anything. I'll bloody well cut it off and make you eat it."

The threat, issued with complete sincerity and no small degree of menace, from Vincent had the desired effect. Simon simply stepped aside and let them pass.

"Gutterborn bastard," Simon whispered.

Vincent nodded. "Aye. I am. Which means I don't give two shites what anyone here thinks of me. I'll beat you till you're bloody and walk away without a backward glance. Do not look at my wife or her sister. Never again. Do not speak to them. Do not even acknowledge them. If you see them out, you will simply turn and walk the other way so that they will not have to suffer your presence."

They had walked only a few short steps from where Simon stood glowering at them when Vincent abruptly stopped. He turned only his head, just enough to see Simon from the corner of his eye and uttered something that made the other man blanch. "Gutterborn as I am, we have friends in common . . . give Ardmore my regards when next you see him."

Hettie had no notion who Ardmore was, but it was apparent from the way Simon reacted that the name was very familiar to him.

Too many secrets. Too many intrigues. Was a simple life really too much to ask for?

Chapter Twenty-Three

MAURICE BATES WAS a creature of habit. He'd work his shift. At the end of it, he'd eat a bowl of stew and a hunk of bread at the tavern nearest his lodging house. He would drink precisely one tankard of ale. No more or less. Then he'd go home. On every other Wednesday, he'd visit a woman who had an apartment on Bedford Ct. Close enough to Bow Street's office and his lodging for convenience, far enough away to avoid any complications. When he visited this woman, he stayed with her for exactly forty-five minutes. No more or less.

It was for those reasons that Joss knew precisely where to find him. Like clockwork, the door to number 47 Bedford Court opened and Bates appeared. He looked pristine. So pristine that Joss was hard pressed to believe the man had spent the past three quarters of an hour swiving some randy widow. But there was a looseness in the way Bates moved, a relaxation that normally was never seen in the man. Maybe, Joss thought, if the bastard visited the widow a little more frequently, he'd be less of an arse.

"Bates," he called out and saw the other man look up. Whatever looseness or relaxation had suffused him prior simply vanished. Instantly, his chin came up, shoulders back, spine ramrod straight—but it was the derision on Bates' face that truly marked his disdain for his former coworker.

Joss didn't give a rat's ass if Bates liked him, respected him, or wished him to the devil on a regular basis. "I need a word with you, Bates," Joss insisted.

"You can make an appointment and see me at Bow Street," Bates replied.

"I don't think so. I'm here to talk to you about Lady Ernsdale."

Bates's expression shifted into a grim smile. "Ah, the murderess. I take it her brother-in-law sent you. Always the Hound's errand boy. What do you get out of that arrangement with him, Ettinger? A pat on the head? A nice juicy bone? Or does he toss you scraps like the cur you are?"

He refused to let the man get a rise out of him. "Lady Ernsdale is no murderer. And if you try to make her look like one, it'll be the end of the career you prize so greatly. If you are wise, you will heed this and turn your investigation in a different direction. The person who had the most to gain from Arthur Dagliesh's death is his nephew Simon."

"His own nephew cut him down in the street?"

"It's as sensible an explanation as his wife doing so," Joss pointed out. "Simon Dagliesh is in deep with the worst money-lenders in all of England. He owes his fucking soul to Ardmore."

Bates paused. "Ardmore?"

"Yes. Ardmore. Look, investigate as you will. But do not be so single-minded in proving that Lady Ernsdale is a murderer that you let an actual one go free."

"Bring me proof. I need more than just your word, after all. You're not exactly the most trustworthy sort, are you? The entire time you were working for Bow Street, you were in the Hound's pocket. Feeding him intel and misdirecting us so we wouldn't catch him in the act."

That hadn't exactly been the way of it. Yes, he'd turned a blind eye to what the Hound did in many instances. But the Hound had also helped them to put some of the worst criminals in a noose or on a ship bound for distant lands. It had been a mutually beneficial arrangement, and the London streets were safer for what they had done. Even if it had required bending a few rules. But Bates wouldn't give a damn about that. He was all about the glory.

"I'll bring you proof. In the meantime, leave her the hell alone," Joss warned.

"Or what? The Hound will make me disappear? His teeth have been pulled and his claws clipped . . . he made that choice when he walked away from his criminal enterprise for nothing but a skirt."

Joss looked Bates dead in the eye. "It's not the Hound you have to worry about. Not when it comes to her. Do we understand one another, Bates, or do I need to spell it out for you more clearly than that?"

"A murderess and an adulteress. It hardly makes her look less guilty."

"Don't make an enemy of me, Bates. Don't put me in a position where I'll have to show you which of us is the better man. I'm not asking you to ignore a crime. I'm asking you to be certain you have the right of it before you lay something that ugly at her door."

Bates looked at him. Then he shrugged. "Forty-eight hours. I'll give you forty-eight hours to prove it. And at that time, I'll take her into custody, and I'll get a confession from her one way or another."

Joss knew then that it didn't really matter. Bates wanted her to be guilty because getting her arrested, getting her convicted, would be the way to make a name for himself. "You won't build your career by putting a noose around her neck. I'll see to that."

Walking away from Bates, he headed for Vincent's and Honoria's home. His home, at least temporarily.

Chapter Twenty-Four

DINNER WAS A decidedly awkward affair. The foursome seated around the table spoke of the mundane and the inane. No one touched upon the dangerous and tenuous situation that faced them. There was no talk of Arthur's murder, of Simon's plots, or Inspector Bates's apparent vendetta against all of womankind. In short, it was like so many society events. Nothing of consequence or substance was discussed, and everyone pretended to be completely unaware of the tension that existed between the parties present.

For Hettie, it was a relief when it finally came to an end. She and Honoria retreated to the drawing room while Vincent and Joss went to his study. Not a one of them cared that it was the proper or done thing. They all simply wanted to be away from one another for a moment.

"You must talk with him, Hettie," Honoria said as she perched on the edge of the settee. "The two of you have to reach some sort of understanding. The sooner the better. Or, if you should decide to marry, do you really want to face the scrutiny of everyone attempting to determine whether or not you are with child? And of course, this child will be born far less than nine months from the date of the marriage. Which means that everyone will be wondering whether the child is his or Arthur's."

"Do you honestly imagine that I've thought of anything else?

But I cannot make decisions about marriage until we've done something to deter Inspector Bates. If he gets his way, he'll see me hang, and then it won't matter, will it? None of it will matter then."

"That will not happen," Honoria insisted. "If I have to put you on a ship to Italy to myself, you will not see the inside of a cell. Wretched places."

Hettie laughed. There she was, an adulteress carrying her lover's child, while her sister—who was always proper and circumspect and moral—was the only one of them who had spent any time under arrest. "I will happily take your word for the conditions. I have no wish to ever gain firsthand knowledge of what those facilities offer."

Honoria shuddered. "I pray that your wish to remain ignorant is granted. What will you do, Hettie? Mr. Ettinger—Joss— had his reasons for whatever transpired between you after."

He did. And he'd touched on them briefly. It rang true for her that he would do something out of some misguided sense of nobility. He might cast himself as the villain, but he was anything but. "I know that he had his reasons. I simply have to decide if they are enough. And it isn't—I am tired of being at the whim of a man. First with father, then with Arthur. I never had any power of my own. I existed solely at their mercy. I will not be with another man who feels he has the right to make all of my decisions for me. And as a widow, I've earned that right. Haven't I?"

"You have," she agreed. "But it can be a very lonely way to live. Men are high-handed by nature. All of them. Some will use that tendency to protect you, and others will use it to hurt and exploit you. Which of those two is the case with Mr. Josiah Ettinger?"

Hettie didn't answer. In truth, no answer was required. They both knew he fell into the former category rather than the latter. "I am very tired, Honoria. I think I shall retire for the night if you don't mind."

Honoria rose and briefly embraced her. "Rest, Hettie. To-morrow is soon enough to tackle the many problems to be faced."

Hettie nodded and then left the drawing room. Taking the stairs slowly, a sign of her exhaustion, she made her way to the room that she had been given for an indefinite period of time. But as she reached it, she paused. Directly across the corridor, opening the door to his own chamber, was Joss.

Hettie allowed her gaze to roam over him, drinking in everything about him. She knew his kiss. She knew the calluses on his hands and how they felt against her skin. She knew the power and strength of his body moving against hers. But she knew very little else.

"We should talk," he said.

"Must we?"

He sighed, his head dropping. "Not tonight, no. But soon. You should get some rest." With that he reached for the doorknob to walk away from her.

"I didn't say that I had no wish for your company. I simply said that I've no wish to talk," Hettie offered those very bold words before opening her own door and stepping inside. But she didn't close it behind her.

⤜⤜⤜✳⤛⤛⤛

JOSS STARED AT that open door for a moment. Bemused. Bewitched. Possibly even bedeviled by her, that open door tempted him. And he was not the sort to resist temptation when it was something he truly desired.

With slow, languid steps, he crossed the hall and stepped into her room. Pausing there, he closed the door quietly behind him. "If you've no wish to talk, what is that you want instead?"

"Is it really so hard to guess?"

"No," he answered softly. "But I don't want to guess. I want to know, beyond even the faintest shadow of doubt, that I'm here because you want me in your bed."

"I want you, Joss. In my bed. Tonight."

"Only tonight?" Her response mattered to him far more than it was safe to admit. Certainly more than he wished it to.

She gave him an assessing stare. "I don't know the answer to that. Not yet. But I don't want to be alone. And I don't want to lie here sleepless, plagued by racing thoughts about how many things could go wrong in my life. It's a terrible thing to admit, but I intend to use you as a distraction."

It wasn't what he'd wanted to hear. He wasn't even certain what it was he'd hoped she would say, only that his disappointment at her response was both surprising and worrisome. After all, theirs was not a romantic entanglement. Physical attraction did not make for love, not that he believed in such a thing. It was nothing more than a foolish, sentimental fancy. The world that had shaped him had been too ugly to leave such fine sensibilities behind.

Not that he didn't admire her honesty. Hettie, he was realizing, was a woman too practical in nature to further complicate their already fraught situation with lies. The only question left to answer was whether or not he was bothered enough by her reply to refuse her. But a glance at her, taking in the utter perfection of her face, gave him the direction he needed and perhaps a bit of clarity. He wanted her. She wanted him. Whatever madness it was that made him think there was more—could ever be more— to it than that was something he would simply have to control. Ruthlessly, if need be. He could protect her. He could take care of her. But he wouldn't make promises of feelings that simply weren't in him to give or receive.

"No. It's only terrible if you aren't honest about it. We have a lot of decisions to make. And they don't have to be made now. But that doesn't mean we shouldn't take our relief and our distractions when we can."

She turned her back to him, presenting the row of buttons at the back of her dinner dress. "I gave Foster the evening off. Help me with my gown?"

Stepping forward, he closed the distance between them, not stopping until he was close enough that her skirts brushed against his thighs. Rather than simply unbutton her gown, he dipped his head, pressing his lips to the tender spot at the nape of her neck. When she shivered in response, it emboldened him to continue.

Hettie had never had the benefit of being seduced. He couldn't even say that if he'd known of her innocence, things would have been any different that night in the Mint. Danger tended to erase any hint of refinement or tenderness, and they'd both been very aware that night of how close to death they had both come. But this was something altogether different. This was a chance to show her all the things that she had missed. All the things that had been denied her.

"You don't need to persuade me," she murmured. "I know what I want."

"No," he said. "You do not. Not entirely. But you will."

✦

Chapter Twenty-Five

HETTIE COULDN'T SUPPRESS the shiver that raced through her. His words were laced with sensual promise. And every touch only proved that he was correct. As his lips moved along the back of her neck, down to the curve where it joined her shoulder, she felt her skin prickling with awareness and anticipation. But he would not be hurried. Languid kisses and caresses that both soothed and inflamed followed. Her breathing became ragged, and soft pleasured sighs escaped her even before he'd removed a stitch of clothing from either one of them.

It had been two months since their night together. And she'd relived it in her mind countless times since then. But the power of mere memories could not compare to the reality of his touch, to the pounding of her heart and the way the blood raced in her veins.

As each button at the back of her gown slipped free, she felt the cooler air of the room against her fevered skin. But only for a moment. Then it was replaced by the warmth of his mouth as he kissed and licked every inch of her flesh that he bared. It wasn't until he finally reached the impediment of her chemise and stays that he halted. From that point, he made quick work of her gown. It skimmed past her hips to pool on the floor, and her petticoats followed seconds later.

"You are shockingly adept at getting me out of my clothes,"

Hettie whispered.

"I am highly motivated," he replied, the whispered words skittering along the sensitive skin of her neck. "You are a feast for the eyes, Hettie."

"And is that all you'll be doing? Just looking at me?" she challenged.

She felt the rumbling of his chest as a soft chuckle escaped him. "Oh, no," he answered. "It's a time for action, I think. Even if looking was my only intent, the flesh is far too willing and my resolve far too weak."

Before Hettie could respond, he simply lifted her in his arms and bore her to the bed. When he'd placed her gently against the pillows, he stretched out beside her and his hands continued their exploration. He touched her everywhere. There were parts of her body that she had never imagined were so sensitive. There were certainly parts of her that she had never imagined could offer such pleasure. When he kissed the inside of her wrist, goosebumps erupted on her skin. And after, when he pressed a tender kiss to the center of her open palm, the tenderness of that gesture rocked her in a way that she had not expected.

Wanting Joss was bad enough. But having more tender feelings for him, having feelings for him at all, might well destroy her. But she didn't protest. It was as he had said. The flesh was willing and her resolve far too weak. She lacked the fortitude to deny herself pleasure in the moment to spare her pain in the future.

He sat up long enough to shrug out of his coat. Then he unbuttoned his waistcoat before discarding it and his shirt. Then it was only his broad chest with his lightly bronzed skin and the massive shoulders that she had placed her burdens upon.

Thought fled altogether when he returned to her side and pressed his mouth to hers. The rasp of his whiskers, the hunger in his kiss, and the intoxicating taste of him flooded her senses, rendering her mindless. She clung to him, straining against him in an effort to get closer still, even when there was not even air between them.

Hettie wanted to beg him to hurry. To beg him to end the misery of wanting that she had suffered since their first night together. But she lacked the words. Instead, she simply kissed him back with all the desire that she felt for him, all the desperation and hunger that had been her constant companion since then.

SHE KISSED HIM like she was starved for him. And he supposed that was true enough. He'd certainly starved for her. From the first moment he had touched her, he hadn't looked at another woman. Not a single woman that he encountered had even tempted him to look twice. Because no woman would ever be all that she was. In one night she had altered him forever.

Having another opportunity to touch her, to feel her silken skin that was far too fine for someone like him to ever touch, and to taste the sweetness of her lips—that was something he hadn't accounted for. She wasn't for him. He'd thought it then, and he still believed it. But nothing he'd achieved in life had been for him. He was a street rat from the rookeries. He shouldn't have survived, much less thrived. He shouldn't have learned to read and write and then be able to parlay those skills into a career. Nothing that he had was something that, based on the way his ignoble existence had begun, should be his. But he would claim her anyway. And even if the devil unleashed hell itself on him, he would not let her go. If that meant seduction, if that meant locking them away somewhere together, sheltered from the rest of the world, he'd do it.

Her hands moved over him, exploring, tracing the lines of muscles and the more than occasional scar. But if she continued, it would all be over before it had begun.

Taking both her hands in his, Joss lifted them above her head, holding them imprisoned in one of his. "Don't rush me. Not tonight. I can't think when you touch me—and I need to think tonight. I need to make this perfect for you."

"I don't need perfect. I just need you."

All his carefully laid plans of seduction, of using pleasure to bind her to him, those faded. Washed away by the naked hunger in her gaze and the vulnerability she had shown him in uttering that confession. If any woman had her reasons to be guarded, it was Hettie. That she chose not to be so with him . . . that humbled him.

Joss slid his free hand along her body, over her ribs and the swell of her hip, then along the supple flesh of her stocking-clad legs. All just to reach the hem of her chemise, to draw it up to her waist and reveal the dark curls nestled between her thighs. It was an irresistible sight.

"Open for me, Hettie. Let me please you," he urged her, pressing his lips against her ear.

She drew in a deep shuddering breath, then parted her thighs, opening herself to him in blatant invitation.

Joss kissed her once more, taking her mouth even as he slipped his hand between her parted thighs and stroked her fevered flesh. And all the while, he savored every sound she made. Every whimper and cry was a victory for him.

Chapter Twenty-Six

HETTIE LAY AWAKE with him sleeping beside her. All the while she thought of all the things she'd heard people say about lovemaking. And she thought of all the things she'd heard from the women she encountered through her charities and their much more realistic, if crude, understanding of physical intimacy. Not a single one of those conversations had prepared her for him. For how he'd made her feel.

The passion and pleasure of their first night together had not been an aberration. If their activities from earlier in the evening had proven one thing to her, it was that Josiah Ettinger knew her body perhaps better than she did herself. It left her feeling disadvantaged in some way. She didn't have the same level of experience to draw from. She didn't know all the things to do that would even the field of play between them. Right now, it felt as if he held all the cards and she was simply being buoyed along by the current he created.

There was one undeniable truth that she would admit, at least to herself if not yet to him. No other man would ever be the perfect combination of dangerous and protective that he was. No other man would ever make her feel safe without also making her feel smothered. That was only him. The man who had fathered her child and whom she was once more counting on to save her life.

He turned over in bed, one heavily muscled thigh draped over her and his arms tightening about her, pulling her back against his chest. And yet he slept on. His deep, even breathing was proof enough of that.

Rather than try to extricate herself from his slumberous embrace, Hettie settled into it, allowing the warmth of his body to seep into her own. It calmed her racing thoughts and eased the grip of fear that held her so firmly in its sway. And that bit of relaxation allowed her to both accept and admit one undeniable truth: There was a sort of inevitability about them. It felt as though they'd been moving in concentric circles about one another, caught up in the currents of their own lives until they were finally brought together. Was that enough?

She had wanted love. Having married once for position and rank, only to suffer terribly for it, she'd clung to the notion that one day she might marry again—and marry a man who cherished her. She wasn't certain that Joss could ever give her that. He could offer her protection. Heaven knew he could offer her pleasure and passion.

"Your thoughts are troublesome enough to keep the whole house awake," he murmured against her ear.

"I thought you were sleeping."

"I was," he said. "But instead of holding a warm and pliant woman in my arms, I find myself holding a tense one—your body is all but rigid with whatever turmoil is brewing in your thoughts."

"I can't help it. There are so many things happening—and I feel like I'm barely keeping my head above water. And you know how I feel about water!"

She felt his smile as his lips pressed against her neck.

"We have time. We have time to figure things out for us," he said. "So that goes on the shelf, at least for a while. And we focus on the things we are not yet fully in control of. Simon and Bates. Once we have them where we want them, then there will be time enough to figure out the rest."

Looking down at her already slightly rounded belly, she made a sound of derision. "We don't have that much time."

"Two weeks," he vowed. "Give me a fortnight, and all of this will be gone from your life. These burdens they have put on you will be lifted. I promise."

"Do not promise things that you cannot possibly deliver," she rebuked softly.

"I do not. I never have," he said. "Two weeks, Hettie. Then we look to the future and what it means for us both."

IT TOOK SOME time before she finally drifted to sleep. Gradually, the tension seeped from her and her eyes fluttered closed. And in the faint light that filtered in through curtains they'd not bothered to close, he studied the delicate lines of her profile. The slim, straight, and slightly upturned nose was the sort that most women bemoaned not having. He'd never met a single woman in all his life who was satisfied with her appearance. Yet, Hettie seemed to be. As well she should. In spite of her awareness of her beauty, she lacked any conceit or vanity about it. Likely because she understood it to be a double-edged sword.

His gaze then drifted to the fullness of her lips, slightly parted in her repose. And yet even in the boneless sleep of exhaustion that had finally claimed her, her chin jutted forward in display of her enduring stubbornness. It wasn't a flaw to his mind. It was simply part of her, and perhaps one of the best parts.

Extricating himself from the bed was not exactly easy, at least without doing so in a fashion that would not wake her. Finally, he rose and retrieved his clothing, dressing silently in the dim light. With one last lingering look at her, he turned and left the room. He was about to do something he hated, something that galled him beyond belief. He'd be getting his hands dirty once more, whether he liked it or not.

Padding silently to the door, boots in hand, he exited to the corridor and then made his way downstairs. He didn't question for a moment that Vincent would be awake. He might have sought his wife's bed and her company for a time, but the man rarely slept.

As predicted, the Hound was in his study, sipping a brandy and staring at several documents spread out on the desk before him. He looked up as Joss entered.

"I rather thought we'd seen the last of you for the night. Surely you have better things to occupy your time!"

"The same could be said of you," Joss retorted, taking a seat across the desk from him. "I can only presume we are both awake because of the situation Hettie finds herself in."

"The one where her nephew and a corrupt Runner are trying to pin a murder on her? Or the one where she's having a child that is most decidedly not her late husband's?"

Joss shrugged. "Both warrant an equal amount of urgency, I think."

"So they do. What is on your mind, Joss? You wouldn't be here unless there was something particular you have thought of."

"Bates has a mistress. To my knowledge, she's not a light skirt, not some third-rate courtesan . . . but they aren't married. And she lives alone in a rented apartment. We need to find out who is paying that rent. Because it can't be her, and it can't be him. Not on what a Runner makes."

"You think he's being paid off?"

Joss nodded. "I do. Maybe not now, but certainly at some time in the past."

"What's the address?"

"Number forty-seven Bedford Court," Joss said.

"Alright. I'll speak to an agent tomorrow about acquiring the property."

"You don't have to buy the bloody building!" Joss protested.

"Maybe, maybe not. If it's a good investment with reasonable and legitimate returns, there is no reason not to do so. Regardless, as a prospective buyer who wishes to retain tenants, I'd certainly be entitled to ask questions regarding how rents are paid and by whom."

It was a solid plan, and one he certainly should have thought of. One he might have thought of had he not been so distracted by other things. "Right. I'm off to the Cock and Crow."

"Why the devil would you go there? If you want to drink something to rot your innards, no doubt Mrs. Ivers will have some poisonous cleaning concoction that would do the trick."

Joss laughed then. "Not going for a drink. There's a fellow I know, someone who used to feed me quite a bit of information when I was still with the Runners. It's a meeting place, as you know. A place where contracts of a diabolical nature are often struck. I doubt very much that Simon Dagliesh managed all this on his own. If I can find someone to place him there, and to place him with known thugs for hire, then I can cast enough doubt on his motives that Hettie would at least not be the only suspect."

The silence in the room stretched, becoming quite uncomfortable. "That's your only destination?" Vincent finally asked.

"Do you mean will I be stopping by the opium den that is operated next door? No. I will not. I mean to visit the tavern, speak to my man there, and return here—hopefully before Hettie awakens to find me gone."

"At what point, if you haven't returned, should we be concerned?"

Joss didn't take offense. He knew that Vincent wasn't only thinking of the temptations that lay ahead of him. "If I'm not back by breakfast, then you should worry."

Chapter Twenty-Seven

HETTIE AWAKENED ALONE. She was disappointed initially. But then a wave of nausea overtook her. As she had no desire to suffer the indignity of casting up her accounts in front of Joss, she conceded it was for the best. Not to mention that the servants were already up and about. While Honoria's household might be less than conventional, having her very recently widowed sister entertain her lover in their home might be pushing the limits of what certain staff members would tolerate.

When her stomach was entirely empty, she lay back on the bed, exhausted and pale. Once she had caught her breath, she sat up again, moving slowly, testing the degree of dizziness and nausea very cautiously. Finally, when she was certain she wasn't about to retch or fall over, she moved to the wash basin and began her morning ablutions. She preferred to dress her own hair and see to her own toilette. But she did ring for her maid when it was time to dress. Foster had come with her. The girl's loyalty to her would have made her a target had she remained in the house after Simon assumed the title. *If* Simon assumed the title. Though she supposed it did not matter, as someone, even if Simon was proven to be responsible for Arthur's death, would be taking possession of the house.

A moment later, as Hettie placed the very last pin in her hair, Foster came bustling in with another black gown. Honoria was slowly giving up her widow's weeds and Hettie was inheriting them. Not that she minded. In truth, if it wouldn't be such a scandal, she wouldn't don black at all. But at least for the time being, it was to her benefit to appear the grieving widow. Otherwise, she would simply be fueling the fire of Inspector Bates's suspicions.

Once she had donned the latest of her hand-me-down gowns, she moved toward the door. "Foster, I won't be needing you for the remainder of the day. Why don't you take the rest of the day off? I know you'd like to see your mother and sister. And it might be best if you inform them in person of the recent changes in our situation."

"Will you be keeping me on, my lady? I know that things will change for you . . . financially, now that you're a widow."

"You'll be staying with me, Foster. I'm not paupered by Arthur's death. My social calendar will become very slim, I'm afraid. And depending upon where I wind up living, your duties may change, but you will always have a position with me if you desire it," Hettie reassured her. "You were very brave in retrieving the ransom letter and taking it to Honoria. I will not forget that. You saved my life as certainly as Mr. Ettinger did."

The maid blushed and ducked her head. "I been with you ever since you married Lord Ernsdale . . . it weren't right the way you was treated. I'm not the only one what thought so. But my mother raised me not to turn my back on someone in need. I reckon when they took you, you was definitely in need. I did what was right."

"You did. But at great risk to yourself, and that is what courage means, Foster. Do not ever think that I am not grateful to you."

"Go get your breakfast, m'lady. I'll tidy up in here and then go to see my mother."

Hettie would have said more, but it was very apparent to her that the young woman was embarrassed by the praise. So she kept her silence and exited her chamber, making for the breakfast room. But when she entered that room, it became immediately apparent to her that something was terribly wrong. Vincent and Honoria had abruptly stopped speaking, and the tension in the room was palpable. The fact that neither of them would make eye contact with her was far more revealing than they might have realized.

"What is wrong?" she demanded, her stomach knotting with fear.

"Possibly nothing," Vincent answered. "Or possibly, Joss may be in trouble."

Hettie's steps faltered. "What sort of trouble?"

"That is undetermined at this point," Vincent said. "He wanted to visit a particular establishment where Simon Dagliesh may have procured assistance in his scheme."

"Where he hired someone to kill Arthur, you mean," she fired back rather pointedly.

"Yes, that is what we suspect. If not kill him, then to watch him and alert Simon to any opportunities to do so. After all, no one can watch a man twenty-four hours out of the day. Especially not if he is forbidden entrance into his house. Why did you inform your late husband that Simon was not welcome there?"

There had been any number of reasons. His drinking. His gambling. His leering glances and grasping hands. For the duration of her marriage, she'd endured his advances—his offers to provide her the passion her aging husband had been unable to. Repeated refusals had not curbed his efforts. It had gotten to the point that Hettie had always made certain she was never alone with him. She didn't know that he would have forced the issue, but she'd certainly been smart enough not to give him an opportunity to try.

"He's a cad. A worthless libertine who does not understand the meaning of the word no or that every woman who crosses is path is not available to him," Hettie explained. "And that is all I mean to say about it."

Vincent said nothing for a moment. Honoria's spine had

stiffened to a degree that Hettie feared her sister might actually do herself irreparable harm. "I see," Vincent finally managed. "So, in short, the death of your husband was to line his pockets and give him a title. Pinning it on you is petty revenge for having been denied what he saw as his right."

Hettie blinked in surprise. "It had not occurred to me, but I suppose that is possible. Convenience and a bit of vengeance all in one would certainly appeal to him. Are you going after Mr. Ettinger?"

"I have men scouring that area of the city. If he's there, he will be found."

"Alive?" Hettie demanded.

Only silence greeted her question. Sometimes no response was all the response that was required.

Wordlessly, Hettie sank into a chair at the table. And there they all remained, silent and waiting. Waiting for him to return or waiting for the awful possibility to be confirmed that he would never return at all.

Chapter Twenty-Eight

HIS HEAD ACHED. That was the first thing Joss realized as his eyes opened in the very dimly lit room. Glancing around, it didn't take a great deal of mental acuity to determine that he was still very much within the premises of the Cock and Crow. The cellar, most likely, given that the floors were damp earth, there were no windows at all, and the only light was what managed to pierce gaps in the floorboards above his head. Around him, barely discernible with the meager illumination, were stacks of barrels and shelves likely filled with bottles of watered-down whiskey.

Sitting up, he touched his hand to the side of his head and felt the stickiness of blood. Then memory came rushing back. He'd come in, asked a few questions, and as he'd been preparing to leave, someone had jumped him. Two people, in fact. He might have made it, had a serving wench who worked for the establishment not bashed him over the head with a heavy crock. He couldn't imagine that she was anything to Dagliesh or that he was anything to her. But it was likely she had some connection to the man he'd hired. Now, he just had to figure out how to get himself out of the cellar so he could find out.

Struggling to his feet, he cursed when he bumped his already abused head against the beam above him. When the pain subsided to a tolerable level, he moved forward carefully, keeping his shoulders hunched to avoid repeating his previous mistake.

There were stairs in the far corner, though calling them that was generous. Steep and impossibly narrow, he had to turn his feet sideways to stay on the tread. At the top, he banged on the door, but no one answered. He had no notion what time it was, but based on the lack of noise coming from above, he had to assume it was morning. Even drunkards and criminals slept sometime, and it was typically when the rest of the world was awake.

There was no way to break the door down. With the stairs as they were, he'd never get the leverage required. His only hope was to wait for someone to open that door and then rush them. "Fuck," he whispered in the darkness. "I hope you were listening, Vincent, when I said to send help if I didn't make it home by morning."

Settling down on the steps, resting his aching head in his hands, he cursed his own arrogance. He should have known better than to come to such a place alone. It had made him vulnerable, and he was paying the price for that hubris.

But the sound of voices abruptly ended his reverie. And one of those voices he recognized. "Bates!" he called out as he banged loudly on the door. "Bates, get me the hell out of here!"

MAURICE BATES DIDN'T like to be wrong. If there was one thing that goaded him beyond anything else, it was the prospect of looking like a fool. With what had been disclosed to him about Simon Dagliesh, particularly the man's indebtedness to a notorious criminal, he'd decided it would behoove him to at least look in the direction of Ernsdale's heir.

What he'd discovered thus far had fallen perfectly in line with everything that Ettinger had told him. He wasn't foolish enough to simply take the man at his word, but in this instance, he had to concede that he'd been speaking the truth.

"Do you know this man?" Bates asked the sleepy-eyed proprietor who had been dozing in a room upstairs with a girl that was most assuredly not his wife. He held out a news sheet bearing a sketch of the newly named Lord Ernsdale. "Has he been here?"

"I seen him a time or two, but he's not a regular," the man said.

"When did you see him last?"

"How the bloody hell should I know?" the proprietor groused. "Don't mark the date when I see someone darken my door. Why would I? Don't much matter to me anyway!"

"It matters because he likely came here to retain the services of a murderer for hire. This could make you an accomplice," Bates informed him sharply.

"Not an accomplice to nothing. I pour the ale, and I keep my mouth shut. I don't hear nothing, I don't see nothing, and I don't damn well say nothing!"

Bates opened his mouth to retort, but another sound gave him pause. From somewhere within the building, he could hear thumping. Someone was banging on a door. And amidst the muffled shouts, he could make out his name. "Where's that coming from?"

"Don't know," the man said, still resolutely looking at a point past Bates' shoulder. He hadn't made eye contact from the first.

Bates looked back at the two inspectors he'd had accompany him. After all, everyone knew that the Cock and Crow was a dangerous place, especially for Runners. "Wait here and watch him. I'll yell out if I need assistance."

With those parting instructions, Bates began searching the lower floor of the establishment. In a small corridor tucked back behind the stairwell, he found the source of the noise. The heavy oaken door was solid and locked from the outside.

"Wait a moment, and I'll get the key," he shouted.

Returning to the main room, he pulled the billy club—standard issue for every Runner—and smacked it into the palm of his hand. The threat was obvious, and he'd long ago figured out that sometimes the threat of violence was more effective than violence itself. No point in fighting when one didn't have to. "Now, I'm going to give you one chance to tell me what I want to know before I make you tell me what I want to know. What is that room?"

"It's the cellar," the other man answered, his voice barely above a whisper as he eyed the billy club warily.

"Get me the key."

The proprietor looked momentarily mutinous, but Bates raised the club, just enough, and the man capitulated. With a muttered curse, he produced a heavy iron key from the pocket of his coat.

Key in hand, Bates returned to that locked door. It took a bit to work the lock, as there was considerable rust on both it and the key. That made it quite clear that securing the room beyond was an unusual occurrence. So it was highly unlikely that anyone imprisoned inside had come to that outcome by accident.

When at last the lock sprang free, he released the hasp and stepped back. Seconds later, it swung open and Josiah Ettinger appeared. Hunched over due to the low ceiling and looking more than a bit worse for wear, he emerged from the darkness of the cellar.

"Why are you here, and how did you come to be detained in a makeshift cell?" Bates demanded.

IF THERE WAS one person in the world Joss did not want to aid in his rescue, it was Maurice Bates. But he didn't have the luxury of looking a gift horse in the mouth. "I came here to ascertain whether or not Simon Dagliesh had hired an accomplice from the bevy of criminals that utilize the Cock and Crow for their enterprises. Two men jumped me as I started to leave, and someone, a tavern wench, I believe, bashed me over the head . . .

that's the last thing I remember before waking up in the cellar."

"Did you find anything?"

"Nothing of note. But clearly someone does not like me asking questions here. If we identify the two men who jumped me, it may lead us to whomever Dagliesh hired to assist him in killing his uncle."

Bates's eyes narrowed. "You still think her entirely innocent?"

"I do. If she'd wanted out of the marriage, she had other ways to get out of it." *Or she'd had other ways out of it, until he couldn't keep his cock in his bloody trousers.* "And after the ransom refusal, had she elected to remain with her sister and the Hound, no one would have questioned it, and Ernsdale wouldn't have dared brave the scandal to demand she return."

Bates was silent for a moment, considering those things. "Those points do have a certain degree of logic. But there has to be more."

"Hettie would never have harmed him. She's not the sort to plot out a murder for hire. It's not in her nature."

Bates drew back. "Hettie . . . not Lady Ernsdale. You are more than simply a hired inquiry agent to her! You have a personal relationship with the woman!"

"I do," Joss admitted. "Just as you have a personal relationship with the woman residing at 47 Bedford Court."

"Do not dare threaten her!"

Joss shook his head in denial. "I'm not threatening her. I'm just pointing out that if the situation were reversed, and she was facing such accusations, you'd do exactly as I am to prove her innocent."

"Fine. I'll take it on account," Bates admitted. "You're a lot of things, Ettinger, but your ability to read a suspect has always been spot on."

Because he'd been raised in a place where reading someone's intent and capabilities had often been a matter of life and death, he'd learned early on what the cost of inaccuracy could be. "Speak to her. Speak to her without any sort of bias. After all, it was Dagliesh who pointed you in her direction . . . ask yourself why he would do that. And how the hell did he even know that his uncle was already dead and had likely been murdered?" That was the thought that had been niggling at his mind from the beginning. The man had time to seek out the Runner, pass along his accusatory tale, and set something in motion that would cast suspicion on anyone but him. Still, Simon had known before anyone else did that Ernsdale wasn't only dead but had been murdered. If that wasn't some proof of his guilt, what could be?

Bates nodded. "She's no longer my primary suspect. But I'll not be taking her off the list altogether. Not until I know for certain who the guilty party is."

It was a gamble to confess it, but Joss didn't feel he had any choice. They needed Bates on their side. "That's all any of us want, Inspector Bates. To find out precisely who did this . . . because Lady Ernsdale is with child. And if the person who murdered Lord Ernsdale did so to gain the title, that makes her a potential victim rather than a suspect."

"Is the child Ernsdale's?"

Joss did not lie. But he answered without answering. "Under the law, any child conceived during a marriage is considered to be the progeny of the husband. And that's what we're up against here. The letter of the law."

"I'll ask around about Dagliesh."

"Find out if he has any connection to the Walpoles," Ettinger suggested. "I can't help but feel there is something there."

"Is this one of your hunches or based in fact?"

"A hunch," Joss admitted. "But you know they are never wrong."

Bates cursed. Because he did know.

Chapter Twenty-Nine

SIMON ENTERED THE solicitor's office in high spirits. As quickly as the man had summoned him, he could only imagine that things had gone smoothly with Henrietta and she had capitulated to his demands. It didn't take long for his spirits to flag. The grim-faced solicitor appeared quite put out.

"What's happened?"

"Your aunt is with child," the solicitor replied. "And there is naught to do now but wait. Perhaps the child will be female and it will have no bearing on your claim to the title. But if she gives birth to a son—I do not need to tell you how disastrous that would be for you."

Simon sank into a chair. "With child? It cannot be my uncle's! He was impotent!"

"Who knows that? Who can testify to it? Only his wife, and it is in her best interest to say nothing!"

Simon cursed bitterly. "I'm a dead man. Ardmore will not give me any more time. If I cannot repay him, it will be the end of me . . . and you. You're just as indebted to him as I am!"

"You think I do not know that?" the solicitor snapped. "There is one possibility . . . women lose their babes all the time. Just because she's with child is no guarantee. If Lady Ernsdale were to suffer some sort of accident . . . perhaps a fall?"

"It won't be easy. She's moved in with her sister and that

criminal! I'll not be able to get to her."

The solicitor shook his head. "Not you. But a servant perhaps? A maid or a footman who could be swayed to see our way of things?"

Simon nodded. Remembering the maid who had been Hettie's constant companion and a constant thorn in his side, he smiled. The girl's mother and sister lived in town. The mother was not well, and the girl—she was young. Very young. Not even fifteen. Foster would do anything for her mistress, true. But would she do those things if it meant the life or death of her family?

"I'll take care of it," Simon replied. "By the end of the day, we'll have the situation in hand."

HETTIE WAS BESIDE herself with worry. And guilt. If Joss was in danger, she had placed him there. She'd gone to him for help. Demanded it, in fact. Now, she had no notion where he was or what sort of trouble he might have encountered. Simon had proven himself to be above nothing when it came to getting what he wanted.

Pacing the length of her room furiously, she could feel the hot sting of tears. It wasn't sadness, though she certainly felt it. It wasn't anger, though that was present as well. It was frustration. Frustration because there was nothing she could do besides wait. Whether she waited until Joss finally—hopefully—returned or whether it was until Vincent could provide some information about what had occurred, then she was well and truly stuck.

"There is no hell greater than uncertainty," she muttered.

Just then, her chamber door opened and she jumped, startled by the unexpected intrusion. But her shock gave way to relief so quickly that she nearly collapsed from it. Joss stood in the doorway, his large frame filling it entirely. And while he was a bit dirty and a bit banged up, he was very much alive and he was there with her. There where she could touch him and know that he was real and safe and hers. Hers.

Hettie had thought she had not made a decision regarding her future. It would appear there was no decision to be made at all. Had it ever been in doubt that she would concede to his will in the matter? Not really. Certainly not to anyone who knew either of them.

"What happened?" she asked.

"Jumped by two brutes in the tavern and whacked over the head with some sort of crock by a serving wench. Knocked over the head, bundled off to a cellar, and locked in . . . until Bates showed up. I think the good Inspector has had a change of heart where you're concerned. He admitted that you are no longer his lead suspect, but that is not the same thing as not being a suspect ad all," he warned. "You still need to lay low for a bit, keep the gossips and well-meaning gawkers away."

"But it's a step in the right direction, though it clearly came at a high cost," she observed.

"I've had worse. And not so very long ago," he replied. "Now, Hettie, I mean to have a bath and get myself clean. And when that is done, we are going to have a long talk about what we need to do to secure your future—our future."

She nodded. That was perfectly fine with her. The prospect of losing him altogether had brought home to her one very key fact: she'd likely fallen in love with Joss the first night he'd plucked her from the filth of the Neckinger River. And maybe he didn't love her in return, at least not yet, but someday he would. And until then, she'd love hard enough for the both of them. "I'll be waiting."

— ❧❦❧ —

Chapter Thirty

JOSS FINISHED HIS bath. He shaved. He dressed in clean clothes that had materialized seemingly out of nowhere. But then, Stavers had always taken care of anything they might need, often without a word being said. When he was done, he headed back across the hall to Hettie's room. He knocked but did not wait to be asked inside. He was done with waiting altogether. Hettie was reclining on a chaise before the window, staring out at the weak sunlight which filtered in.

"I'll be applying for a common license. Sadly, I lack the status to procure a special license. It will be a few days before we can make our appointment with the vicar, but I will make you my wife. And any child we have will be mine. Both legally and by blood."

Her head swiveled slightly until she could look at him. Only silence filled the space between them. It might have been a moment or an eternity. It all felt the same to him just then. Finally, she answered. "So quickly? It will be a scandal."

He raised one eyebrow. "Worse than bearing a child to a man whose impotence wasn't nearly as well concealed as he thought? Any bawd that had attempted to get a rise out of him in years had failed. Impotent husband. Pregnant and possibly murderous widow? Hettie, scandal is something you'd better accustom yourself to."

Another moment of silent consideration, then she gave a slight nod, more to herself and whatever thoughts were racing through her mind than to him. Then she met his gaze once more, "You'll need a better suit of clothes. I'm not marrying you in something that is so ill-fitting."

"Is that your only requirement?" His attempt to sound casual was a terrible failure.

"Yes . . . but I will warn you now, if you ever go off on your own like that again and place yourself in harm's way, I will kill you myself."

"You sound as though you might actually care for my wellbeing!"

"I do. Much as it pains me to admit it and unwise as it is, I am unable to help myself in the matter," she confessed. "I suppose if nothing else, I can blame it on my present condition. I am given to understand it makes most women emotionally volatile and completely irrational."

"You'll never be those things," Joss observed. "You are too fond of order. And you dislike losing control of yourself because controlling your own actions and responses to what occurs around you has been the only form of control you have ever had in life. And I know that because I see the same thing in myself."

Hettie rose from the chaise and walked toward him. She stopped when they were toe to toe. "I don't want to talk about my past . . . or yours, for that matter. What I want, more than anything, is to focus on my future. The one we will build together. But for now, you have a license to obtain. And once it is in your possession, I'll be waiting for you here."

"Naked in your bed, I hope," he said.

"I would have suggested it myself if you had not," she answered with a smile.

"I'll hurry."

And then she laughed. "I know. You've been given proper incentive."

She was close enough that he could reach out and touch her.

And that was a temptation he could not resist. Taking her hand, he pulled her closer still, close enough to wrap her fully in his arms. All else was forgotten. His aching head, the bumps and bruises, and even the numerous threats that hovered around them. Dipping his head, he pressed his lips to hers. It wasn't a kiss about hunger, about desire. But it was filled with something just as powerful. Promise.

SIMON WAS IN hiding, sleeping in a squalid room over a shop. It had taken the last bit of coin he had to persuade the shop owner to let him stay. Not that he could hide anywhere in all of London that Ardmore wouldn't find him. He just needed time. It was Henrietta or him. His life was on the line, after all. She was his only obstacle to claiming his uncle's estate. Eliminating her entirely would erase any questions about potential heirs. And the money would revert to his uncle's estate. Even if it did not, with possession of the estates he could get a mortgage that would at least keep him alive, keep Ardmore from fulfilling his threats. Now, it was all about opportunity—when and where he could actually get to her to see the deed done.

He'd thought Bates was the answer. His whispered allegations to the Runner had seemed to do the trick initially, but now Bates was asking questions about him. He was breathing down his neck, as was Mr. Ettinger, the Hound's lackey and, apparently, Henrietta's lover. How would he get to her? His mind circled back to the same conclusion he had reached earlier: her maid.

Henrietta had a very close relationship with the servant. It was not a surprise, as the girl had been her only ally in his uncle's house. Henrietta might be well guarded, but the maid would not be. She'd be out, running errands for her mistress, or enjoying her half day. There was no guarantee that Annie Foster would turn on her mistress, whatever threat he made. But Henrietta was loyal to a fault. She owed the maid her life, after all, and would likely do anything to keep the girl safe.

Yes. That was a better plan. The girl would be bait and nothing more. But with no money left, he'd have to do the dirty work himself. He didn't mind it. It was simply a complication he hadn't anticipated. Caution would be a requirement if he meant to keep himself hidden from Ardmore or the massive bruisers who worked for him.

Pacing the room, he kicked at a pile of clothes heaped on top of a trunk. Then inspiration struck. They were all—Ardmore, the Hound, and Ettinger—looking for a well-dressed gentleman. If he shed the trappings of his station and camouflaged himself as one of the teeming mass of impoverished wretches that roamed the rookeries and dens that surrounded the city of London, no one would recognize him. He could move freely without being detected at all.

Reaching up, he loosened the knot of his cravat and tugged it free, dropping the silk onto the dusty floor. Once he had divested himself of his perfectly tailored clothing, he donned the disgusting and dirty garments left behind by the room's last resident. Checking his reflection in the grimy glass of the window, he hardly recognized himself.

"Perfect," he murmured. Then he headed out, slipping down the stairs and out the back door of the shop into the narrow alley. He was a world away from Mayfair in status, but in distance it was only a mile. "I'll get her. One way or another. And I'll get that leech off my back."

Chapter Thirty-One

ANNIE FOSTER MOVED through the crowded streets with a spring in her step and a smile playing about her lips. It always made her happy to see her mother and sister. They lived in a modest set of rooms that her pay helped to provide for them.

Getting a position as a lady's maid had been a stroke of luck for all of them. But her smile faded. Because there was James. He was a terrible footman, but he was a very good man, and he took his responsibilities very seriously. Even though she knew he was attracted to her, that he wanted to be much more than simply a friend to her, his job was to keep her ladyship safe, and he wouldn't let anything else get in the way of that. At first, she'd only thought him handsome. But then she'd begun to see him as kind and caring. That had changed things.

She hadn't said anything to him yet, and she wasn't even certain she should. Just because she caught him watching her, that didn't mean anything. Lots of men looked even when they already had wives at home or when they had no intention of having a wife at all. And she wasn't the sort of girl to accept anything less than that.

Turning onto a bustling street that ran between St. James Park and Hyde Park, she saw a man up ahead of her. Clearly, he was watching her. At first, she thought he was one of Mr. Carrow's fellows, but something about him seemed a bit off. He was dressed rough, rougher than most of the men that worked for Mr. Carrow. And there was something about the way he stood there, his shoulders back all straight and tall. Most men from her class, from the working class, didn't move that way, didn't stand that way. They slouched or leaned. He stood like a gentleman would.

A frisson of fear snaked down Annie's spine. There was something about it all that didn't sit right. But it was too late. She'd kept walking, and now she was close enough to see that it was no mere laborer there. It was the nephew of her late employer, Lord Simon Dagliesh. Before she could turn away, he was on her. One of his arms was around her, that hand gripping her upper arm bruisingly. His other hand pressed something cold and metal against her ribs.

"This blade is a good six inches in length. Make a sound, and I'll bury it to the hilt in your lung and leave you here to die," he warned.

"What do you want?"

"Your cooperation," he said. "You're the bait in the trap, Annie. All you must do is be quiet and let the plan unfold. And if you don't . . . I know where your mother and sister are. I know everything . . . their names, their direction. I know that your sister is a pretty young thing and this world can be very unkind to pretty young girls. Don't make me be more of a villain than I have to be."

Annie knew that she didn't have a choice. No one would turn their hand to help a girl like her. Serving class were invisible to their betters and those in service were too reluctant to make a scene and lose their positions. Even if she called out for help, it was unlikely that anyone would bother to help or risk their own livelihood for her.

A glance around made her realize how true that was. No one was looking in her direction. A few, she realized, were clearly avoiding it. They'd not stick their necks out to help some unknown girl. He could tell them anything—that she was a pickpocket, that she was his wife. They'd believe him because he was a man. And it was very much a man's world.

"I'll cooperate. I'll do as you ask. But I can't imagine what you think to accomplish with this."

"Your mistress is very loyal," he answered. "And she'll do what she must to save you because that is what you did for her. Be a good girl, Annie, and you'll get out of this just fine."

With a sick feeling in her stomach and no trust for him at all, Annie allowed him to lead her down the street, far from the safety of the Hound's residence. How strange it was that the man the world called a criminal was the one a woman could count on.

HETTIE HAD LOST track of time. It wasn't until late afternoon that she looked up from the book she'd been using primarily as a distraction from all the things weighing on her mind. Realizing she would need to dress for dinner, she rang for her maid. But moments later, when the door opened, it wasn't Foster who greeted her but one of the parlor maids.

"Has Foster not returned?"

"Annie—pardon, m'lady, Foster has not returned from her half day," the maid said.

It wasn't like her. Foster had never been late returning from her half days. The girl was prompt to the point of compulsion. "Did she say anything before she left that she might be late returning?"

"No, m'lady. She said she was taking her half day and would go to visit her mother and sister in Lambeth. She ought to have been back by now. I hated to say anything. I didn't want her to be in trouble, but I'm so very worried."

"As am I," Hettie replied. "Is Mr. Carrow here?"

"He's in his study, m'lady, with Mr. Ettinger."

Hettie nodded. "Go back to the kitchens. And don't say anything to anyone else. I don't want to raise a fuss if there's truly nothing to worry about. I'll let Mr. Carrow and Mr. Ettinger know that Foster hasn't returned. They'll take care of it and get her back here safe and sound."

The maid nodded and then bustled from the room. Hettie was not far behind. But their paths diverged when the maid disappeared into the servants' stairwell and Hettie made her way down the grand staircase to Vincent's study on the second floor. She could hear the soft murmur of voices within. Knocking softly, she waited for permission to enter.

A moment later, she heard her new brother-in-law's voice calling out. Opening the door, she stepped into that very masculine enclave.

"Is something wrong?" Joss asked immediately.

"I'm not entirely sure. Foster, my maid, has not returned. I gave her a half day to visit her mother and sister who reside in Lambeth. And she's never tardy. It's simply not in her nature. I'm afraid something may have happened to her."

"Something . . . or someone?" Vincent demanded.

"Again, I'm not entirely sure," Hettie answered honestly. "But I cannot imagine that Simon would have any reason to harm her. She's a lady's maid and hardly a threat to him."

"No, but she does have your loyalty. She risked life and limb to bring Honoria word of your abduction," Vincent stated. "And Simon may well be counting on your selfless nature. He's certainly not above using her to force your hand in some way."

Hettie swayed on her feet. "Oh, no. No. I should not have sent her away this morning. I thought—well, she's been working so hard that she had earned a bit of respite. It never occurred to me that I might well be sending her right into the face of danger!"

"It shouldn't have had to occur to you," Joss protested. "It should have occurred to us. We've been chasing our tails trying to tackle this on both fronts—Bates and Simon. We should have focused on Simon and let the Bates business work itself out. Do you know her mother's direction?"

"Yes . . . I have it in my ledger. Foster has me send half her pay there every month," Hettie exclaimed. "I'll get it for you."

"No," Joss protested. "Tell me where it is, and I'll get it. You're near to falling over. You do not need to be going up and down the stairs given the state you are in now."

She wanted to protest, but honestly she could not. The possibilities of what might have happened to Foster had left her quite shaken. "It's in my writing box, next to my dressing table."

Joss nodded and then marched from the room to retrieve the item.

"Sit down, Hettie. You look as though you might topple at any moment."

The directive from Vincent had her shaking her head. He wasn't wrong. But she was also far too nervous to sit. So she paced. "I can't. If something happens to her because of me—"

"It isn't because of you. It's because of Simon. Do not take his sins upon yourself."

"No . . . but I should have considered that he might be desperate and do something horrid."

Vincent shook his head. "Or maybe she's just late? Possibly her mother or sister were ill and she is tending to them? Let us not assume the worst until we have no other option."

Hettie knew he was right, but she couldn't shake the feeling that something horrible had happened. Because in her life something horrible had always happened. Before she could say anything, Joss returned, her ledger in hand.

Hettie opened it to the correct page and then passed the book to him. "That's where they live. Do not go alone. I cannot help but feel that is precisely what he wants. It could well be a trap."

"I've no intention of going alone," he replied. "I'll take some of Vincent's men with me. And in the meantime, you are to stay here with Vincent. I do not trust Simon. This could be simply a diversionary tactic, intended to leave you unprotected. That is not a chance I am willing to take."

Chapter Thirty-Two

J OSS WATCHED THE house for a good half hour before giving a quick nod to Arliss Batson, who then jerked his chin in acknowledgement. They didn't need words to communicate. Arliss was a former military man, and had been working for the Hound for many years. And what he'd gleaned from his service to king and country had been well utilized during his tenure with the unofficial king of London's underbelly.

Crossing the road, Joss knocked loudly upon the door. "Mrs. Foster?"

The door opened, but only by a scant inch. Even that was enough for him to see that the young woman inside was not Annie's mother. The sister then.

"Lady Ernsdale sent me," he explained. "My name is Mr. Joshua Ettinger. I'm a private inquiry agent . . . and Lady Ernsdale is quite concerned because your sister, Annie, did not return as scheduled."

The girl's eyes widened and she opened the door, not to invite him in but to step outside herself. "Annie left ages ago. She should have long since returned by now. But please keep your voice down. My mother is not well. She tried to put on a brave front when Annie was here, and it's left her very fatigued, Mr. Ettinger."

"I understand . . . Mary, is it?"

"Yes, sir. Mary Foster. Annie is older by four years."

It was a strange bit of information to offer, but that was a mystery for another day. "Did Annie say she intended to stop anywhere before returning to Mayfair?"

"No, sir. Annie intended to return straightaway. She's quite worried about her ladyship, though she didn't say why. And given what she's said in the past about the late Lord Ernsdale, I know it's not her ladyship's grief that was cause for her concern."

Was there a soul alive who didn't know what an utter arse Ernsdale was? It seemed unlikely. If they were ignorant of it, then it was likely that they were also entirely ignorant of him. "Does she take a certain route home that you're aware of?"

"She takes the Westminster Bridge and then cuts through St. James Park. If she's any bit of extra coin, she'll buy old bread from the baker down the street and feed it to the swans."

"I'll check there to see if she stopped on her way home, and I'll try to retrace her steps to see if I can find anything of note. If you think of anything, anything at all, do not hesitate to send word to me . . . but do not come by yourself. I will leave a man here to watch your door. You may give the missive to him, and he will see it delivered."

She frowned at him. "You do not think that Annie has taken ill or had some sort of accident. You think someone has hurt her."

"I suspect it," he admitted, sensing that the girl would surely know if he lied. She seemed to have an uncanny insight. "But I have no proof of that as yet. I hope, with all my heart, to be wrong."

"I pray you are wrong, as well, Mr. Ettinger. If something has happened to my sister, it will be the death of our mother. She could not bear it."

Joss felt the weight of that pressing on him. "I will do everything in my power to see your sister safe. Beyond that, I can make no promises, Miss Foster. I will not lie to you. I strongly suspect that I could not even if I desired to. It's very possible that Simon Dagliesh, the nephew of the late Lord Ernsdale, may have had a hand in his murder and now means to see an end to Lady Ernsdale's life, as well. Annie may be a tool he means to use against her."

The girl's face paled. "Annie has spoken of him before. She does not like him. Not at all. And she's hinted that he . . . well, that he could be very dangerous to any woman."

Joss bit back the curse that sprang to his lips. "I'm not surprised to hear it. Thank you, Miss Foster, again for the information. I will send word when I have learned anything of note."

HETTIE WAS SEATED in a well upholstered chair in the morning room. Honoria was seated across from her. Each of them had a sewing basket before them and some halfhearted attempt at embroidery. Neither of them was particularly good at it or particularly interested in it. But it gave them something to do with their hands other than simply wringing them with worry.

"If there is any clue to be found, Mr. Ettinger will find it," Honoria offered with complete conviction.

"You seem so very certain of that," Hettie replied.

"He found you, didn't he? And with a much greater delay from the time of your abduction to the beginning of his investigation . . . if she can be found, he is the man for it."

Hettie didn't bother to explain that it wasn't her lack of faith in Joss. It was her certainty in the wickedness of others. After all, they'd seen it firsthand on numerous occasions with their respective husbands—well, former husbands. They had also seen the aftermath of it countless times as they tended to women who were at the mercy of brutal men and a society that left them with no power at all.

"I know he'll do what he can. But I also know that Simon will stop at nothing to get what he wants. He's reckless with money and wagers on everything far beyond his means. That reckless-ness is matched only by his ruthlessness. It will not matter to him who he must hurt or kill in the name of what he wants," Hettie explained. "I truly believe, had there been even a slim chance of having a child during my marriage, that he'd have done away with me long ago. I was only allowed to live because I posed no threat to him in that regard."

"But you are with child, and legally that child will be recog-nized as Arthur's," Honoria surmised.

"Precisely," Hettie concurred. "I think there may be only two men in all of London who care if I actually live or die . . . your husband and Joss. And Vincent only cares because of how it impacts you."

Honoria sighed. "It pains me that you lived in such fear and such loneliness. That kind of isolation is devastating. And I should know."

"We have both known our fair share of those particular emo-tions. At least now our fear is generally reserved for others than ourselves . . . I suppose that might be considered an improvement in our circumstances, but it does not feel that way in this moment. All I can think about is how remarkably brave and selfless Foster was in her efforts to save me. What if he doesn't find her, Honoria? What if Simon has done the unthinkable?"

"We will deal with that if it comes. In the meantime, we must discuss what you and Mr. Ettinger mean to do about the child you carry."

"We mean to marry," Hettie said. "By common license and as soon as possible."

Honoria let out a sigh of relief. "Oh, thank heavens!"

"Do not . . . not yet. We are not marrying out of love. This is not some romantic notion that has overtaken us. It's the most expedient way to make me less of a threat to Simon. Once we marry, the child I carry will be Joss's in every way . . . by blood and by law."

"Surely that is not the only reason!"

Hettie hoped it wasn't. But she was not ready to own that yet, to admit it either to herself or to her sister. She wasn't ready to admit the depth of her feelings for him when she had no notion if those feelings would ever be returned. Oh, he desired her. But she was very aware that, if not for the fact that their fateful night together had resulted in conception, he would likely never have spoken to her again, much less be planning to marry her.

Funnily enough, the thought of one day marrying for love had sustained her through the worst days of her marriage to Arthur. All her hopes and prayers had centered on such a thing. She had just never specified that the love should be mutual. Now, she found herself hopelessly in love with a man who felt obligated to marry her, and she had no notion of what his true feelings were for her or if they would ever be anything beyond desire and perhaps responsibility.

Chapter Thirty-Three

J OSS HAD RETRACED the maid's steps. Ultimately, the endeavor offered up precisely what he had anticipated—nothing. She'd purchased some of the old bread, taken it to the park, and fed the swans, per the account of witnesses, and had then headed into the heart of Mayfair. From there, she had simply vanished, not unlike the events that had transpired when Hettie was taken.

Hettie's assertion that she suspected Simon Dagliesh had been involved with the Walpoles was seeming more and more likely by the minute. While she had not been the initial target of the crime, someone, after the fact, had been providing them with information from within the Ernsdale household. Recalling the former footman who had aided the Walpoles in Hettie's abduction, Joss realized that it was highly unlikely that the disgraced servant would have remained in the good graces of any staff member still employed by Arthur Dagliesh. There was no loyalty among thieves or among poorly paid servants scrabbling to keep their positions. Someone had fed the man information. And that pointed directly back to Simon.

Any member of the "quality" would make a poor if not out-right hostile witness. They would deny seeing anything. Mostly, he thought, because they chose not to. A serving class girl on the street was beneath their notice unless she picked a pocket or an unscrupulous gentleman wished to get under her skirts. While

Annie Foster was a pretty girl, indeed, she wasn't the sort to give any man such ideas or to tolerate any foolishness from one. But there were servants walking the streets of Mayfair and the City of London. Governesses and nannies played with their charges in the parks. Footmen and other maids on their half days walked out together, likely in secret. They'd be protecting themselves by denying any sight of her.

But that didn't mean he was without recourse. There were carts manned by young women selling flowers and other sundry items. Boys who were hawking news sheets and gossip sheets alike. Those were the people to ask. Those were the people who watched and paid attention. They were also the people beholden to no one except themselves. They wouldn't intervene because those from the streets knew to mind their own business or pay the price. But they could be incentivized to reveal what they might have witnessed if the reward was worth the risk.

Strolling up to one of the carts selling posies near the park entrance, he nodded to the girl. "That bunch there," he pointed to a random bouquet. "How much?"

"A ha'penny, sir," the girl replied.

Joss retrieved the coin from his pocket and placed it in her outstretched palm. Then he held up a guinea. "I need information more than I need flowers."

The girl's eyes widened as she looked at the coin. It was likely more than she earned in a month. Hell, it was more than he earned in a month. Luckily, Vincent was footing the bill. "About the girl?"

Joss nodded. There was no point in asking which girl. It went without question.

"A gentleman took her. He weren't dressed like a gent, but he moved like one," she said. "He stood there on the corner, yon . . . waiting for a good while. Watching for her. A dozen other maids and serving girls walked past him, and he paid them no mind at all. It was her he wanted. Her and her alone."

"Did you see where he took her?"

The girl nodded. "She walked off with him. Not happily, of a certain . . . but he had his arm around her shoulders, and they headed toward Piccadilly."

Joss leveled an assessing stare at the girl. She was painfully young, but poverty and the cruelty of others had already made her wary. "You know who lives at 124 Curzon Street?"

The girl's eyes widened. "Everyone knows that, sir."

"The girl he took . . . she works there as a lady's maid. If you talk to the other flower girls or any street vendors that you feel safe asking, to see if anyone else saw them, you bring the information back to me at that house, and you'll get a guinea for your trouble. If we find her safe, you'll get ten guineas. That's more money than you'll see in your lifetime."

"Aye, sir. It is. I'll let you know as soon as I find something."

It wasn't in his nature to simply offer aid without there being some sort of reciprocity in the bargain. But something about her compelled him to do so. "This is hard work for little pay. And eventually it'll not be enough." He didn't name the sort of work she'd have to turn to then. He didn't have to. "If you're interested in doing something more respectable and less dangerous than taking your chances on the street, his lady wife will find you better work."

Joss watched the girl as she closed up her flower cart and began making her way down the street. She stopped at the first corner and spoke to a boy selling apples, then turned left, heading for Piccadilly.

He signaled to Arliss Battson to follow her. When Arliss nodded, Joss headed for home. It wasn't a task he looked forward to, telling Hettie that her maid had been taken by Simon. And there was little doubt that was exactly what had transpired.

ANNIE DID EXACTLY as he told her. She wasn't so foolish as to be outwardly defiant of a man who was both desperate and madder than a March hare. But fear had a way of making one forget even the most reasonable of cautions.

"Get in," he demanded.

Annie looked at the heavy barrel. "No. No, I won't do it."

"Then I'll cut your throat and put you in it," Simon retorted, flashing the blade he carried. "You're going in the barrel, Annie Foster. It's up to you whether you do it dead or alive."

Annie wanted to protest, she wanted to shout for help. But the docks were busy. They were teeming with men, most of whom were no more trustworthy than the man before her. If, and that was a very great if, someone deigned to help her, it would take them ages to determine where she was in the rabbit warren of warehouses that lined the quay. That was assuming they'd be able to hear her screams and shouts over the noise of goods being loaded from ship to barge and sailed further upriver into the heart of London.

"How do I know you won't just leave me in there to rot?"

"You do not," he said. "But you'll rot quicker if you're dead going in."

Annie shivered. He was right enough about that, and the very thought of it made her shudder. Her only chance of surviving was to do as he said, hate it though she did.

Taking a steadying breath, she stepped up onto the crate and managed to hoist herself over the lip of the barrel. She was a small woman, slight of frame and very short. Sinking down into the barrel, she could sit on her bottom with her knees drawn up to her chest. There was plenty of room and plenty of air, she assured herself. But as the lid went on the barrel, and she could both hear and feel the hammer strikes as it was sealed tight, she found it harder to breathe. Her heart raced in her chest until it was a wonder it didn't simply give out.

"Be a good girl, Annie. Not a sound until I come back to let you out. I'll ransom you back to your mistress, and once I've been paid, I'll set you free."

No, he wouldn't. She could hear the lie in his voice. He'd kill her either way, money or no. But at least this way, he was leaving her there and heading off to do whatever it was he felt compelled to do. She'd have a chance, while he was composing his ransom demand, to perhaps get herself out of that barrel and away from him.

Chapter Thirty-Four

THEY HADN'T STAYED at the house very long. Taking just enough time to inform Hettie and Honoria of what they'd found, he'd headed out once more with Vincent at his side. Now, he was inordinately grateful for having the foresight to request his presence.

The room, upon their entrance, was unnaturally quiet and still. Rather like a predator lying in wait, Joss thought. It was an apt comparison. Beside him, Vincent was deceptively relaxed, but beneath their coats, both of them were armed to the hilt. It was a necessary precaution when walking into a den of thieves and cutthroats. If they were lucky, they'd get out without having to use any of those precautions, but that wasn't really up to them. They were behind enemy lines. *When needs must.*

"You're invading my territory, Hound," Ardmore observed from behind his massive desk. The marble top was so heavy it was a wonder the floor could withstand its weight. Not even the laws of science and nature defied his will, it seemed.

"I'm not here for trouble," Vincent said. "Oddly enough, I'm here to solve one of your problems. In return, I hope you will help solve one of mine."

Ardmore shoved back the stack of papers he'd been perusing and then eyed them both speculatively. Finally, after a long moment, he waved a hand toward an empty chair. Only one. Joss knew he didn't qualify as a guest, so he'd be standing. *Relegated to the position of lackey.*

"I don't have any problems," Ardmore said softly. "Anyone who told you otherwise is mistaken."

"Simon Dagliesh will never be able to pay you what he owes. Contrary to what he might have led you to believe, there is no money. He gets the title, he gets the house—which is entailed— but the money isn't his. It isn't even really in possession of Ernsdale's late wife. It's in trust for her and overseen by the bank with an eye toward caution and moderation."

Ardmore remained silent, likely expecting Vincent to fill the silence with more information. But it was an old trick, and no one played it better than the Hound himself. So the stony silence stretched on interminably.

Then, without preamble, Ardmore uttered a single curse. It reverberated in the silence of the room like a shot. "Lying shite," he finished.

"One of his many sins," Vincent concurred. "I'm prepared to pay his markers."

"You don't know how much they're for!" Ardmore protested. "And why the hell would you do that?"

"Because I need your men to help find him. Mine can search Mayfair and other areas, but we can't very well look in your territory without starting a war. I'm not here to challenge you or to squabble over what bits of the city we get to lord over."

"Thought you was retiring anyway."

"Delegating. Not retiring," Vincent corrected him.

Joss watched the exchange and not merely with idle curiosity. There was the very real possibility that they might have to fight their way out. Ardmore was unpredictable at best. At worst, he was a madman.

"Delegating, hmm? Is that what this giant looming over your shoulder is here for? Because you've delegated to him?"

"He's here because he has a vested interest in the fate of Lady Ernsdale . . . a fate that is threatened by the continued existence of

Simon Dagliesh."

Ardmore stroked the mostly silver beard that covered the lower half of his curiously unlined face. "So that's the way of it . . . she's sister to your wife, isn't she, Carrow?"

Vincent's only answer was a nod, but Joss tensed, waiting for the other man to say something so heinous that it would be impossible to ignore.

"They seem to have a preference for gutter-born bastards... but then, given what I know of Ernsdale—and I can only assume your wife's late husband was of similar ilk—they are entitled to that preference."

Joss bit back a sigh of relief. It wasn't as if the comment had been entirely inoffensive, it was simply that the offensiveness of it was directed more at Vincent and himself than either Honoria or Hettie. It was that fact which allowed it to go unanswered.

"Find Simon Dagliesh, find out what he has done with the maid he has abducted in effort to force Lady Ernsdale's hand— and you shall be paid in full. It will likely be the only way that you will be paid in full, or at all, for that matter," Vincent countered coolly.

Ardmore, with a simple jerk of his head toward the door, set in motion a manhunt. The bevy of guards shrank down to only two, but those two were roughly the size of mountains. "We work together this once," Ardmore said. "Then it goes back to how it always was. Me on one side of the Thames and you on the other. Agreed?"

"Agreed," Vincent said.

"I'll send word to your club when we find him."

"When . . . not if?" Joss asked.

Ardmore smiled, the expression utterly terrifying. "Oh, yes, Mr. Ettinger. It was always a question of when. Good evening, gentlemen."

HETTIE WAS WAITING in the morning room with Honoria. Neither of them knew precisely what it was they were waiting for, but there was a sense of dread hanging over them both. The anticipation of something awful lurking—lying in wait—building with every tick of the clock was a feeling they were both far too familiar with.

It had been hours now since Annie had last been seen. Hours in which anything might have happened to the girl. The feeling of responsibility and the awful amalgamation of blame and shame that roiled within her was dizzying for Hettie. On the one hand, she desperately wanted news, and on the other she was so fearful of what that news might be that it defied all reason.

The sound of footsteps in the corridor had her tensing. And when the door opened to reveal a footman holding a simple silver tray with a single missive on it, Hettie instantly knew that it was what she'd been waiting for and what she had been dreading. That sealed note contained Simon's demands . . . and the conditions by which Annie might be spared whatever fate he had dreamed up for her. There was little doubt in her mind that Simon would be unspeakably cruel if necessary, simply to bring her to heel. While greed was his primary motivating factor, there was the same streak of cruelty in him that had existed in Arthur. Perhaps even to a greater degree.

"What is it, Hettie?" Honoria asked.

Hettie scanned the contents and sighed wearily. "He's demanding that I surrender myself to him in exchange for Annie Foster. Obviously, I cannot do that—not because I am unwilling to aid her but because he cannot be trusted. If I give myself over to him, he will simply kill us both."

Honoria nodded. "Indeed, he would. You need not surrender to him . . . you need only allow him to think you are. But neither Mr. Ettinger nor Vincent will approve."

Hettie folded the note and placed it in her pocket. "I do not require their approval—but Joss is not yet my husband. If you fear how Vincent will respond, I understand. I would never ask you to jeopardize your happiness with him."

Honoria laughed softly. "Nothing will jeopardize my happiness. It may well jeopardize the peace in our home, but only temporarily. We, my dear sister, are not shy, retiring violets. It is not in our nature to allow men to handle matters for us."

"Primarily because we've never known men who could do so with any degree of aptitude." It was a pithy rejoinder, but it rang with sincerity. They had both seen the worst of men. Perhaps it had jaded them to some degree.

"Indeed. And while these particular men are cut from a very different cloth, sitting idly by while that poor girl suffers torment in heaven only knows what manner is not something either of us could live with. But we cannot do this alone. We will require a small amount of aid . . . and I know just who to ask."

"Stavers?" Hettie asked. The former pugilist turned butler was a remarkably capable individual. And that capability seemed to carry into every possible sort of situation.

"Not necessarily. He would only attempt to stop us. We will inform him, but not immediately," Honoria replied cagily. "We may not have a battalion of soldiers at our disposal, Hettie, but we are not without allies. There is a veritable army of women out there who feel no small degree of gratitude for us. I am certain that if we were to ask for their aid, most would give it. But there is one in particular who has the necessary skill that we will need for this plan to work."

"You have a plan already? Have you become some sort of mastermind by association now?

"Half-formed plan," Hettie corrected. "And no, I am no mastermind by association or otherwise. But I do know of a way for you to meet him that would not necessitate you go alone. For now, we must secure the assistance we require, and we will work out the particulars on our way. First, we need to go to Vincent's study."

"Whatever for?"

"Weapons," Honoria replied. "He keeps several braces of

pistols there and a few blades. We will, both of us, be well armed when we meet with Simon."

Hettie considered that for a moment. Then she gave a jerky nod. "You're quite right. We cannot wait. Foster likely does not have time to waste."

Chapter Thirty-Five

JACK COLLINSWORTH EYED the case of brandy with some disappointment. "That's all you could get?"

"No, sir. That's all I could sneak this way for now. I'll be sending the rest of it one crate at a time. Seven in total," the captain said. "There were things going on at the docks what made me nervous."

Jack started to lift his head, remembered they were in the cellar beneath his club, and quickly corrected before braining himself on a beam. "What sort of things?"

"Lots of blokes about. Some looked official, and some looked—well, they looked like me, sir. Criminal," the captain explained.

Thinking of the note he'd received earlier from Joss Ettinger, Jack took a shot in the dark. "You didn't happen to see one escorting a pretty-ish young woman . . . a proper one? Works as a lady's maid and has been taken as a hostage of sorts. Incentive might be a better description, I suppose."

"Did see something that was a bit odd," the man said, scratching his beard thoughtfully. "He were dressed rough, clothes soiled and ragged. But he moved like a gent, if you ken?"

Intrigued, Jack put down the bottle he'd been inspecting. "I do *ken*. Go on."

The captain nodded. "Had a girl with him. Didn't pay much

mind to how she was dressed, except to note she looked out of place. Not exactly the sort a man looks at twice. Pretty-ish, as you said, but not available, if you get my meaning. Weren't no doxy, for certain."

"Your meaning is quite clear, and your information most welcome. You'll be getting a hefty bonus on your seven crates of contraband," Jack said, feeling that very familiar tingle. Perhaps it was instinct, perhaps it was something more than that. He could not say. But he could predict the turn of a card or the roll of the dice. He could, at a glance, know whether or not he ought to walk down a certain alley. It was more than street sense, though he had that in abundance. And in that moment, he knew, without question or hesitation, that the smuggler had seen Dagliesh and the maid. "Where did you see them?"

"They was near Fincham's, the textile mill and warehouse."

"If you see either of them again, send me word immediately. As for the remainder of the brandy, just hold onto it for the night. We'll settle up tomorrow. This takes precedence . . . and if I'm not here, get word to the Hound."

The captain nodded vigorously. "Oh, aye. It's big doin's for the both of you to be in the thick of it!"

"That it is, Captain. That it is." Jack climbed the steps out of the cellar and went directly to his office. There, he dashed off a note to Joss Ettinger directing him to Fincham's but with the need for discretion. After all, they didn't want to spook the man and send him running once more. It was very likely that he'd find the man before the note did, but as he couldn't be in two places at once, it was the best option. Giving a boy a coin to deliver it to the Hound's club, he made his way toward the docks and Fincham's.

HETTIE MET SALLY Dawson's worried gaze. "All will be well."

The only slightly older but significantly more weary woman shook her head. "With respect, my lady, it rarely is. And when dealing with the sort of man the new Lord Ernsdale is, 'tis even less likely. But I'll help because I owe the both of you." She jerked her head toward Honoria. "I know what you've both done for me. And for the other girls. They'll be marching and rioting in the streets of Mayfair if aught happens to either of you. On that score you need not worry."

Hettie breathed a sigh of relief. "Thank you, Sally. I cannot tell you how grateful I am to know that I will have your assistance."

"Never doubt it, m'lady. Never doubt it."

Hettie rose from the small and rickety wooden chair that flanked the table. It was one of the only bits of furniture in the squalid little room. "I fear, Sally, that we have not done enough for you. Do you have money for food? Money to heat the room when it grows colder?"

"I'll be all right," Sally insisted. "And if I'm not, I'll not be taking to the streets again. I'll come to Mrs. Carrow or yourself before I take such a risk. This world is hard enough even with a mother's love and protection. I can't take the risk of leaving my wee ones to fend for themselves."

It was an instinctive thing for Hettie to place her hand protectively over her still-flat stomach. But it was a gesture that spoke volumes. "I can't imagine it."

Sally's eyes widened, and then her expression settled into one of knowing. "I suspect you'll be finding out soon enough."

Hettie did not confirm or deny it. But there was no need. They all, every person in that room—from the youngest to the oldest—understood the ways of the world very well. "I suppose I will. One hour, Sally. And not a moment later. Timing must be precise."

"It will be, ma'am. It will be."

Hettie walked toward Honoria, where she cuddled the youngest of Sally's children. The little girl was an angel-faced hellion of four, and Honoria adored her.

"It's time to go," Hettie said.

Honoria sighed and gave the little girl another squeeze. "I will come visit you again very soon, Mary, and I will finish telling you the story of the princess with yards and yards of golden hair."

"I like that story very much," the little girl said. The word very sounded like "vewy," and it was impossibly endearing.

Honoria rose and settled the little girl on the simple pallet on the floor that served as her bed—a bed she shared with her two sisters and one brother. For all that they lived in poverty and for all that the world had been beyond unkind to Sally, she managed to give her children the kind of love that both Hettie and Honoria had been denied as children. *And as adults.*

Honoria raised up and took Hettie's hand. "Let's go. Before I lose my nerve entirely."

"You're not the one who will be going into that house," Hettie pointed out.

"No," Honoria said. "And that's rather the problem. I can't be with you. I can't protect you. Not from Arthur Dagliesh and not from his rotten nephew."

"It's a good plan," Hettie insisted. "A solid one. He won't dare harm me in that house, for then he'd have to explain it. One death, certainly. But for both Arthur and I to meet such an end? No. He'll force me to go elsewhere, and that is where you and Sally come into play."

"If we survive this, Vincent and Mr. Ettinger may well kill us for it. And rightfully so . . . but I couldn't live with myself if we did not at least make an effort to save Annie Foster. We'd be the worst sort of hypocrites then," Honoria reflected.

"And you are many things, sister, but hypocritical has never been one of them."

Chapter Thirty-Six

J OSS FOUND HETTIE'S room empty. Down the corridor, Vincent appeared at the top of the stairs. He could tell from the set of the other man's shoulders that things were only going to get worse.

"They're gone," Vincent said, and there was a growl in his voice that hinted at just how dangerous he could be when provoked. "And so is the carriage. Meanwhile, the coachman is passed out drunk, having been given the night off. That tells me they're doing something foolish and reckless that they didn't want the servants privy to, lest they warn me and prevent it." He paused again, his jaw clenching and unclenching with barely suppressed fury fueled entirely by fear. "I'll wring her bloody neck for it."

There was a tightness in Joss's gut, a feeling of danger. It was a feeling he'd had more than once. A feeling, he thought, that had saved his arse more than once. "They are. The question is, where have they gone and why?"

Vincent strode past him. "Let's find Stavers. Perhaps they will have sent him word, though if they had he would most certainly have stopped them."

Joss felt a frisson of unease. More than a frisson, really. It rolled through him like waves, each one cresting a bit higher than the last. He wanted to think that Hettie wouldn't be so reckless, but then he recalled the night of their first meeting, watching her leap from that ship into the filthy water. "Assuming that whatever scheme they've cooked up wasn't already in motion by the time such a message was delivered, both of them have the ability to be quite cagey and terrifyingly independent. But isn't that why you're hopelessly in love with her?"

Vincent whirled on him. "What about you? I knew you, Joshua Ettinger, before your ballocks even dropped. I've never seen you so enthralled with a woman as you are with Henrietta. Do you deny that you are in love with her?"

Instantly, the comment had his back up. The denial sprang quickly to his lips, but he couldn't just say no. Even as he wanted to, the word would not pass his lips. So he offered an answer that was not an answer at all. "What the fuck does that even mean? To be in love? People like us, people who come from where we do—such fine feelings aren't for us. I want her. I like her. And I'll do right by her. But I'm not going to pretty it up with sentiment that is nothing more than fodder for novelists and poets."

Vincent shook his head, laughing mirthlessly. "Deny it all you like or call it anything you wish—I know the truth, Joss. Be certain that you do not discover it too late, or you will never be able to salvage even a hope of happiness. These women are maddening . . . but they're the only thing that makes this life worth living." With that, the Hound of Whitehall turned on his heel and made his way toward the stairs, leaving Joss to follow him or be left behind.

Cursing the man, cursing his wife, and cursing the woman who was proving to be the very devil to him, Joss fell in step and headed for the club and, he hoped, a reasonable answer from Stavers. If it was anything else—well, that didn't bear considering.

It was quicker to walk than to take a carriage. They could cut through the mews and be at the club in a matter of minutes, so that is precisely what they did, dodging piles of dung as they did so. The streets of Mayfair might be swept clean frequently, but the hidden parts of it held the same dirt and shit as every other alley in London.

Entering the club, Stavers raised one eyebrow at their appearance. One was all he could raise. The other one hadn't moved in decades, not since it had been split open in a boxing match. It gave him a fearsome appearance, and the man often used it to his advantage.

"You were not expected tonight, sir," the boxer turned butler said.

"We've had some unexpected alterations of our plans," Vincent said, signaling to a footman to watch the door. "My study. Now."

HETTIE LOOKED OUTSIDE, peering through the carriage window. Sally was on the box, dressed in borrowed livery that disguised her as a coachman. There were other women present—friends that Sally had pressed into service. They carried baskets of flowers and meat pies. One was selling oranges. In truth, they were there simply to stand watch. Where they had come by such things was anyone's guess, but they'd given themselves the perfect cover.

"They are remarkably resourceful," Hettie noted.

"They are women . . . they are women who live in poverty. Resourcefulness is as necessary for them as the air they breathe. Perhaps even more so," Honoria answered sadly.

It was as sad a truth as it was an undeniable one. "If this works as I hope, and if we all come out of this in one piece, I want to change that. However we can. A school to train women for vocations, better housing, food that they need not beg for nor barter their bodies for . . . and not in the way we have done it. Not piecemeal. I want an organized effort."

"You mean starting our own charitable organization rather than supporting others or simply helping them on an individual basis?"

"Yes. That is precisely what I mean. I know you want to return to the country with Vincent, and you should . . . but I would hope that you might find it in your heart to offer a bit of aid. At least as I attempt to start such a herculean effort."

"Oh, I will. Of course I will. But there might be someone even more suited to such an endeavor. The Duchess of Clarenden—the founder of the so-called Hellion Club."

"Do you know her?"

Honoria smiled somewhat enigmatically. "I do not. Not personally. But Vincent does . . . as does your Mr. Ettinger."

Hettie wanted to correct her. Joss Ettinger wasn't hers. He felt obligated to her by honor—something he would deny he even possessed. He would label it too refined for the likes of him, though he was more a gentleman than the majority of nobles she had encountered. Regardless of his reasons for committing himself to her, that didn't make him hers. Not in the ways that really mattered.

Taking a deep and steadying breath, Hettie opened the carriage door and climbed down. She glanced back at Honoria, who remained concealed within the darkened interior. "Be careful."

"You be careful. There is far more at stake for you than for me."

"Then let us hope we both come out of this on the winning end," Hettie stated. Then she closed the carriage door behind her and made her way across the street to the house she had once shared with her husband, the place that held so many sorrows. And she prayed desperately that she would not be adding to that list.

* * *

Chapter Thirty-Seven

"I'VE NOT BEEN told of any plans, Hound," Stavers insisted. "I can't imagine what they're thinking."

"They, wrongheadedly, are thinking they can handle this on their own," Vincent said, sounding impossibly weary for once.

"When I get my hands on her—" Joss didn't finish the statement. He was interrupted by a knock at the door. Stavers opened it to find a footman there with a silver tray.

"Two letters have arrived for you, Mr. Stavers. The messengers said they were both quite urgent."

Stavers took the missives and sent the servant on his way. He opened the first one, scanned it, and frowned. The second one only deepened the lines that crossed his forehead and made his scowl even more fearsome. "You'd be right on that score. They're headed for the Ernsdale house to meet with Simon Dagliesh."

"And the other note?" Vincent asked.

"Jack Collinsworth thinks he knows where the maid might be . . . or at least where she was. Fincham's down by the docks."

It was Vincent's turn to scowl. "No one is working off the books. Not now. Not after last time."

Joss shook his head. "Dagliesh can't pay anyone to work for him. His pockets aren't simply to let, they're so empty they'd echo like a cavern. Whatever has been done to Annie Foster, he's done it himself. Which do you wish to take? Mayfair or the docks?"

"I'll go after Annie Foster. And if you find my wife, Joss—no. Nevermind. I'll deal with Honoria myself when all this is settled. Just get them somewhere safe and put them in shackles, if need be, to keep them there. Stavers, send for that bloody inspector, Maurice Bates. He'll need to be in on this or he'll never be satisfied of Henrietta's innocence."

Joss wasn't listening. He was already out the door, taking the stairs in a rush. He had one thought and one thought only: Get to Hettie. Get to her, gut Simon Dagliesh, and damn the consequences. Lord or not, the man wouldn't see the dawn.

HETTIE ENTERED THE house and found it dark and quiet. There were no servants, which did not bode well.

"They've all been instructed to make themselves scarce."

The voice, an all too familiar one, had come out of the darkness. Hettie fought back a shiver of fear. She hadn't expected all the servants to be present, but she hadn't thought he would have dismissed them all for the evening. It didn't change her plans, but it did infinitely increase the level of danger she presently found herself in. "Of course they were. What is all this really about, Simon?"

"It's about the bastard in your belly. It's certainly not dear Uncle Arthur's," he mused, slowly stepping forward.

Hettie took him in. Dressed in rough, dirty clothing, his face unshaven and his hair unkempt, it was quite clear that Simon was spiraling out of control. The stress of his current situation, his debts, and the threat she posed to the security of his future had clearly taken their toll on him. "Simon, you do not look well."

"Concerned for me, Auntie? I don't think so."

"No," Hettie agreed. "It's merely an observation. What is it that you have planned? Naturally, it will be something dastardly."

"Indeed it is. You're going to die. Whether it is quickly and as painlessly as possible or whether I make you suffer greatly will depend entirely upon how cooperative you are."

Hettie laughed. "Dead is dead, Simon. Whether it is painful or painless, the end result is the same and undesirable. But I shall cooperate with you on one condition—"

"Do you really think you are in a position to make demands?"

"It's a simple enough one," Hettie continued. "You will take me to wherever Annie Foster is. And I know she is not here. You would not risk her having an ally in this house, nor could you persuade all the servants to vacate the house if you brought her here with you."

"All your association with criminals has apparently given you remarkable insight . . . but I've no wish to traipse all over London with an unwilling woman who might throw me to the wolves at any moment."

"We need not traipse. I have a carriage. You take me to Annie, put her in the carriage, and send her on her way. Then you will have my full cooperation."

"And if I do not?"

"Then I shall scream this house down around our ears. While the servants here have been given the night off, they have not been sent away next door, nor across the road. Someone *will* hear me. Perhaps that will not be enough to save me, Simon, but it will be enough to see you hang."

He stepped forward, one menacing step after another until he stood there, nose to nose with her. "Do not try me, Henrietta. And do not defy me. You want to see your maid? Fine. I'll take you to her, but her face will be the last thing you see."

Chapter Thirty-Eight

JACK MOVED ALONG the docks looking for the warehouse in question. They were not well signed, but asking for the location was not really an option. Discretion was vital, and announcing his presence by asking someone to direct him there was hardly the way to go about that.

When he finally found the building, he noted that it was locked and deserted. Not surprising, given the hour. What was surprising were the footsteps he heard approaching. Ducking into the shadows, he reached for the knife tucked into the concealed holster at his waist, prepared to meet any potential threat. But the footsteps halted nearby.

"Who's there?"

Jack recognized the voice instantly. It was none other than the Hound himself. Tucking the blade back into place, he stepped forward. "I see you received my message."

The Hound visibly relaxed as another man stepped forward. Jack knew him instantly, not by name but certainly by vocation. He was a Runner for sure. There was a look about them, a watchfulness.

"I did, and I thank you for your assistance," the Hound replied. "Have you found anything yet?"

"Sadly, no. I have not found any purloined lady's maids just lying about the place. Who is your associate, Carrow?"

The Hound laughed even as the other man bristled. "Careful, Collinsworth. You don't want to end up on the wrong side of Bow Street. Oh, too late for that. But you don't want to draw their ire."

"I'm Inspector Maurice Bates, and I'm here to determine whether Lord Ernsdale was murdered by his wife or his nephew. That is all. I do not, as a general rule, associate with criminals."

Jack couldn't stop the chuckle that escaped him. "No, I don't imagine you do. You'd be in a better mood if you did, though. We're right fun, we are."

"Enough chatter. Let's search inside." The Hound stepped forward and retrieved a tool from his pocket. He made quick work of the lock while the Runner simply stared steadfastly in the opposite direction. Once the lock gave, he pushed the heavy door open. The interior of the space was dark. There were crates of fabric stacked nearly to the rafters. There were bolts of cloth draped across tables and benches. There was not, however, a single sign of life within. The place was empty, and he would stake his life on it.

"He only said he saw them near Fincham's. Not in Fincham's," Jack mused. "Where else might he have taken her?"

The Hound gazed out through the open door toward the Thames. "I fear the answer to that question, Collinsworth."

The river was unforgiving. It carried bodies away so that some might never be found. Others sank to the bottom only to be discovered later in a state that no human should ever be in. "Let's not jump to the worst conclusion just yet . . . but we should check the wharfs just in case."

"We'll go left. You go right."

Jack nodded then headed off. He walked down the first quay, checking the water on either side. There was nothing. But as he started down the second quay, he heard something that sounded off. It was not the sound of the water lapping at the pilings. It was different, lacking that same lulling rhythm. Between those laps, there were distinct thumps.

He acknowledged that it might be nothing. There could be a piece of debris caught up around the pilings. *Or a body.* Finding the earthly remains of some poor unfortunate girl who happened to wind up on the wrong side of Simon Dagliesh was the very last thing he wanted, but he had to accept that it was a very real possibility.

Heading back toward the bank, he stepped off the boards. His feet sank into the silt, and he struggled to retain his balance as he moved deeper beneath the quay. The water was already over the tops of his boots and rising by the second. Whatever searching he meant to do under there would have to be done quickly.

There was little light as he moved from one set of pilings to the next. He didn't see the barrel until he nearly fell over it. It was half submerged, the water lapping at the sides.

Feeling foolish, he rapped softly on the top of the barrel. "Miss Foster?"

There was a muffled scream from within.

"Christ," he muttered. Retrieving the blade from his waist once more, he began prying at the staves, taking chinks out of them until he could finally pry the top free. Ignoring the splinters that sank into his fingers, he ripped it away and peered inside. His heart lodged in his throat as he stared down into wide, frightened eyes that gleamed with tears in the dim light.

Jack had always had quite the soft spot for ladies. He'd never met one he didn't like. Young or old, fat or thin, pretty or plain. It didn't matter to him. Women were almost mystical creatures to his mind, and as such, he had a kind of reverence for them that would never permit him to act violently against one or to tolerate that sort of violence from others. And Annie Foster, quietly pretty and entirely terrified, had suffered greatly.

"Let's get you out of there," he said, trying to keep his tone gentle, trying to hold back the anger he felt at seeing her so abused for nothing more than the selfish agenda of a spoiled boy who lacked honor and a conscience.

Holding out his hand to her, she placed hers in his. It trembled like a bird's. When she rose to her feet, her knees buckled. She would have fallen back into the filthy water that was slowly filling that barrel had he not caught her. Realizing that she was too weak, too frightened or possibly injured from being cramped in that small space for so long, he simply lifted her out of it.

"I've got you," he said. "The Hound is waiting up there to see you home. Can you stand?"

"I think so," she said, her voice hoarse from having screamed for so long. "But don't let me go. Please."

"I won't. I will not let you go," he promised.

IN THE COMPARTMENT beneath the carriage seat, Honoria remained silent. With every bump and rut in the road, she bit her lip to stay quiet. Above all, she stayed quiet to listen, to hear everything that Simon Dagliesh said to her sister.

"How much money is there?" Simon demanded.

Hettie's answer was soft and but audible. "I wouldn't know. Men never deign to share such pertinent information with a mere woman. I doubt Arthur swayed the trustees to part with too much of it."

"You must have some notion. Ten thousand? Twenty?"

Honoria knew the range was significantly higher. But that was not information Simon needed to have. Anything that would make him more determined to see Hettie dead in order to claim the remaining fortune was something that should remain secret for as long as possible. He was a lord, after all, and the law very rarely made men of such position pay for their misdeeds.

There was a loud rapping sound. Simon had ordered the carriage to stop.

Honoria held her breath. Sally was not a coachman. Putting her in livery did not make her one. Handling a matched pair of carriage horses was a far cry from driving a farm cart. If she fumbled the reins or revealed herself in any way, that would be the end of all of them.

The carriage wheels slowed as Honoria's heart sped up in opposing proportion. When at last it rolled to a stop, smooth as silk and in no way belying that it was not an experienced driver on the box, Honoria barely held back the sigh of relief. It was time. And failure was not an option.

HETTIE TRIED TO remain calm, tried to keep her gaze averted from the boot compartment where Honoria had secreted herself. She tried not to glance out the windows to see if the women Sally had gathered were now in place. If the plan was to work, he had to get her out of the carriage and take her to the place where Annie Foster was being held.

When the hoofbeats faded and the wheels finally stopped, she gathered the last bit of her courage for the part that would come next. She made no move to exit the carriage. Instead, she remained there quietly waiting for his command to do so. Appearing too eager to meet her fate would only rouse his suspicion, and he needed to think she was compliant and docile. At least for the time being.

"Get on your feet," he commanded her.

"I'm not going anywhere until I know that Annie Foster is safe."

"If you want to see Annie Foster again, you'll get on your bloody feet and you'll shut your mouth."

Hettie had no doubt that he was capable of violence. She'd always known that of him. But he seemed to be teetering precariously on the edge of it, as if he might lose control of his temper at any second. Given the scheme he was attempting to pull off, his desperation was glaringly apparent.

"You won't get away with this. You will be pursued to the

ends of the earth," she said. "Even if you manage to take my life and secure your position as Arthur's heir, you won't benefit from it. There are those who will see that you do not."

"They have no power over me," he said dismissively. "I have a title. They are naught but squalling gutter rats no matter how much wealth they may have amassed! You and your sister were barely clinging to your status as genteel with your continued association with the worst sorts that this city has to offer. And in the end, Henrietta, those poor unfortunates who feed on your generosity will be the only ones who miss you. Even then, they will only miss what you provide for them. In short, no one will miss you when you are gone. Your sister will be too busy with her criminal husband to be bothered."

Hettie smiled. "You do not know my sister. Or her husband, for that matter. And you would be surprised at how many people will miss me . . . and the lengths to which those people will go to make certain you regret your actions this night."

His answering grin was chilling. "I'll take my chances. You want to see your maid? Fine. You can change places with her. It's a fitting way for you to shuffle off this mortal coil. Though perhaps after your brave escape from Walpole, you've overcome your fear of water."

Hettie suppressed a shiver. Her fear of water remained and might, in fact, be stronger than ever. But she couldn't let him see that. Giving him any hint of weakness would only make it more difficult. So she climbed down from the carriage with him right behind her. When he reached out and grabbed her arm, locking his fingers around it in a bruising grip, she uttered not a complaint. But as he walked her toward the docks that faced the row of warehouses, she dared a single glance over her shoulder. Sally was no longer perched atop the box, and the carriage door stood open. She couldn't see them, but she knew they were there, hiding in the shadows and watching over her as Simon led her into the darkness.

Chapter Thirty-Nine

T HE HACK STOPPED and Joss climbed out, tossing the driver a coin. He could hear the water lapping at the banks as he approached the wharf. Searching the house for Dagliesh and Hettie had taken minimal time. The entire place had been empty. Even the servants were absent.

Up ahead, he could see the Hound and Arliss Battson along with Maurice Bates. There were other men there as well, all of them being assigned specific areas to search and monitor. Approaching them, he noted the grim expression on Vincent's face.

"What is it?"

"Collinsworth found Annie Foster. He's seeing her back to the house. She's in a bit of a bad way. Cold and frightened. The bastard had her in a barrel, under the quay . . . just waiting for the tide to come in and finish her off. Another five minutes, and we'd have been too late."

Joss winced. It wasn't just attempted murder. It was mental and emotional torment. For her to have been locked in that small tight space for hours, waiting for the water to swamp her—he couldn't imagine that such an event would not leave her irrevocably altered. But there were other matters that required immediate attention.

"Are you convinced now, Bates?"

The detective looked at him. "I am. And given what he's done—the particularly fiendish manner in which he nearly killed that girl—I'll have no trouble at all getting him convicted. We just have to catch him."

That was, Joss thought, at least one of their many problems solved. Hettie was no longer a suspect. Now, if only he could ensure that she remained alive long enough to thrash her for being so reckless. "If Dagliesh finds that Annie has escaped, that puts Hettie in more danger than ever. He'll feel threatened because he will not believe she might ever have escaped on her own. The moment he realizes that we're onto him, Hettie's life will be forfeit."

Vincent nodded. "I have men stationed there already, watching for him. And that is where we will go now, as well. Because wherever Hettie is, Honoria will be right with her. I may well throttle them both for this harebrained scheme!"

For his part, Vincent would have to get in line. But he said nothing further as they made their way along the row of warehouses, keeping to the shadows and watching for even the slightest hint of trouble.

HONORIA HAD WAITED until they were far enough from the carriage that she wouldn't be overheard. Then she slowly extricated herself from the small compartment concealed beneath the seat. The coachman, Sally in disguise, was inside the carriage, concealed from view but watching through the open door.

"Which way did they go?" Honoria asked.

Sally pointed straight ahead. "Down that way. I'm coming with you."

"No. If Hettie should escape him or Annie, they'll come straight back to this carriage. Your job is to get them back to the house on Curzon Street as quickly as possible."

"I will not just leave you here!"

Honoria shook her head. "Vincent has men working all over this city. I will be able to find someone to give me aid should I require it. But Hettie, as soon as we free Annie, needs to be as far from Simon's reach as possible. She'll have no chance of that on foot. Promise me, Sally, that you will not take unnecessary risks. Your children need you too much."

Sally made a sound of distress. "I don't like it. I don't like it none at all."

"None of us like this," Honoria said, checking the weapons she'd liberated from Vincent's office. The pistols were primed and ready. She had one blade tucked into her boot and another up her sleeve. "But I won't lose her. I will not lose my sister. No matter what I must do."

With that, Honoria slipped down from the carriage. She could see Hettie and Simon walking only a few yards ahead. Ducking quickly into the shadows, she followed behind them with a stealth worthy of even the greatest of spies. There was too much at stake to risk even the smallest of errors.

From one darkened alcove to another, concealing herself behind stacks of crates and barrels—Honoria never let Hettie and Simon out of her sight. When their steps slowed before one of the warehouses, her breath caught and held even as her heart pounded furiously in her chest. Then arms reached out of the darkness, snatching her back even as a hand closed over her mouth, muffling the slightest of sounds.

"When I get you home, I have a half a mind to turn you over my knee . . . and not in a way you'd particularly enjoy."

That familiar voice hissing a harsh warning in her ear belonged to Vincent. With recognition came instant relief, and she sagged against him. "Thank heavens you are here! We had to act quickly when Hettie received Simon's demands."

"That's no excuse for behaving so recklessly," he admonished. "If I lost you . . . Honoria, do not ever place yourself at risk this way again. There is a darkness inside me that you cannot conceive of, and your presence in my life may be the only thing holding it at bay."

The furious pace of her heart had not slowed, but now there was a cause beyond fear for its rapidity. "We couldn't just leave Annie to his mercy. He does not have any." She turned back to where Simon was leading Hettie down the embankment toward the river. "I presume that you have men stationed to wherever it is he's leading her?"

"Joss is waiting under there along with Arliss Battson. What bloody coachman brought you here? I'll have his head."

"We told the coachman to take the night off. Do not blame him for our actions. And as for who brought us, if you'd like to read Sally Dawson the riot act, feel free . . . but I wouldn't expect her to take it quietly."

He muttered a word under his breath that had her smiling. She knew she'd won the argument, at least for the moment.

Chapter Forty

J OSS WATCHED THEM approach from his position deep under the quay. Crouched in the shadows, he could see Hettie clearly only because the paleness of her face was a perfect foil for the darkness around them. Her skin caught every small fragment of light and reflected it back. Beside her, Simon was less distinct. His face was shadowed with beard and perhaps with dirt, as well. Given the obviously rough state of his dress, barely visible as it was, it seemed that Simon Dagliesh's financial woes had finally caught up to him.

He moved toward the barrel where Annie Foster had been imprisoned, now almost entirely submerged by the rising water of the river. Dagliesh was all but dragging Hettie along with him. Somehow, Joss managed to tamp down his fury at seeing him handle her so roughly. It infuriated him, but precision was key. If he acted too quickly, Simon could flee with Hettie, and they'd be chasing him once more. They needed to wait for him to be in a position where he would be completely surrounded by them before alerting him to their presence. There would be only one chance to catch him truly off guard, and that would be the moment he discovered the barrel was empty.

"What have you done to her?" Hettie asked, her voice rising with panic. "You've murdered her! She could not have survived in there!"

"No," Dagliesh said with smug satisfaction as he began to pry at the lid of the barrel. "And you will not either."

He should have known. That phrase would echo in his mind for the rest of his days, Joss realized. Because Hettie would not simply be docile and cooperate with him. It was not in her nature. Her days of bowing to any man were long over. She wrenched away from him, staggering backwards and sending water splashing in every direction.

Simon cursed and grabbed for her, but she was just out of reach. Still, she stumbled, falling backward into water that, in her seated position, was neck deep. And with the weight of her gown and the soft silt beneath her, Joss knew she'd never be able to get to her feet in time to avoid further attempts to capture her. At that moment, Bates emerged from his position, a pistol trained on Dagliesh.

"Do not move, sir. I mean to take you into custody for the murder of Lord Ernsdale, the abduction and attempted murder of Annie Foster, and now the abduction of Lady Ernsdale. You may never see the inside of a cell and you likely won't swing for it, but I'll make sure all of England knows you for the criminal you are!"

As Bates pontificated, Joss slipped deeper into the water, moving silently. He timed his advances toward Dagliesh with the waves lapping at the pilings. He only moved forward when the cresting water pushed him in that direction. Only when he was close enough to make his move with complete accuracy did he spring up from the icy water and grab Dagliesh from behind. With his arm wrapped around the other man's neck, squeezing with just enough force to subdue him, did Joss speak.

"You will never touch her again. If you ever attempt it, there will not be enough left of you to stand trial," he warned with a low growl.

Other men began to step forward, some lowering themselves from the wharf above where they'd been concealed amidst stacks of unloaded cargo or empty crates. Others still were concealed in the water, hiding behind pilings or buoys. It was Arliss Battson who helped Hettie to her feet as Maurice Bates moved toward them and placed a pair of handcuffs on Simon's wrists.

When he knew Dagliesh was subdued, Joss moved toward Hettie. He wrapped her in his arms and whispered in her ear, "You are the most reckless, willful, obstinate, maddening woman I have ever known. Do you have any idea what might have happened to you?"

"I have a very good idea of it. Is Annie . . . is she in that barrel?" Hettie asked softly.

"No. Jack Collinsworth found her earlier. He's already returned her to Vincent's house to be cared for. She is frightened, but otherwise well enough."

She sagged against him then, her relief evident. "I couldn't let him harm her because of me. I never imagined that he would have devised something so diabolical as this."

"Desperation creates ingenuity. He's out of funds entirely. There's not a soul in London he can beg, borrow or steal from now . . . not when he's hunted by Ardmore and his band of cutthroats. With no accomplices, he had to get creative," Joss surmised. He didn't add that he had an inkling it wasn't the first time Simon Dagliesh had tormented a woman. Knowing what he did of the late Lord Ernsdale and the various establishments that had banned him for his treatment of the working girls, it stood to reason that both of the Dagliesh men were poisoned fruit from a very rotten tree. "Let's get you out of the water. I know it's your vision of hell."

HETTIE ALLOWED HIM to lead her from the water via the same steps she'd taken down with Simon. The source of her fear had been eliminated, but still her heart raced, and it felt as if she could not breathe in enough air. The chilly night air and her sodden clothes did not help the matter. By the time they reached the quay, Vincent and Honoria were there. From somewhere, a heavy cloak appeared and was draped about her shoulders. It did little to dispel the cold.

"I need to get her back to the house and warm. We haven't time to waste."

"Sally Dawson is waiting to drive you home," Vincent said, clearly nonplussed by it all.

"Sally?" Joss repeated and then looked at her. "What were the three of you planning?"

Hettie looked at her sister and nodded. Honoria then proceeded to pull a brace of pistols from her pockets and also two wicked-looking blades. "We did not come unprepared," she said. "I have a blade of my own. It's tucked into my boot. We did not come here to die. Nor did we intend to leave here with Simon Dagliesh still drawing breath."

The admission, that they'd come there with the intent to do murder, was met with complete silence. Neither Vincent nor Joss spoke a word. But they exchanged a look that seemed to say the pair of them were the banes of their respective existences. For her part, the feeling was quite mutual. The man was maddening. Did he care for her? Sometimes she thought so. He desired her. Had his concern been only for the child she carried, or was there some tenderness in his self-proclaimed hard heart for her? Hettie had no notion. And pride would not let her ask.

In that moment, she found herself weary of it all. So weary, in fact, that she swayed on her feet. Immediately, his arm about her tightened, holding her upright.

"Home. We'll discuss your schemes and desire to resort to a life of crime at a later time when you've had a hot bath, hot tea, and dry clothes," he said.

She might have argued on principal had the things he suggested not sounded so terribly divine to her.

Chapter Forty-One

Simon Dagliesh looked up from the plate of bread and tankard of water that had been given to him. While it had only been hours since his arrest, it had been some days since he'd eaten anything of real substance. The fresh baked bread had smelled heavenly, and the young guard, who looked little more than a boy, had taken pity on him with his rumbling belly. But now, halfway through the hearty chunk, the other guard—the brutish one—was standing in the doorway, slapping a billy club against his palm, as if waiting for an excuse to use it.

"Come with me," the guard demanded.

"I'll finish my meal, thank you," Simon said, and picked up the hunk of bread to take another hearty bite.

The guard laughed. "Oh, you've had enough, you puffed-up bastard. Preening like a peacock when you're in rags not fit for the dust bin."

Simon's eyes narrowed, and without any warning he rose from the bench where he'd been sitting, hurling the plate and tankard at the guard as he charged toward him. It had been an impulse. Not well thought out, nor particularly stylish in execution. It also landed him flat on his back, the guard's boot on his throat and the man leaning menacingly over him.

"Give me a reason," the guard taunted. "Just one. A strong enough kick to the head, and you won't even be fit to hang."

Before he could reply, the guard jerked him up, and he stumbled as he gained his feet, the manacles digging into his ankles as his boots had been "confiscated." More than likely taken to the nearest pawnbroker or rag seller.

Yanked upward by the neck of his shirt, once he was on his feet, Simon jerked out of the guard's reach. Even then the guard used the billy club to prod him along the corridor to the dim, dank cell.

It was will alone that kept him on his feet. He'd enter that cell under his own power. He wouldn't crawl before any of them. The very idea of being manhandled by those he found to be utterly beneath him was inconceivable to him. It didn't matter that they were, at present at least, dressed better than he was and significantly more well groomed. They were still inferior to him.

"Get in there, your majesty," the one intoned sarcastically. "Welcome to your new abode . . . the very height of luxury!"

Simon smirked. "I may have been arrested. My guilt might even be proven. But I will not be imprisoned for long. Men of my standing rarely are. And when I am free, I shall make you regret every insult you visit upon me."

"Will you now?" The guard chuckled even as he gave Simon a harsh shove, pushing him back from the door. As it clanged shut with a horrible grating sound of metal on metal, he peered through the bars. "I'll be wishing you the best of luck with that . . . *m'lord*. It ain't the trial you need to worry 'bout."

"Ill-bred brute," Simon muttered as the guard ambled off, leaving him locked in the damp, wretched place. The only light spilled in from a single lamp burning in the corridor beyond the door. It did little to dispel the deep shadows in the corners. He dared not think of what sort of vermin might be inhabiting the place with him.

Even as that thought occurred to him, there was a slight shuffling sound. He shivered with distaste. "Rats."

"Rats are not your greatest cause for concern, Lord Ernsdale."

Simon's blood ran cold in his veins at the sound of that voice coming out of the darkness. Not even the iron bars of the gaol could keep him out. "Ardmore."

From the shadows, the man leaned forward, resting his forearms on his knees. "You're lucky in one regard, Dagliesh. The Hound has covered your debts in exchange for my aid in searching for you. Not that I helped much. But then I didn't need to. I knew you'd do something reckless and foolish . . . something to draw attention to yourself. Why? Because you're incapable of setting aside your own vanity and conceit, even in the face of certain death."

"If my debts are paid, why are you here?"

Ardmore made a tisking sound, clucking his tongue over and over in a way that was intentionally grating. Largely because it was quite terrifying. "Simon, you know me better than that. Your debt is paid. The money has been returned to me. But you've taken something else from me that the Hound, with all his resources, cannot return to me. You've made me a laughingstock. If I let you get away with your attempts to dodge me, what message am I sending to others? Oh, no, Simon. My pursuit of you was never about the money. While it was an astronomical sum to you—it is a mere pittance to me. My reputation? Now that is worth something."

"So you intend to murder me in my cell?"

Ardmore smiled. "Oh, it's done already. Didn't that kindly young officer give you bread and water?"

Panic raced through him. His skin prickled with it and his lungs tightened as the breath refused to expel from him. "What do you mean?"

Ardmore simply rose and walked toward the door, passing within arms reach of him. With a snap of his fingers, a guard appeared and opened the heavy door to let him out. Casually, as if he were not talking about having poisoned him, Ardmore said, "I'm not a religious man. I don't think you are either. But you have a very limited amount of time to change your mind about that. It wouldn't be the worst idea to hedge one's bets a little."

Ardmore vanished into the dimness of the corridor, the cell door clanging shut behind him once more, and Simon was alone in the cold, dank space. It felt as if the walls were closing in on him. Every beat of his heart sounded like a drum as he weighed and measured each one. Was his heart speeding up? Slowing down? Was it panic making it difficult to breathe or something more sinister?

He fell to his knees, his fingers shoved down his throat as he tried to force the poison out. He gagged and wretched to no avail. Even when he scraped his knuckles against his teeth with enough force to make them bleed, the contents of his stomach refused to be purged. The coppery taste of his own blood filled his mouth as he felt a faint twitching in the muscles of his legs. He tried to get to his feet, to call for help that likely wouldn't come anyway. But he couldn't get his feet under him. The more he tried to move, the more stubbornly ungainly and uncooperative his limbs became.

Sprawled on the floor without a shred of dignity left, Simon felt those tremors in his legs moving upward. They passed through his entire body. And then the tightness in his chest began. It was subtle at first, but grew progressively worse until only a hoarse rasp escaped him. Ardmore had spoken truthfully. The bread and water he'd been given had been poisoned. Death was coming for him sooner rather than later.

For a split second, he was tempted to pray for forgiveness—to beg the Lord for mercy. But as he wasn't entirely certain he believed in the Lord at all, it would have done him little good. If the Lord did exist, and he knew every man's heart as the church insisted, it would have been a wasted effort. Simon wasn't the least bit sorry or repentant for anything he'd done. His only regret was that he'd failed.

Chapter Forty-Two

I T WAS LATE when Hettie awakened. The sun was streaming in through the curtains, oddly bright for London. And she was alone.

Of course, she had been alone when she retired for the night. She had simply assumed that at some point Joss would join her. However angry he'd been at her for taking the risks she had, surely it would not keep him away? Or so she had thought. Clearly, she had been mistaken.

Getting out of the bed, forcing one foot in front of the other, she saw to her morning ablutions. Annie Foster had been returned to her mother's home the previous night. After her ordeal, she'd wanted to be close to her family. Hettie could understand that. After all, when she'd been in that dark hold on the ship, had she not only wished for her sister?

With her hair brushed and pulled back in a simple chignon, one that required no assistance, she dressed in one of the borrowed black gowns from her sister. Her figure had been more generous than Honoria's to start, and there was no denying that her body was beginning to change. They were subtle changes to the outside observer, but unmistakable to her. Stays that didn't quite cover her as they once had, chemises that no longer fit quite as they should—and the reality of her situation had altered quite dramatically.

Simon was in the gaol. Inspector Bates no longer considered her a suspect in any of the crimes he might have once accused her of. All the reasons for them to marry, save for the child itself, had been eliminated in one fell swoop. The truth was that it would be to her benefit to remain a widow. Her child, if it was a boy, would inherit the title. But she didn't want that. She wanted her child to have a father, and for better or worse, that was Joshua Ettinger.

Unable to hide in her room any longer, Hettie left her bed-chamber and made her way down the stairs. Breakfast would long since have been over, so she bypassed the breakfast room entirely. Near Vincent's study, she heard the low hum of hushed voices. As one of those voices belonged to her sister, she felt assured enough of her welcome to knock softly.

Almost immediately, the door opened and Honoria smiled. "Come in. We were just discussing . . . things."

"Things?" Hettie asked, puzzled at her sister's odd tone.

"Simon is dead. Discovered in his cell this morning. Strychnine, most likely, based on the evidence," Joss explained from where he stood staring out the window.

Hettie blinked. "Oh. Is it . . . did he . . ." She trailed off, uncertain if she wanted to know.

"I don't think it was suicide," Joss said, looking at her for the first time. "He wasn't the sort for that, was he? It was Ardmore, most likely, or one of his men. I say good riddance."

Vincent shook his head. "It's too bold, Joss. Ardmore's power is growing every day. If he takes control of the various illegal enterprises in this city, rather than just controlling the bulk of the cent-percenters, no one will be able to stop him. I hesitate to think what the consequences of that might be."

The room grew quiet then as the potential ramifications of it all sank in. Vincent, for all his protestations of not being a good man, of being a criminal, still operated within the confines of his own moral code. Ardmore had no such constraint. Though Hettie had only learned of him recently, what she had heard was enough to terrify her. Morality was fluid for him, if it existed at all.

"What can we do?" Honoria asked, rising from her seat and crossing to where Vincent was seated at his desk. She placed her hand over his. "You have said that you wished to step back from this life. If you mean to do that based solely on the belief that I require it or even wish for it, then you are wrong. I fell in love with you for who you are and who you were and whomever it is you choose to become. If I'm willing to follow you into hell, surely Newgate is not much of a stretch."

It felt wrong to observe such intimacy, such devotion. As if her presence was an intrusion, Hettie thought. For the first time, she recognized that she was no longer the thing that mattered most to her sister. Like all younger siblings, there was a moment of resentment for that. As a woman, there was something else. A moment of the purest envy. She wanted to be loved that way, but she also, desperately, wanted to *love* that way. The very idea of having such deep and abiding feelings for another human being was both terrifying and exhilarating. It was also out of reach. Because Joss Ettinger would never love her that way, and she didn't have the strength to give him her heart when she'd never hold his in return.

"On that note, Hettie, we should go. We have an appointment with a vicar," Joss said.

At least one question in her life had been answered. He intended to go through with the wedding. Hettie wasn't certain whether to be relieved or reluctant.

HE DIDN'T BELIEVE in love. So why he felt envious of the connection so evident between Vincent and Honoria was a mystery to him. Mysterious or not, it didn't change the fact of what he felt. Nor did it change the fact that the woman whom he wanted such an expression of devotion from was the very woman he was on the verge of marrying for reasons that, while morally correct, still felt wrong. *Or not enough.*

On the surface of it all, it'd be better if she remained a widow. There would be no shame or outcry over having a child within nine months of her husband's death. The child, if male, would inherit the title. But he couldn't. He couldn't let his child carry another man's name. *Their child.* But would he feel that way if it were any other woman?

During the night, he'd toyed with the idea of not marrying her at all. Not because he didn't want to, but perversely because he did. He wanted her too much, and that terrified him. He was man enough to admit that. Then there was the other side of that coin. He wanted her too much to simply walk away and let her go. Altruism of that sort was foreign to him.

There was a possessiveness in him when it came to Hettie that was also quite foreign to him. In all his life, he'd never felt that connection to another person. There were people who had his friendship, who had his loyalty. But there was no one that he couldn't simply walk away from. *Until her.* She was his. But for a man who didn't believe in love or other such fine, sentimental feelings, what did that mean exactly?

He wasn't certain but there would be time enough to figure it out. The rest of their lives, in fact.

Chapter Forty-Three

*T*HE BRIDE WORE *black.*

Joss could only imagine what the vicar must be thinking. Hettie in her widow's weeds and he in clothing that clearly indicated the disparity in their class.

Despite the unusual circumstances, it was a simple enough ceremony. They married at St. James's in Piccadilly. It was the church that Hettie typically attended. As he didn't attend church with any regularity, it was at least a location that might have significance for her. There should be something about their wedding that was normal.

When it was done, they signed the register, as did the witnesses the vicar had provided. Once outside, they climbed into a hack, and it was only then that Hettie spoke without it being at the direct instruction of someone else. "Where do we go now?"

"For the time being, we return to Vincent's and Honoria's. Then we will make a decision as to where we wish to go next. Obviously, I cannot provide the sort of home for you that you are accustomed to." It goaded him to admit it.

She laughed bitterly. "You mean one where I have to live in fear daily? I'll thank you to never provide such an environment for me."

"That isn't what I meant, and you know that. I do not expect you to live at the standard my present income would provide. But

I do have a certain amount of pride, and it goads me that we should have to live off your fortune."

"Then we will live on the income that your new endeavors with Vincent will provide. He does mean to make you a partner in several of his enterprises—lucrative enterprises at that. I don't need society, Joss. I don't need to be dressed in the first stare of fashion, nor do I need to live on Grosvenor Square in a house staffed with dozens of servants. If that is what you think of me—"

"It isn't. If anyone knows that you are not what others expect you to be, it is I. I've seen you both at your best and your worst. Could you be content in a modest house with only a maid and a cook?"

"Content," she mused. "I cannot say whether contentment is something I am even capable of feeling. I've never experienced it. But I shall endeavor to be so. I would not want this to be a miserable marriage where we spend the majority of our time avoiding one another."

"Is that how it was with Ernsdale?" he asked. Part of him wanted to know and part of him did not.

"In the end, it was. In the beginning—well, Arthur could be very cruel. It was prompted by his wounded vanity. Whenever he failed at something, whether it was losing heavily at the tables or his inability to consummate our marriage, he would be violent. In the beginning that was fairly mild, but as things do, it escalated over time. It was only after he refused to pay the ransom that I had some sort of leverage. I could hold the threat of exposure over his head and force him to be, if not pleasant, at least inoffensive."

It occurred to him then that much of her life had been no different than what he'd endured as a child. Oh, the clothes had been finer and the food more plentiful, but the slaps and kicks and insults—those had been her daily existence for far more years than he'd been forced to endure them. "There are certain things that I can promise you. I will never be intentionally cruel to you. I hope to never hurt you in any way. But life is very messy, and those sorts of promises are destined to be broken. I will try to be the husband . . ."

"The husband I deserve?"

He shook his head. "Such a man does not exist. I will simply be the best that I am capable of."

IT WAS A fairly short journey back to her sister's home. After their initial conversation, they'd fallen into silence. Not necessarily companionable, but at least not awkward and fraught with tension. They'd simply been lost to their own thoughts.

Now, as they entered the house, Hettie felt the weight of it all on her. It had been a momentous day, and it was not yet noon.

"Ah, they've returned!" Honoria called out as she stepped into the foyer. "It's simple fare, but a wedding breakfast has been prepared. There is cake at least."

It was an attempt by her sister to make everything feel normal, and Hettie was not unappreciative of the effort. At the same time, it was terribly difficult to be in the presence of her sister and Vincent when they were so obviously painfully in love with one another. And when she was facing the unfortunate truth that she had feelings for Joss that he would likely never return. But she wouldn't hurt Honoria's feelings for the world, and given how much thought had been put into it, it would have been churlish to decline.

"And cake," Hettie managed with a smile, "is always welcome."

The celebration, subdued though it was, did not last long. They ate and talked, generally maintaining a jovial air for just a few moments when suddenly the doors flew open.

A footman, not from the house but from Vincent's club, entered the dining room. He handed Vincent a folded note and waited for him to read it. Hettie knew instantly that something was wrong, and as she looked at her sister, she realized that Honoria did as well. She was incredibly tense while Vincent emanated cold fury, coiled like a serpent prepared to strike.

"What's happened?" Hettie asked.

"Ardmore has essentially declared war," Vincent said, addressing the statement more to Joss than her. "He sent several of his men to the docks today . . . my docks. And they 'liberated' a large quantity of cargo to which they had no entitlement."

"It isn't an insurmountable loss, surely," Honoria protested softly. It was fear that motivated the question, and perhaps a vain hope that the entire situation might just go away.

"The cargo isn't," Vincent agreed. "And if it had been a storm or a fire or some other such event, it would not matter. But Ardmore did this as a challenge, my love. If I allow it, then it will be the first of many things he takes. He will not stop until everything I have built in this city is under his rule . . . and for many reasons, both obvious and more opaque, that cannot be permitted."

"It'll be only the beginning. Ardmore will chip away at everything piece by piece until he has it all," Joss concurred. "And there will be casualties. He's not a man who understands the concept of mercy."

It was as if they were trying to communicate something to one another without stating it baldly. But Hettie was tired of men trying to shelter her with enforced ignorance. "You think we are in danger."

Both men looked at her, but Vincent looked away first. Joss's gaze remained on her for a moment, silent and measuring before he spoke. "It would not be the first time Ardmore has used a man's family to force his hand. In fact, it's his most common tactic. He'd have used it on Simon if the bastard had cared for anyone but himself."

It was said so matter of factly. He was being completely honest with her. This was no attempt to make her panic or to scare her into compliance. He was trusting her with the truth and trusting her to make the right decision with that truth.

"And that," Vincent said, "is why you are both going to the country and Stavers is accompanying you. Do not argue with me about it. Joss and I need to be able to deal with him, and we cannot do that if we are distracted worrying that the two of you may become a casualty of this debacle."

"I don't want to leave you," Honoria said. "And Hettie and Joss are newly married!"

"He's right, Honoria," Hettie said, surprising even herself with the agreement. "If that man could get to Simon while he's in a cell under guard . . . I would rather be apart and reunite later than be the cause of a fatal distraction."

"You'll leave at first light," Vincent said. "Be ready. I'd advise you to make good use of the limited time you have to enjoy your newly embarked-upon connubial bliss."

Honoria rose to follow Vincent as he strode from the room. "I've had the servants move your things into Mr. Ettinger's chambers, Hettie. They are the larger of the two rooms you've been occupying. I do hope that is all right." Then she sailed out of the room behind him, leaving them to sort out what should happen next.

"The pair of them are many things, but subtle is not one of them," she noted.

"Indeed, they are not," Joss agreed. "But in this instance, is subtlety a requirement? Neither of us are virginal, though some of us left that state behind only recently. It is our wedding day, Hettie, and we will only have today. I cannot say how long it will be until these matters with Ardmore are settled. What happens next is entirely up to you."

"How fortunate that I am aware darkness is not a requirement for such activities. As I currently have no lady's maid, do you think you can manage all the buttons and pins?"

His lips curved in a half smile. "I'm certain I can muddle through."

Chapter Forty-Four

HE'D BEEN THINKING of kissing her all morning. And all the night before, if he were honest. And each and every night since he'd first met her. Those desires were ever present in his mind, always hovering on the periphery of conscious thought. Wanting her was as inevitable and instinctive as taking his next breath. The moment the door closed behind them, he reached for her, hauling her against him.

She came to him eagerly, without a hint of hesitation. As she molded her body to his, he could feel every lush curve, all the glorious crests and valleys that made the female form such a delight. And somehow, despite having enjoyed those intimate delights with so many others, with her it was an entirely different experience. As cliche as it sounded, every time was like the first time. There was a wonder to it that he had thought himself too jaded by all that he'd experienced and all that he'd witnessed to ever feel such a thing again.

Trailing his lips from hers, he pressed kisses to her jawline, the delicate shell of her ear, then down her neck to the arc of her collarbone that was barely visible above the neckline of her gown. As he did so, he worked the buttons at the back until the fabric sagged, falling from her shoulders to her waist. The undergarments she wore were not intended for seduction. They were serviceable, practical, and for all that were still undeniably alluring.

"It isn't exactly how one dresses for their wedding night . . . or day, for that matter," she mused.

"If you find your present attire objectionable," he suggested, as he freed the simple bow to loosen her stays, "there is only one solution . . . discard it. All of it."

It didn't surprise him in the least when she accepted his challenge. With a shrug of her shoulders, the restrictive undergarment fell away. Her petticoat followed, and then her chemise. She was nude, save for her stockings and garters, while her hair was still neatly pinned back. But he wanted it free. He wanted to feel it tangling around their bodies, brushing against his skin, feather-light and all the more arousing for it.

Joss plucked one pin from her hair and then another, until the mass of it tumbled down her back. Then he retreated one step, just to look at her, to take in all of her. "Beautiful . . . too beautiful for some battle-scarred wretch like me."

She shook her head. "Your battle scars tell the story of your life, of who you are. That makes them beautiful to me. Now, it's time you removed your clothing. I refuse to be the only one so exposed."

Joss shrugged out of his coat, then his waistcoat came next. The simple neck cloth he favored followed close behind. He didn't stop until he was stripped down to only his trousers.

"You won't offend my maidenly sensibilities," she offered.

"No, but I might severely damage my own pride if . . . if I were too eager." He settled on that wording with no small degree of thought. Hettie wasn't a virgin, but that didn't mean she understood all the particulars of carnal relations. And some things were better learned from exploration than explanation.

He pulled her against him again, marveling at the silken texture of her skin, the suppleness of her flesh. It spiked his hunger for her to an almost unbearable degree. He claimed her mouth in a searing kiss and, even as he did so, walked her backward toward the bed. Once they reached it, he spun them around until he could sit. She followed him down, sprawling across his lap as he'd intended. It gave him access to every part of her, and he intended to exploit that benefit fully.

HETTIE SIGHED IN delight as his hands roamed over her body. He touched her everywhere—stroking, caressing, teasing. And every touch only served to make her more eager, more desperate for him. When his mouth covered the taut peak of one breast, his tongue swirling over her sensitive flesh, she arched against him, offering herself more fully. She wanted to seduce him. She desperately wanted to be the kind of woman who could lure and ensnare a man . . . but he would be the only one she would use such wiles on. Indeed, he was the only man she could ever imagine having such intimacies with.

"Is there some reason why you do not feel inclined to hurry?" she asked him.

He laughed, his breath fanning over her skin in a way that made her shiver. "It's a rare thing for a woman to complain that a man is taking his time."

"We can take our time . . . next time. I've spent my whole life waiting to feel this. To feel anything." It was a painful admission, but an honest one. She'd wasted years in a loveless farce of a marriage to a man who was as incapable of being a husband to her as he was unworthy of being one. And while she had no illusions of love between herself and Joss, they did have passion. He desired her. Surely that was a place to start.

When he lifted her off him and bore her back onto the bed, the weight of him pressing down on her so gloriously, she knew that she had succeeded in her efforts of persuasion. Within seconds, her stockings and garters vanished, discarded somewhere in the room along with the remainder of their clothing. His trousers were gone, as well. She could feel the rigid length of him pressing intimately against her.

If, Hettie thought, she were a more morally upright sort of woman, she'd have been appalled at her own eagerness. But she wasn't, and appalled was the furthest thing from her present feelings. She gloried in it, savoring the sensuality of his nearness, of the startling contrast of their bodies and the glorious ways in which they simply fit together.

Slipping her hand between their bodies, she gripped him gently and guided him to the part of her that ached so desperately for him. Words were no longer needed as he pressed himself inside her, filling her up and soothing the emptiness that seemed to gnaw at her.

Hitching her legs higher on his hips, she let her head fall back as a soft cry of pleasure escaped her. She gave herself up to it, to him—allowing herself to be swept away on that haze of passion until they both found that perfect moment of release.

Chapter Forty-Five

"ARE YOU IN danger?" Hettie posed the question with her head resting on his shoulder as he rubbed a strand of her silken hair between his fingers.

"It is not without danger. But I am certain that we will come out of this well. Vincent will not allow for any other outcome, and neither will I," he said reassuringly.

"Good," Hettie said. "I have no wish to be widowed twice."

"I've no wish to make you a widow." He could feel her hesitation. "Whatever you wish to ask, just do so."

"What will you do after all these things are settled with Ardmore? I know Vincent wanted you to manage the club, but . . . I fear that with what is happening, he may decide to remain in London and see to his businesses himself."

"As you have a fortune I cannot fathom, I know you're not worried about my ability to support you. So what is this, Hettie?"

She sighed, sitting up and putting space between them. She couldn't think clearly otherwise, much less articulate her concerns. "I know you want a purpose. If we live off my fortune entirely, I know that you will grow to resent it and perhaps to resent me. We have enough obstacles before us."

"I will find a way. I rather like being a private inquiry agent. It's not especially lucrative, but as we are not dependent upon that income, it need not be. I'm man enough not to be threatened by you having money. I'm also man enough that I fully intend to earn my own."

It was not what she'd expected him to say. She'd thought, perhaps foolishly, that he would approach it as most men. That he would assume control of her fortune and dole out an allowance or pin money to her. "You're not worried that I will bankrupt us? That by virtue of being a woman and therefore too stupid to manage anything on my own I will squander the entirety of it?"

"No. And even if you did, I'm no worse off than I have been. Besides, you're accustomed to wealth. It stands to reason you'd be more capable of managing it than someone who has barely ever had more than a tuppence to his name. So, tell me, Hettie, what it is that you wish to do with your fortune?"

"I wish to make a difference . . . a real one."

He nodded. "And what does that mean to you?"

"Honoria and I have talked about starting a charity . . . there are so many that exist already, but to access them these women must go in with their heads hung in shame, be preached at and pontificated over as if their entire existence were naught but a cautionary tale. I'd like to do something that allowed them not to simply keep their current degree of dignity but to expand upon it. Train them for jobs and to run their own businesses, even. Women are just as capable as men are of such things."

"I'll not disagree with you. Most of the pleasure houses in London are run by women and run quite well. I don't see why women should have a head only for that business rather than running their own shops or other enterprises," he said softly.

Hettie couldn't quite believe it. Her whole life she'd been fighting to make men hear her, to acknowledge her as a person in her own right. "You really do not believe that women are intrinsically less capable than men?"

Joss chuckled. "I've known many people that were inept in many ways, and that was dictated solely by what they had between their ears and not what that had between their legs."

A feeling of immense relief washed through her. And perhaps even a feeling of hope. "You are a remarkably forward-thinking man, Mr. Ettinger."

IT WAS HIS turn to broach somewhat difficult subjects. Difficult because he found the answer mattered more than he'd thought it would, certainly more than it ought to. "Will you miss being Lady Ernsdale? Trading that for being a mere missus must be something of a let down." He hated himself for even asking the question, for allowing even a hint of the vulnerability he felt on that score to be evident. He could hardly admit it to himself, after all.

Hettie's smile grew. It was no longer simply a bemused curve of her lips, but a full smile that spread across her face, crinkling her nose and showcasing a dimple in her cheek. "I've already had more happiness as Mrs. Ettinger than I had cumulatively in all my years as Lady Ernsdale," she mused softly. "I think I will not miss that at all."

The relief that washed through him at her response was beyond gratifying. And that terrified him. It terrified him enough that he needed to immediately quash any hopes she might have of this becoming the love match that poets and novelists all spoke of. "I can't offer you the kind of marriage you deserve," he said. "I'm not a romantic man. I'm not one given to sentiment or fantastical emotion. I like you. I respect you. I want you. But love, if it exists at all, isn't something I have any experience with. I cannot imagine that will change any time soon."

The smile, so bright and genuine, shifted subtly. It became tighter, more guarded, and he saw a bit of the light in her eyes fade.

"I'm sorry for that," he offered.

"No. No, you are not. I think that you are sorry I might be

hurt or disappointed by it, but you are not sorry for the way that you feel. Nor should you be. This is a practical arrangement, Joss," she said. "We married because I am carrying your child. And we are simply making the best of it."

It was what he'd wanted. It was certainly all he wished to give of himself. So why the hell did it sound so awful when she said it?

Chapter Forty-Six

Two Weeks Later

SHIFTING IN HIS seat, Joss peered out the window for likely the hundredth time. The carriage seemed to be crawling at a snail's pace. The closer they came to Eastvale, Vincent's estate, the slower each mile seemed to pass.

"The view has not altered significantly since last you looked . . . a mere five seconds ago," Vincent observed, sounding at once amused and annoyed.

"Your eagerness to see Honoria has had you looking out the window with no less frequency." There was perhaps more snap to his words and tone than Joss had intended, but he was more than a bit on edge.

"Oh, I do not deny it. I cannot wait to see my wife again. But I love her. Is your eagerness to see Hettie an indication that a shift has occurred in your stance on the existence of that particular emotion?"

The question, posed in a very bemused tone, grated on his nerves. "You know better than that. I'm happy that you have found what you believe to be love . . . and perhaps for you and Honoria it is real. But it's not for me. It'll never be for me."

Vincent shook his head in exasperation. "If you do not love Hettie, why such eagerness? No, not eagerness. Longing. It's a far different thing than simply the need to slake one's lust."

"For fuck's sake, must you poke at everything?" The exasperation in his tone was unmistakable. "We're not all sentimental fools under the surface, Vincent. Some would say, based on your current behavior, that the Hound of Whitehall has been turned into a lapdog."

No one said that. But it was a low blow and one that he hoped would end the conversation. The truth was, that might have been speculated as a possible truth two weeks earlier, before Ardmore had made his play. Before Vincent had once more established why he had control of so many vast enterprises, both legal and otherwise, in London. The unscrupulous moneylender, while not broken, was still beaten. The lines demarcating the territories ruled by each of them had been reestablished quite firmly. There had been a few injuries. A bit of blood shed and a couple of teeth on the floor. But in the end, the Hound of Whitehall had kept all that he'd earned over the years.

It had come down to a singular challenge. A boxing match. The two competing lords of the underworld squared off toe to toe and pummeled one another until one submitted. Obviously, it hadn't been Vincent. Courtesy of Stavers's many lessons, each of them could more than hold their own in the ring. Ardmore had conceded defeat and retreated to the east end of London, and Vincent would continue running everything west of the bridge. Hardly a lapdog.

"I'm merely pointing out, Joss, that for a man who proclaims himself incapable of love, you do seem to have missed your new bride a great deal."

Rather than continue the debate, Joss remained silent. Primarily because he could not refute Vincent's assertion. He had missed her. While they'd been focused on finding Arthur Ernsdale's murderer, they'd spent more time together. Almost daily in fact. And somehow, even in that short time, he'd grown quite accustomed to her presence. Sharing a word or two in passing, seeing one another at meal times, and, on a few occasions, slipping into one another's room for more intimate encounters—and for two weeks, he hadn't laid eyes on her. Was it any wonder he was eager to see her?

But missing someone was not the same as loving them. One could miss things and people that one only liked or had a fondness for. Those were perfectly reasonable feelings to have for someone. Liking or fondness for someone or something meant that losing that someone or something would not be devastating. No attachment meant no loss, no grief. Because the pain of losing things—or people—that truly mattered was something he had no wish to endure. Not ever again.

"Why are you so determined not to feel anything?" Vincent asked. "Or is it the other way around?"

"What the hell does that even mean?"

"It means that perhaps it isn't that you think yourself incapable of loving someone so much as you think yourself completely unworthy of being loved," the other man mused. "I should hope such a foolish thought, if it ever entered your mind, would be dismissed as being both asinine and baseless."

It had. That thought had plagued him for all of his life. Try to dismiss it as he might, he had never succeeded. "You do not know when to quit."

"Are we going to brawl in the carriage, then? I think not. Answer the question, Joss."

"Because I don't bloody well deserve her, do I?"

Vincent was quiet for a moment. "No one does. Not a man alive is worthy of a woman like Honoria or like her sister. But that's not stopping me from seizing what happiness I can. I very nearly cocked it up too, you know? It's a hard thing—to just hand someone the power to break you. But if you hand the power to the right person, it will only make you stronger."

"Shall I confess my feelings for her to you so that you'll shut the hell up?"

Vincent shrugged. "I'm not the one who needs to hear them, am I?"

Banging on the roof of the carriage, Joss shouted, "Can't this bloody thing go any faster?"

With a satisfying jolt, the horses shot forward and the carriage picked up speed. And neither of them spoke for the remainder of the journey—Vincent because he'd said all he needed to, and Joss because he was digesting all that had been said.

HETTIE SQUIRMED ON the settee. It seemed to have happened quite overnight. She'd woken up one morning and her belly had grown quite round. Not large, and certainly easily concealed beneath her gowns, but still very present. And not entirely comfortable. She felt thrown off balance by that small bump. But perhaps it was that it made the very abstract notion of her child far more substantive. It wasn't just something in the distant future. It wasn't just being nauseous or any of the other symptoms associated with early pregnancy that could just as easily be some other illness. It was now an undeniable physical presence, even if still in her womb.

"Why are you so antsy?"

"Likely because my clothes have grown too tight," she replied balefully. "Why else would I be?"

"Because you miss your husband?" Honoria voiced it as a question, but it didn't feel like one. It felt as if her sister knew the answer already.

Hettie simply elected not to answer. There was no need. If she admitted the truth, she'd only be confirming Honoria's suspicions. If she denied it, then her sister would instantly recognize the lie.

Honoria, after receiving no response, simply forged ahead. "I've received word. Vincent sent a courier ahead of them. They will be here this afternoon."

The relief Hettie felt at that bit of news was overwhelming. "Well, that is wonderful to hear. I know you've been terribly worried about Vincent."

"Yes, I have. And you've been worried about Joss. I know because you've moped around here looking utterly miserable. You are pale and have shadows under your eyes," Honoria observed.

Hettie was well aware of her appearance. She'd looked at herself in the mirror, after all. The sleepless nights she had endured for the last fortnight had taken their toll on her. But it stung to have it pointed out. "Your flattery will go to my head, sister."

Honoria waved away the sarcastic rejoinder. "You are lovely, as always. But I am worried for you. This cannot be good for you or for your baby."

"I am fine. And so is my child," Hettie snapped. It was a reflexive action, to be so defensive, mostly because she had been worrying about that matter herself. But giving it voice made those fears far too real for her.

"Perhaps I can have the housekeeper prepare a sleeping draught for you?"

"If I feel I need one, I will ask for it myself. I am with child, Honoria. That does not mean I am one!"

Honoria grew quiet then. That quiet was almost worse than her helpful suggestions because her silence allowed Hettie to stew in her own guilt for lashing out at her sister for simply caring about her well being.

"I apologize. I fear my temper is quite short and . . . well, I do have a great deal pressing on my mind. But that is no excuse for being short with you," she admitted somewhat grudgingly.

"I know. I know you're worried about what happens when Joss joins you here. I know you're worried about your child. About your marriage. About all the things that could possibly go right and possibly go wrong. But you are not alone. I am here for you. Always. Whatever may occur."

"I appreciate your support, but it is my dearest hope that it will not be needed. But I have no notion what is on his mind. His correspondence has been limited and perfunctory at best."

Honoria seated herself beside Hettie and took her hand. "If it is any great consolation, Vincent's letters have indicated that your husband is quite surly and put out."

"Why would that be a consolation? The last thing I wish to deal with is a surly man!"

Honoria shook her head. "Have you considered that perhaps he is surly only because he is absent from you?"

No. She had not considered it. In truth, she couldn't imagine that to be the case. Surely if it were, his letters would have indicated some degree of emotion—that he missed her, that he wished to see her. The salutation was always direct, the body of the letter was short and succinct, and they were signed, very simply, J. Ettinger. They might have been business associates for all that the letters indicated any sort of relationship between them.

"He writes to you every day?" Hettie asked the question with a pang of envy. While Vincent and Joss had been in London taking care of the threat to Vincent's empire—in ways she had no wish to know of—Honoria had still been ever present in Vincent's mind. That much was clear from what he wrote to her. A pang of jealousy swept through her, followed by a wave of guilt.

O, what a bitter thing it is to look into happiness through another man's eyes. The quotation wasn't quite right for the situation as her sister was the one whose happiness highlighted her own dismal state, but the sentiment of it certainly was. No one had a greater understanding of the follies and feats of man than William Shakespeare. And Hettie was honest enough with herself to admit that she envied her sister. She did not begrudge her the happiness she had found with Vincent Carrow, but there was a part of her that desperately longed for such happiness herself.

"He does . . . Joss has written you. Surely that indicates something of his feelings."

Hettie nodded. "He has written . . . briefly, almost to the point of curtness, and has done so with such infrequency that it indicates I am little more than an afterthought."

"I had thought your sleeplessness and worry were simply out of fear for his safety. Now, I wonder if it isn't something else altogether. Are you happy, Hettie? Truly happy?" Honoria asked, her concern evident in the gentleness of her tone.

Hettie considered the question carefully, sipping her tea to bide her time until she could answer both honestly and reassuringly. "I am not unhappy. My expectations have been carefully managed. Content is, I suppose, a more accurate description."

Honoria's eyebrows lifted, her eyes wide with incredulity. "Content? Hettie, contentment is a feeling for fat puppies with full bellies and old men dandling grandchildren on their knee. It is not how a woman ought to describe her life when she is newly married to a man . . ." Honoria trailed off.

"To a man that she loves?" Hettie suggested.

"You haven't said so. I have assumed," Honoria admitted.

A sigh escaped her. "Not everyone is destined for a great love story. Sadly, as we both know, not every marriage is built on a grand romance or even romance at all."

"Do you deny that you are in love with him?"

She wanted to. But lying to her sister was not something she had ever done with any real degree of success. "No. I am not denying it. I am merely saying that I have made peace with the fact that he does not love me. He is kind to me—unfailingly. Considerate, mostly, if somewhat distant, and, by every measure that one could count, a good husband. Our relationship is passionate." *But not loving.*

"Clearly passion is not lacking. Otherwise you would not need to have married one another at all!" Honoria said, quite miffed at the whole thing. "Hettie, can you really live with him this way? Loving him when you feel he does not return the sentiment?"

"I may not have what you do," Hettie said softly. "But very few people do. We both know that there are far worse fates than to have a marriage that is . . . simply satisfactory."

Chapter Forty-Seven

THE ROADS HAD been better than anticipated, and they had arrived, despite the carriage's seeming slowness, sooner than expected. Joss had been far more eager to return to his bride than he wished to admit, which was why he'd sought her out first rather than going upstairs to clean the road dirt off himself first. But as he stood outside the drawing room door listening to the conversation taking place within, that eagerness was tinged with . . . with what? Regret? Sadness? Anger? If it was anger, it was directed solely at himself.

Satisfactory. The word reverberated in his mind. It was his own fault for eavesdropping on a conversation that was not meant for his ears. But the hushed voices from within had piqued his curiosity. And even when he'd realized the conversation was not one he should be privy to, that same curiosity had rooted him to the spot.

A marriage that is satisfactory. Was it satisfactory when she said so with such obvious disappointment?

Joss was puzzled by his own violent opposition to the description. It was what they had agreed upon, after all. They may not have used precisely that term, but he had made it clear that theirs would be a practical arrangement. He'd thought she had accepted it, and according to what she told her sister, she had done so. And now that seemed to be the very last thing he desired.

Recalling how he'd laid it all out, he flinched. They would marry to give their child the benefit of legitimacy. *They would live together and make the best of their situation, but love would never be part of the equation.* Thinking back to the moment when Hettie had tried to open up to him about her feelings, he knew he had not responded well. He'd known it then. And in two weeks of being without her, he'd had to accept that maybe his attachment to her was greater than he'd intended for it to be.

How could he explain to her that his objection to hearing her tell him that she loved him was not because he did not love her in return, but that he felt unworthy of her love entirely? He was a gutter rat, born and bred. All the fine manners and education in the world would not change that he was born with nothing and everything he had currently was solely based on the generosity of a man the world saw as a criminal. Who would want to be loved by someone like him?

Turning away, Joss made for the stairs. He would clean himself up first, and then they would talk. They would have a conversation about just how satisfactory their marriage would be . . . for both of them. Whether it was Vincent's goading or the obvious unhappiness he'd heard in Hettie's voice, something had shifted inside him. He wouldn't allow his fear to hurt her. Never again.

WHEN HETTIE ENTERED her room, she was quite stunned to find that it was occupied—by the same man who occupied her thoughts. And he was standing before the wash basin with his shirt off and his wonderfully broad shoulders bared and little droplets of water rolling down his very muscular chest. Scars and all, he was a remarkably well formed man.

Realizing that she was staring far too intently, Hettie turned away. With as casual a tone as she was capable of, she remarked, "Oh . . . I didn't realize you'd returned already."

"Only just," he said. "The journey was not as difficult as anticipated."

"And things in London are settled? If such things are ever settled, of course."

He nodded. "For the time being. Ardmore may be a problem for another day, but for now, he is suitably bowed. I do not foresee that he will make a nuisance of himself again for some time. But I could be wrong. I've been wrong about many things."

There was something about that last statement that made her breath hitch. There was a degree of emotion infused in those words that she had not heard from him before. "'Tis a rare thing for a man to admit. What else have you been wrong about?"

"Walking away from you after that first night in the Mint. Keeping my distance from you every day since. Telling you that ours would only ever be a marriage based in practicality rather than feeling . . . I heard you—downstairs—when you were speaking with your sister."

Hettie's heart sank even as her face heated with embarrassment. "That was not a conversation you were meant to hear."

"No. It was not. But I think it is a conversation I very much needed to hear . . . because I had no idea how disappointing a *satisfactory marriage* could be until I heard you describe ours as such."

"You expressed yourself quite clearly on the subject," she replied with a healthy amount of haughtiness. She needed to make some effort to salvage her pride, after all. "I have no expectations of you."

"I think it might be better to say that I had no expectations of you. I never expected that a woman such as you would ever feel anything for me. Nor should you, honestly. But a thing can be improbable and still be possible. Can't it?"

Hettie shook her head. "I have no idea what this is about or what you're trying to say, but I very much wish you would just say it directly. I cannot simply guess at it or presume that I understand your meaning when you are being intentionally vague and cryptic!"

He was silent for a moment, simply staring at her in that enigmatic way of his. Finally, he spoke, his voice soft and low, "I no longer want a practical arrangement. I no longer want you or anyone else to think that what has passed between us is only because of this child . . . because I love you, Hettie. I think I have loved you from the first moment I saw you."

"In some hovel in the Mint covered in the filth of the river?" she demanded, her voice rising with a hint of hysteria in it.

"No. Running across the deck of the ship with your hair flying behind you. Seeing the stark fear on your face and watching you jump into the river anyway . . . because even if you died, it wouldn't be their choice but yours."

Tears burned her eyes and on a choked cry, she demanded, "Do not do this to me."

"What am I doing to you?"

She shook her head, dashing away the tears that simply would not be held back any longer. "Giving me hope. I can live with anything but disappointment. Do not offer me love and then be unable to support the words with your actions."

Chapter Forty-Eight

JOSS CROSSED THE room to where Hettie stood. "You are everything I could have ever dreamed of in a woman, and that is why I was so afraid to love you. I've lived my whole life with the notion that I didn't deserve good things because good things never came my way. But you . . . what man could ever deserve you? I'm a baseborn gutter rat who never knew my father and who has only the barest memories of his mother."

"And Arthur Ernsdale was a titled gentleman, a peer of the realm, who drank, wagered, and tormented his way through life. The station of your birth does not define your character!"

"No, it does not. But there are others who do not share that belief and . . . it isn't simply that I climbed up the social ladder with this marriage, it's that you have climbed down. They will all look at you differently. They will look at me with contempt. Contempt that is more than likely well deserved," he confessed. The admission was more troubling than he wished to consider. But what he wished to do and what he had to do were very different things.

"You do not deserve their contempt."

"You do not know that! There are horrible things in my past, both distant and recent, that make me the absolute worst choice for a husband."

Hettie merely shrugged. "No. Arthur Dagliesh was the worst

choice for a husband. I was a prisoner in that house. Bought and sold by my father into a loveless marriage to a cruel man who would slap, shove, or otherwise abuse me for the slightest infraction and took every opportunity to belittle and humiliate me. Will you do those things?"

"Never."

"Then you are not the worst choice, are you?"

There were things that she could only know if he were brave enough to tell them to her. Vincent would keep his secret forever if need be, but it seemed grossly unfair.

"I tried to return to Bow Street after my injury . . . and failed. Not because of the damage to my shoulder, not because I could no longer take down a suspect or subdue a criminal caught in the act. I couldn't do the job, Hettie, because I couldn't stay out of the opium dens." He waited for her to ask him why, waited for her to denounce him for that weakness of character. But she did not. She simply stood there, patiently waiting for him to continue the woeful tale.

"It was the laudanum after I was shot. At first, it was only to numb the pain. But it doesn't just numb physical pain. It numbs everything. And then one day, not having it causes a kind of agony I cannot describe. Your body aches from head to toe. You are alternately sweating and burning up or trembling from a cold that cannot be combatted with a dozen blankets. Puking your guts up—but laudanum, diluted as it is, only offers a small amount of relief. And that relief becomes less and less each time. So you find stronger laudanum, and stronger still when it ceases to have the desired effect."

"Opium is a terrible thing, Joss. It destroys people, their lives, their families . . . but you came back from that!"

"Because Vincent pulled me out of it. Because he dragged me from one of the dens, locked me in a room and then threatened anyone in the area who sold it if they even considered supplying me. It took a week for the worst of the pain to go away. It took another two weeks for the craving to pass. It took more than a month for me to realize that by essentially keeping me as a prisoner, he was saving my life. If he hadn't done what he did, I'd be dead now."

She nodded. "And so would I. Because you wouldn't have been there to save me that night. Do you still crave it?"

There had been times when he did. But he recognized one undeniable truth—he craved her more. "In the beginning, I craved it constantly. Then I began to only crave it most of the time. Then some of the time. Then only infrequently. And since you came into my life—not at all. Because there is something else that I crave, something else that takes up my every waking thought and torments me in my dreams."

She licked her lips nervously, her gaze locked with his. "What is that?"

"Who . . . who is that," he corrected. "And the answer should be quite obvious. It's you, Hettie. From the moment we met, it's been you."

She said nothing, but when he reached for her, one hand cupping the back of her neck while the other snaked about her waist, when he pulled her against him, she came willingly into his arms and let her head rest on his shoulder. He could feel the heat of her tears, and each one, he would atone for.

"I do not deserve you," he said. "And I know that. But it was pointed out to me that there isn't another man who does. And I at least, finally, have the sense to see that. Whether I deserve you or not, I will appreciate you. I will be grateful for you. And I will strive every day to be certain that you know how wonderful I think you. Strong, smart, desirable. Everything. You are simply everything."

HETTIE WAS OVERWHELMED. Speechless, even. She could barely think, much less articulate a response. So she did the only thing she could that might show him how she felt. Even standing on her toes, she wasn't tall enough to reach him. So she grabbed his shoulders and pulled him down to press her lips to his.

She kissed him with everything she had, with everything she felt. Relief. Giddiness. Hope. But above all, she infused that kiss with the love she felt for him. The love she had thought would never be returned and would simply wither away over time.

When he lifted her in his arms and carried her to the chaise lounge that faced the fireplace, unlit given the warmth of the day, she simply clung to him. She was half afraid it was all some beautiful dream and that she would wake up to the reality that the happy ending she hoped and prayed for had not come after all.

"Please don't let it be a dream," she whispered.

"It's not a dream. I can pinch you if you like," he offered.

Hettie smacked his arm. "Don't you dare."

He pressed his lips to the tender skin just below her ear. Then he scraped his teeth over that same spot, biting down just hard enough that it was impossible to deny the reality of it. Even as she shivered at that sensation, she couldn't hold in her laughter. It rang out clearly.

"Do I amuse you?"

She shook her head, still smiling, still trying to hold in her giggles. "No. But you have made me very, very happy. So happy that all I can do to let it out is simply laugh."

"You could," he said, "put me out of my misery and tell me that my affections for you are returned."

That did halt her laughter. "Do you honestly think you are the only one who can fall in love at first sight? Do you really believe that I would have given myself to you that night in the Mint only out of gratitude or the heightened emotion of our situation?"

He shrugged. "Perhaps."

"Well, no. I didn't. I wouldn't. You made me feel safe . . . but you also made me *feel*. And for so long I'd just been numb to everything. I'd had to be in order to survive marriage to Arthur. But with you, simply ignoring my feelings or locking them away—it wasn't an option. Do you believe in fate, Joss?"

"I didn't. Like many things, I'm having to reevaluate my stance on the matter," he admitted ruefully.

"I do believe in it. I believe that we—and what we can have together—that's our reward for all that we've been forced to endure in this life. I don't mean to squander that." Pulling back from him just long enough to release the buttons of her day dress, Hettie shoved the garment down over her arms, to her hips, and then, with more determination than grace, she rose and managed to get herself out of it entirely.

She'd forgotten for a brief moment how much her body had changed in the two weeks since they'd seen one another. When his shocked gaze landed on the swell of her belly, she wanted to hide from him. But somehow she didn't. She made herself stand there before him and let him look his fill. When he brought his large hand up and placed it tenderly over her, cradling the place where their child was growing within her, Hettie felt tears stinging her eyes. "Our child will be loved," she said. "Love grows from love. The more we love one another, the more love we'll have for our child."

"Children . . . let's have a house full of them. They'll never be alone and will always be surrounded by people who love them."

Hettie stroked his cheek. "So will you."

Epilogue

One year later

LIZA ETTINGER WAS a spitfire. She couldn't talk, walk, or manage to get her own fist in her tiny, perfectly shaped mouth. But she was still perfectly capable of making her displeasure known to one and all.

As she released her considerable fury in a wail that could wake the dead, her father smiled down at her, completely and hopelessly in love. In love with her, in love with her mother. Honestly, he was quite in love with life itself.

"You're spoiling her," Stavers warned.

"I have it on good authority that babies cannot be spoiled. They can only be loved," Joss corrected him. "And even if I am spoiling her, so what? She deserves it. She's perfect, after all . . . just like her mother."

Across the room, seated with Honoria, Hettie lifted her head and met his gaze. Her smile, as always whenever it fell on him, was like the warmth of the sun shining on him.

Vincent stepped forward. "Give me my niece before you trip over your own tongue as you gaze at your adoring wife like a lovesick calf."

A profane retort burned on his tongue. Had he not been holding his infant daughter, it would have already been uttered with no small amount of enthusiasm. Instead, Joss replied, "You're certainly one to talk. I can practically see stars in your eyes whenever you look at Honoria. And as for you, Stavers, I've seen you sniffing about after Mrs. Wheaton. Don't think we don't know what's going on there."

Stavers shrugged. "We're both old enough to not have to worry about consequences like the one you're holding. That makes it none of your damn business."

Joss grinned but did hand Liza over to Vincent. "Take her. But do not fill her mind with nonsense. She doesn't need lessons from infancy on how to cheat at faro or land a right hook."

Vincent took the baby with an ease and familiarity that would have been shocking only weeks earlier. But in that time, he'd come to dote on his tiny niece. He whispered close to her ear, "And you don't need a right hook. You'll likely be smaller than anyone you have to hit, so an uppercut will be a better tool in your arsenal. When you're a little bigger, Stavers will teach you."

Joss walked away, shaking his head. He hadn't thought living a life of leisure would suit him. Thought, it wasn't all that leisurely. There had been another smaller house on the estate Vincent had taken in lieu of payment of a debt. That was where he and Hettie currently resided with their child and a small number of servants. He still took on inquiry work from time to time, but for very select clients who paid well for his services. Hettie continued to manage her charity with the aid of Annie Foster, who was no longer a lady's maid but a personal secretary. It was quite the step up for her, and despite her ordeal, the young woman was thriving. In short, the chaos, upheaval, and near tragedy that Simon Dagliesh had visited upon all of them—while not forgotten—was being laid to rest with each step forward all of them took.

"Do not encourage him," Hettie said as he neared her. "The very second you tell Vincent not to teach her something horrid, he only becomes more determined to do so!"

Which was the point, to his mind. Throwing a solid punch,

regardless of one's gender, was a valuable skill to have.

Leaning down, he kissed her cheek then gave her a wink. "Of course. And he played perfectly my hand."

"You'll raise her to be a hoyden if you have your way," Hettie accused, though it lacked heat.

"As if you'd have it any other way."

She sighed wearily. "Of course I wouldn't. You know me too well."

"And love you more with every day."

Honoria rose. "I believe I shall go wrest my niece from Vincent before he offers her a matched pair of white horses and a gilt carriage."

Despite the jest, there was an air of sadness about Honoria. "She wants a child of her own very badly," Hettie observed softly.

"I'm certain it will happen for them. It is certainly not for lack of trying on their part . . . but as your sister is very fond of breaking rules and defying expectations, there are children out there who need homes and who need love quite by the thousands. You needn't bear a child to love it. You need only ask the Duchess of Clarenden. She raised and loved countless young women as if they were her own daughters."

Hettie nodded. "When Hettie and I are alone, I shall speak to her about it. But for now, while our daughter is well tended and completely occupied with everyone else, why don't we take a walk?"

"Where would you like to walk to?" he asked.

"Our chamber . . . we have a rare opportunity to be alone."

Joss took her hand and they slipped quietly from the room, secure in the knowledge that all would be right in their world.

The End

Author's Note

I know that the two-week period in which Vincent and Joss are in London dealing with Ardmore is something of a mystery. And that is for a very specific reason. The Hellion Club may be expanding yet again. Ardmore, Jack Collinsworth, Annie Foster, Maurice Bates, and even Arliss Battson have become very compelling characters for me. So much so that I plan to use the events of those two weeks as a way to springboard their stories going forward. I didn't want to give too much away, so please be patient as you wait for those answers. They are coming. I promise.

Thank you for your continued investment in The Hellion Club and in all of my writing.

About the Author

Chasity Bowlin lives in central Kentucky with her husband and their menagerie of animals. She loves writing, loves traveling and enjoys incorporating tidbits of her actual vacations into her books. She is an avid Anglophile, loving all things British, but specifically all things Regency.

Growing up in Tennessee, spending as much time as possible with her doting grandparents, soap operas were a part of her daily existence, followed by back to back episodes of Scooby Doo. Her path to becoming a romance novelist was set when, rather than simply have her Barbie dolls cruise around in a pink convertible, they time traveled, hosted lavish dinner parties and one even had an evil twin locked in the attic.

Website: www.chasitybowlin.com

www.ingramcontent.com/pod-product-compliance
Lightning Source LLC
Chambersburg PA
CBHW060440310726
48977CB00001B/270